The Key

Relics Series, Volume 2

K. A. Moore

Published by K. A. Moore, 2024.

Book cover design by Betibup33

Editing by Ginny and Judith at Bookhelpline

ISBN 9781957223049 (ebook)

ISBN 9781957223148 (paperback)

Also by K. A. Moore

Relics Series

Relics

The Key

The Chosen

Standalone

Watching Her Sleep

Sentinel

Weeping Widow's Heirloom

One

"No!" Casey's voice sounded through Clint's communicator. He stumbled out of bed and lurched toward his door. Ben loped to the hallway. This was far from the first nightmare Casey had had in the last month, but it had been a week since the last one. They took the steps two at a time on the way down.

The old iridescent light in the hallway hummed from the flow of electricity through the ancient wiring traveling along the ceiling, when they passed under.

Ben eased the door open in front of Clint as Casey tossed from her back to her side. An opalescent shield deployed from her to surround the bed. It shimmered and cast off bits of glitter and diamond flecks as the dome encapsulated the bed and Casey. The shield was just one of the relics they discovered just a little over a year ago in tunnels under an abandoned warehouse as they hid from a terrorist group, the Monarchs, who infiltrated the United States with help from the previous president.

Ben stepped through the shield, one of the perks of being a chosen one, and approached Casey.

Dampness dotted her forehead. "No!" Casey turned.

Ben perched on the bed. His hand hovered over her shoulder. "Casey?"

"Don't make me choose." Her fists twisted handfuls of the blanket in a mass of pale lilac quilted material around her.

"Casey," Ben's hand barely brushed against her skin.

Casey bolted straight up, gasping for air. "Ben!"

"It's okay. It's me." Ben gathered her into his arms. Damp blonde hair stuck to her forehead and down her neck. He rocked her as she trembled. The shield retracted as her breathing slowed and her eyes focused.

"Clint?" Casey latched onto Ben's muscled arm, which was a protective anchor around her. Her wide eyes perused the room.

"Shh, take a deep breath. I'm here. I've got you." Ben kissed her temple.

Clint nodded to him and left to get a glass of water. The cool glass chilled his fingers as he added ice and turned on the faucet. He yawned as he trudged back to Casey, who now sat with her eyes scrunched, clinging to Ben.

Ben's lips brushed her cheek. "I'm here. I'm not going anywhere."

Her hazel eyes flew open and she squirmed from his arms and hurdled over the other side of the bed away from him. She used her hands to manipulate the shield. The bracelet relic that controlled the shield was secured with the parchment in another section of the house. Clint still couldn't get used to the fact that Casey absorbed the shield's energy like she did the healing relic and no longer wore the bracelet to access its abilities.

Chloe swore the scroll never mentioned this before, at least the parts she recalled. She'd stated that the parchment seemed to have written additional elements and chapters including added details about the Key and what Casey would bring with her once she united the Chosen Ones.

They decided to take photos of the parchment periodically and keep them to document and log the changes to the prophecy.

"Casey!" The shield passed through Clint, and the relic weapon on his palm blazed. She pulsed, sending inescapable dread through his heart, overwhelming him. He blew out his breath, set the glass down on the dresser, and took three paces toward her. It had been a while since she'd sent out a pulse like she used to do in the warehouse when it told him and Amanda that she was the key.

"Clint?" Casey's eyes examined the room; confusion clouded her features.

"Babe, it's okay," Ben bolted off the bed and held out his hands to her.

"No, he's here!" Casey scrunched her eyes.

"Casey, it was a nightmare. It's not real. He's dead." Clint inched forward.

"No," Casey gaped around past the two of them.

"Look around. What do you see?"

"He's here." She pressed her palms against her eye sockets. The shield retracted.

"Open your eyes. Where is he? Show us." Clint hunched forward and slightly bent at the waist to look her in the eyes.

She opened them slowly. Ben turned on the lamp next to the bed at the same time Clint turned on the light in the room. Frantic, she scanned everywhere. "Where is he?"

"He was never here. He's dead. He can't get to you. You took care of that." Clint clutched her shoulder. She flinched.

"But what about you two?" Casey scanned the room past the two of them.

"Hon..." Ben locked onto her eyes.

"I thought he was here." Goosebumps prickled up her arms. Moisture dripped from the ends of her hair.

Ben gestured to the bed for her to sit.

Clint made a mental note to see if Chloe could get Casey to talk. He had to do something to help ease her guilt and torment of taking a life.

Two

"I'm okay." Casey glanced around, a meagerly furnished room stood before her, two windows with gray blackout curtains to block out the blinding glare of a rising sun. There was no attacker. She marched across the room and yanked back the fabric; disturbed dust particles swirled through the air. She fanned the dust away with her hand as she sneezed before she yanked them back into place. The window panes only showed their reflections; the dark night showed no signs that the morning was about to arrive. The walls held ancient, yellowed wallpaper with faded flowers curled back at the seams, exposing shockingly bright pink paint underneath.

"Are you sure?" Clint steered her by the elbow to the bed. He stood almost a foot taller than her. His green eyes were etched with concern.

"Oh, my gosh. Did I wake up anyone else?"

"No, I don't think so." Ben held her hand.

"But you were still sleeping. I'm so sorry. Why do I keep having these stupid nightmares?" Casey huffed.

"This is normal. You'll work through this. I promise, it's only been a month and we'll be there for you while you do. Look, it has been a week since the last one, so they are becoming less and less frequent." Clint gave the water to Casey.

"Ben, I want this to stop. I'm tired of being so scared all the time." Casey gulped the icy water as condensation ran down the side of the glass, before landing on the old quilt left by the previous owner.

"It will help if you talk about it. You bottling it up is only going to make it worse." Ben rubbed his hand up and down her back, his piercing blue eyes locked on her, which seemed even brighter in contrast to his short dark hair.

Casey shook her head. "I don't want to talk about it."

"I know you don't, but I think you need to." Clint arched his eyebrow to Ben. "Talking about it helps to take away some of the power it has over you. Admitting it out loud does wonders. Believe me. The military requires their people to talk, especially after hard missions. We all had to talk to a therapist. It helps."

"Clint and I talked about the need to do some major testing on these relics, more than ever with what yours did. We want to go back to the neighborhood. We can sneak around and see what's going on at the perimeter. Then, if there are Monarchs there, we can practice on them." Ben nodded to Clint.

Casey shook her head. "No, I'm too dangerous for you! What if I won't be able to keep you two safe? Also, what about all the houses they blew up? They have massive weapons we can't compete against and live."

She could still feel the skin on her arm as it blistered and charred when the house next to Ben and Clint's blew up and flaming lumber flew in every direction. The board that hit her had lit her arm, and the fabric of her shirt melted onto her skin. The pain was unbelievable, much less the stench from skin literally burning. And there were so many bodies in the street of the friends who fought with them to keep the terrorists from taking over.

"Not if we're careful. And I believe it's *our* job to keep the Key safeguarded, not the other way around." Clint crossed his arms, stretching the material to the limit around his biceps, and sat back against the dresser.

Casey frowned and muttered, "Not according to the new symbols on the parchment."

How her life had changed in the last year. Most people would scoff that she could fall in love with the man across the room from her, the one who claimed she was the key that unlocked their relic's powers.

Relics were specific to certain chosen ones. The healing stone absorbed into her heart gave her the gift of healing even the most hair-raising injuries, although it wasn't enough to save both of the people she had grown to love when they were injured back-to-back. Clint, with his weapon that molded around his hand, was able to send out bursts of power to incapacitate the enemy. Amanda's shield bracelet enclosed them in safety. Ben had the ring of truth. No one was able to withstand the compulsion to speak the truth while under its spell. If they counted just those four, it was a lot to take in, but to also include the small, spiraled communicators that were embedded in their ear canals and the sphere that allowed for traveling through time was a bit much. Not to mention the parchment that told of the relic's powers. Amanda and Chloe helped her learn to decipher the symbols so she became familiar with the prophecy.

Casey realized she wasn't paying attention to what Ben and Clint were discussing. Did they ask her something?

"So, we can keep you safe. Between the weapons I have and the relics, there shouldn't be a problem. It's not like we are going to go storming into the middle of the territory and scream come get us." Clint's lips twitched as he kept a smile from splitting his face and showing his dimples, as he tried to lighten the mood.

Casey slumped her shoulders as she sat on the corner of the bed and faced them. "When did you want to do this revisit to the neighborhood?"

"Maybe in the next couple of days." Perspiration soaked through Ben's shirt where her head rested.

"HOW ABOUT TOMORROW? I really don't want to wait." Her eyes met Clint's and held them. Her anxiety radiated through him.

"I think that's a great idea. Casey, we'll be there with you, and maybe you can confront the people who want you. It may help with the nightmares. And let's discover what else the shield can do. Since the bracelet was absorbed like the healing stone, we need to figure out if it works the same or if you can enhance the abilities without the physical bracelet being attached to you. Plus, it's not like we will be walking down the main street, right into the heart of their territory. We will stay on the perimeter and work from there." Clint understood getting her out there and seeing they were just people, albeit evil people, might help.

Casey lifted her head to Clint; she nodded and closed her eyes.

"I'm going back to bed. See you in the morning." Clint lingered out of Casey's line of sight yet with his eyes still on Ben. The fear that radiated from her ebbed away as she quieted down and he found breathing easier.

"Are you okay?" Ben stood. The damp patch of material stuck to his skin.

"Yes, I'm going to take a shower and try to sleep some more. Do you really think revisiting the neighborhood will help?"

"Clint does and he is more knowledgeable about that than anyone. Who knows, we may discover new ways to use the relics and keep the fighting away from us out here." Ben kissed her on the forehead and moved to the door.

"I can try. What can it hurt?" Casey latched the door behind Ben.

"How is she?" Clint propped against the wall across from Casey's door. He heard her shuffle to her bathroom and turned off his communicator.

"She's okay. Do you think the neighborhood visits will help her? I don't like that she's going through this. Her nightmares are dragging her down. Amanda didn't struggle like this." Ben took off for their rooms.

"Yes, I think so. Getting out there may help her find that they're not invincible and that you and I are okay. What she's struggling with is the thought of one of us dying. Yes, she ended someone's life, but I think there's an underlying issue that she won't admit to us, much less herself. This has gone on longer than I thought. I think the possibility of either one or both of us not being here, is haunting her more than that man's death. We're all she has. She wakes up yelling for you or me, not about her actions. I wish she would talk to us."

"I don't know. Could this set her back and make the precarious situation worse? She's scared but she's putting on a front trying to be brave. Did you see her jump in the garden the other day? At least no one else is aware when she deploys the shield." Ben's fingers curled around the open door to his room. "Do you really think she's more apprehensive about one of us being killed?"

"I'm keeping an eye on her. What do you make of the shield absorbing into her? Do you think one of us can use the bracelet and have two shields working for us? Maybe that will help." This would be a rough road for her, and Clint wanted nothing more than to take the burden for her. He marched into the third room and removed the bracelet from the desk that sat at the far wall. It was missing a couple of sections of the roll-top part, leaving a small gap but not too big to keep them from hiding the relics.

Ben focused on him as Clint slipped the bangle on, scraping the skin on his large hand as he manhandled it through the delicate design. Clint grimaced, expecting the elegant, scrolled filigree bangle to bend or break.

"Clint, how are we going to help her through this? She was so far under and confused she couldn't comprehend she wasn't in the dream. She couldn't see us. She only saw the man she killed."

"Continue to pray for her. Be there when she needs us. I'll pull her to the side and talk to her again. Maybe I can draw out the despair closing in on her." Clint frowned when nothing happened, and the bracelet kept its bangle shape and lay dormant around his wrist. He took it off and relinquished it to Ben. If they could get one of them to operate the shield, maybe that would take some pressure off Casey and give her some relief.

"I've never stopped praying for her since I found her." Ben took the bracelet and thrust his rough calloused hand through. He shrugged when nothing happened and handed it back to Clint.

"I understand, brother, me either. Let's plan on going to the neighborhood tomorrow as today is already off to a rocky start. If she's doing better later, we'll see what we can find out in the old community the next day. Keep the fight from here. I'll have Chloe ask her uncle to verify first by satellite if we risk going back or take the battle somewhere else."

"Sounds good. I'm going to try and get some shuteye before the sun rises and keeps me from getting any more sleep." Ben wandered out.

Clint turned his communicator back on and stared down at the floor. He heard the water turn off in the shower and expected Casey would try to doze. If not, he would double-check in a few minutes. He would let Ben crash. Sleep was scarce over the last couple of weeks. Casey struggled and Ben would never let her labor through this without him by her side. The love between them was hard to miss.

He thought of Amanda. Ben told him when they were kids about reading Amanda's diary. He was shocked Ben had done that and even more mortified to find out that

Amanda had a crush on Clint back then. He was in the awkward teen years so he didn't envision her like that. Now, the head cheerleader, on the other hand, was who he was enchanted with all those years ago. He didn't want to admit the embarrassing fact that someone he perceived as a little girl was enamored with him. Yet after the initial shock, he never admitted to Ben the boost to his ego that her crush gave him. No matter what people say, it's nice to learn when someone likes you, who means so much to you.

All these years later, he had vivid images in his mind of how she blushed and squirmed when she found out Ben told him. He thought of how the coloring of her flushed skin made her look different. Older, prettier. She avoided him for months. He found himself missing her during that time. She and Ben had always been in his life. He told her she was only a sister to him. She agreed he was only a brother to her and she didn't mean what she wrote in the diary. With her now gone, an emptiness ached in his heart for her. More than a sister, maybe something more toward what she wrote about her unrequited feelings.

Amanda's death still shook him to his core. The enemy's bullet found its mark, and he couldn't take it back. He felt as if he was a leader to this group, and he counted Amanda's death as his failure. Oh, her brother and Casey didn't see it that way, but there was no way he could keep those lingering thoughts out of his head.

He tucked his hands under the pillow behind his head. The muscles in his arms bulged at his biceps, stretching the fabric of the sleeves. He stretched his hand to the nape of his neck and snagged the collar of his T-shirt, pulling it over his head and tossing it across the room. Then he lounged, listening to Casey move around. She wasn't going back to bed. But then, she would be tired later since the clock read two in the morning. That was dangerous in the world they lived in. He expected her to be alert and aware of everything around her.

A sheet snapping through the air filtered through his communicator. He pictured her tucking the elastic corners around the edges of the mattress. A few minutes later the old worn bedsprings groaned under the bulk of a person. She had climbed on the bed. The silence was heavy around him. He closed his eyelids, but listened, ready to go to her if she cried out again. Moments later he was asleep.

Three

Casey heard someone in the kitchen. She slipped her legs out from under the heavy homemade quilt. She discovered it in the back of the closet when she hunted for sheets to remake the bed after her nightmare. It replaced the lighter one from the night before. She adored the fabric squares that made up the quilt. The bright purples blended into dull pinks in the pinwheel patterns. Browns and tans edging the quilt only seemed to accent the purple, making them appear brighter. She ran her hand over the light-colored blocks before snatching her robe off the back of the door.

She shuffled sock-footed toward the kitchen. Exhausted from last evening's bad dream, she was happy the rest of the night was uneventful. No dreams visited her when she drifted off after her shower.

Chloe was talking to Clint in hushed tones when Casey joined them. She must have just gotten back from a grocery run. At least they were able to keep up with their previous supplier while they were out in the country.

"How about you guys check out the parchment and see if anything has changed? It's been a week since the last time you did." Clint moved around Chloe to help Ben put away the delivery.

Chloe smiled as Casey walked past her to the small room off the kitchen. "I'm interested to see if there have been any changes. The possibility that it would change and alter the relics in so many different aspects is so exciting!"

Casey couldn't keep a grin from her face when she and Chloe took the time to study the prophecy. "Me either. Yet I am still getting used to the fact the sphere was able to let Ben through to the past and bring me here."

"Explain to me again how the bracelet absorbed into you. I just don't understand that." Chloe had the parchment rolled out and used the chests for the relics to hold down the four corners on the small table they pulled from the garage.

Casey thought back to that day as they were the last to leave the houses they moved to after leaving the warehouse and started relaying everything to her.

As they stood on the lower level of Clint and Ben's house, a rush of warmth radiated from the bracelet. Diamond flecks sailed around the stone as Ben and Clint gaped down at the swirling speckles.

"Casey?" Clint's weapon flickered.

"What's happening?" Casey held her arm away from her body. The flecks spread and swirled around her as the silver in the bracelet amplified into a blinding white light. Blue specks crossed her field of vision as her body temperature skyrocketed.

The blue and silver glitter intermingled, racing up and down her arms and legs until she was a mass of sparkles. Her hair whipped around behind her head as she was encased in the brilliant light. The bracelet sent out a shield engulfing her.

"Your eyes are a bright blue. Are you injured?" Ben's voice was in her communicator that they'd turned on when they started loading. His voice didn't penetrate the shield.

"No," Casey turned her arms over, mesmerized by what was happening. Symbols from the parchment, which told of all the relics' powers and uses, dotted her skin and then covered her arms completely as if she had tatted sleeves from her wrists up to her shoulders. They were the color of hemp ink. She scrubbed her hands over them, but they didn't disappear; instead, they started to glow. Amanda—before she died—and Chloe were helping her learn to read and decipher the writing to become familiar with the prophecy.

"Ben, what's going on?" Clint squinted and shielded his eyes with his hands.

Ben's ring projected yellow flecks of diamonds into the air. Clint held his hand up when ruby particles from his weapon sizzled in and around the room.

"Don't move." Ben squinted at Casey through the light.

She saw them fine through the bouncing specks flying around.

"Trust me."

"Did you hear that?" Ben turned in a full circle.

"Yes." Clint and Casey replied in unison.

"Trust me."

"We do, Father." Ben held out his hands.

Clint clasped one and held his other one out for Casey when she grabbed both of theirs. Red and yellow specks dissipated and flowed back into the other two relics. The blue and diamond dots on Casey flowed toward her heart where they brightened. They absorbed into her skin after a small dance, and their glow dimmed. Her hair fell slack against her back, and the fever subsided in her as a rush of coolness from the concrete basement flowed around them.

"Wow, I could listen to that all the time. I'm so jealous you could hear God's voice. I've never heard it like you have described." Chloe beamed.

"I can't even do it justice just using words for what it sounded like. Then the bracelet turned back into a bangle and slid off my hand. Ben took it and we thought for sure that meant we couldn't use the shield anymore when it exploded around us. He placed it on the table, and it retracted so we thought he was controlling it. Then I just thought about the shield, and there it was again, and the bangle still lay on the table. That is how we knew that I absorbed another relic's powers." Casey was winded as she rushed through her story.

"Okay, so look at this. There's another line that wasn't here the last time. Let's get an image from this to load into the sequencer so we can compare the previous scans and show us what is new." Chloe pulled out the small palm-sized imager and took a series of shots.

Casey still wasn't up on all of the new techy things that had come out in the last thirty-five years. "What does it say?"

"Um, let's see. Once the key unleashes new powers, the prophecy will evolve with those pertaining to those powers. The chosen will still be four." Chloe's head snapped up.

Casey's heart ramped up its staccato beat. "Does that say what I think it says?"

"We have to tell Ben and Clint." Chloe jumped up and started for the door before Casey could get her to stop.

Casey hissed. "Chloe!"

Spinning on her heels, she connected with Casey's frantic stare. "We can't tell them yet. What if it isn't what we think it means? I don't want to give them a false hope that Amanda will be coming back. It would break their hearts."

Chloe scrunched up her face and then let her features smooth back out. "Yeah, you're right. Come on, you need to grab something to eat."

The tantalizing fresh-cut fruit made her mouth water when she entered the kitchen, almost as if she stuck her tongue out she could capture the smallest hints of the flavor hanging in the air. Hot steaming croissants heaped on a plate, while cut fruit overflowed in a bowl in the middle of the table. "That looks delicious."

"How are you?" Clint stopped. His hand poised over the table to get butter for the flakey pastry.

Casey nodded her head. "I'm okay."

"Morning." Ben placed his arm around Casey, kissed her head, and then meandered to the cabinet for glasses.

"Morning." Casey didn't meet Clint's eyes.

"Chloe, are you joining us for this feast?" Ben's hands already held three plates with his hand hovering over another one.

Chloe's eyes darted to Clint and then to the floor. "Nah, I'm going to get going. I ate on the way back from the food run." She disappeared through the back door.

"Did you want to talk about last night?" Clint sank into a chair.

The corner of Casey's mouth twitched. "Nothing to talk about."

"Are you sure?" Ben's arm brushed hers as he set the plates on the table.

"Yup." Casey chose a croissant and piled fruit on her plate. She pulled the bread apart with her fingers and ate the small flakey dough without butter or any other condiment to adorn the light fluffy pastry that melted in her mouth.

"Casey, you can talk to us." Clint speared a strawberry with his fork.

"I'm fine." She drained the glass of milk she poured and pushed her uneaten plate of food away from the edge of the table. When she thrust back from the table, the chair legs skidded and bounced across the old linoleum floor, the noise resonating down the hall.

"Casey." Ben rose.

She had already made it to her room; the latch clicked as she nudged the door behind her. Maybe if she busied herself with other things, she might forget what she did. She slumped forward as she sat at the end of her bed. Her cheeks puffed when she blew out her pent-up breath. Ben and Clint wanted to help her through this, but she didn't know where to go. She hated being a burden to them, knotting her insides and gnawing holes in her already exposed nerves. Not sure what to do, she selected jeans, a top, and a flannel shirt for the day.

Once dressed, she tugged her hair into a messy bun at the crown of her head. Maybe going to the neighborhood today, instead, to find out what the Monarchs were up to would be an option. She trembled at the thought, but she wanted to do this for herself. Her heart ached as she thought about the dangers posed for Ben and Clint if they went back and the Monarchs captured them. It would be worse the second time around if they got their hands on them to lure her out. They wouldn't hesitate to take their lives. She shook her head and laced up the boots Chloe acquired for her. They were more suited for farm life than the old tennis shoes she wore when Ben had come into her life. She snorted. More like kidnapped her, dumping her entire world upside down.

"Are we going somewhere?" Clint eyed Casey. "I thought when we said that it was going to be tomorrow, not later this morning."

"I want to go to the neighborhoods today. I don't want to wait." She stalked past them to the back door and prayed her nervousness didn't show. She looked over her shoulder to make sure they followed.

Out of the corner of her eye, she saw Ben spin on his heels as she marched past him.

Clint removed the gun from the top of the refrigerator, thrust it into the holster at the back of his waistband, and jogged to catch up. "Are you sure you want to go today? We thought maybe we would go tomorrow."

"No, let's just go now." She turned to Ben, who had snuck up on them. She struggled to smile but the pain in her eyes overrode her attempt and showed the secret agony she suffered.

"Alright, let's go. I'll put together food for lunch as we won't be back before then." Ben trotted back to the kitchen.

Four

The cool morning air made her skin flush as the wind whipped at the flyaway hair around her. She shivered and propelled her arms into the jacket she had with her. Clint appeared at her side, and she didn't say anything when he gazed down at her. Almost a foot taller than she was, he towered over her. He was worried about her, but she was doing better with the thought that she took a life. Her eyes became unfocused as she remembered that night.

A shadow moved from the corner. Her bare feet skidded on the floor. She slipped closer to the intruder as she tried to stop and turn around.

"Ben, someone's here!" Casey hissed through clenched teeth.

The shadow struck forward; the silver barrel of a pistol glinted as the kitchen light reflected off the shiny smooth surface polished to an obtrusive shine. Her feet slipped again when she backpedaled, not able to find traction on the slick floor. Her hair whipped around her head as she twisted her body around. The dark shape pounced, hitting her in the back with his entire body. It jostled her several feet forward. They both collided with the floor, and it knocked the wind out of her. She was pinned down by the barrel; the cold metal was pressed to the back of her head. She clawed at the floor. A fingernail bent backward and tore from her effort to escape. Her eyes widened as she gasped against her shocked diaphragm that refused to let her pull in air.

"What have we here?" A male's voice grated through the air. His weight bore down on her as suffocating panic seized her.

The bookcase splintered, shattering into the dark dining room. The guy wrenched Casey off the floor by a hand full of hair, placing her between him and Ben and Clint. Tears streamed down as her heart skipped while she gasped for air. Cold hard steel met her temple while his other hand inched around her. His fingers splayed out before they dug into her skin under the surface of the soft knitted sweater. She winced. Ben and Clint held up their hands to the intruder. The man took a tentative step forward. When Ben and Clint didn't move, he took another footstep, his fingers dug in further, fingernails as sharp claws against the smooth, delicate skin of her belly. She gritted her teeth and was sure they would puncture her skin soon.

Ben and Clint crept forward a single step at a time and were soon within a couple of feet from Casey and the unwanted guest when he stopped, yanking to open the door to the closet. Anger burned in Ben's narrowing eyes as she stood there helpless with the cold metal of the barrel against her temple. Clint flinched; his hand inched its way around his back with every stride.

"Stop if you don't want me to splatter her brains all over this room," the man's hoarse voice hissed, his hot breath against her hair. She shuddered. He pulled back on her, so that she blocked the closet, with him behind her, away from any action the other two would have an opportunity to take.

Clint, with a palm out showing an empty hand, shook his head. "Just let her go."

"Um, let me think…no! Do you realize the price on this one's pretty little head?" The intruder snaked his hand from her waist up to her throat and smiled before he licked the side of her face. Clint held Ben back when he tried to lunge forward.

With his foot on the first rung of the ladder, he hauled Casey up with a tight grip on her neck, urging her to follow. "Which one did you want to say goodbye to? You pick which one dies tonight. Which hero will you choose to save?" His lips brushed her ear as his hot breath made her quiver. "Or do I take them both out?"

When she turned her head, his chipped, nicotine-stained teeth grinned at Ben and Clint. The bracelet shimmered as her anger took hold. Without lifting her head, her eyes held their gaze. A brief look at Clint and he gave a minute nod. She straightened up and screamed as she projected the shield up and behind her. The shield changed into an opaque opal solid mass that propelled back toward the male behind her into the closet. The sickening sound of bones snapping permeated the air.

She blew out a breath at the memory that assailed her and knew in her gut that maybe this was not something that they should risk.

This morning, the thought of the loss of either of them was something she refused to consider. Amanda was hard enough but they had grown so close over the last month since they had moved, nestled in the beautiful grove of trees obscured from sight away from the main road. How do you tell someone you're okay that you took a life and not have them think of you as a monster?

Today, she would do what she could to work past her worry. She may perhaps make sense of a few things about the shield. She couldn't wait to prove her determination to keep these two and everyone with them safe. Clint squinted down at her again, but she didn't acknowledge him. The back door to the house opened on the creaky coiled spring that snapped it closed when Ben let go.

"You guys heading out?" Mark, one of the original group from when Casey joined them, walked around the corner of the house. He was a little on the shorter side and was only a couple of inches taller than Casey, but he was one of the nicest people she had ever met. Never had a negative word to say about anyone.

"Yep. We'll be gone the rest of the afternoon. Did you need something?" Clint put his hands on his hips.

"Nothing that can't wait. I was just going to talk to you about the idea of you three splitting from the group. I've had time to think about it since you brought it up a couple of months ago, and I have to say I think it's a bad thing. What if something happens and we need you? I know you have skills and weapons to defend against our enemy, but if you leave and take that all with you, then how do we defend ourselves? I can shoot, but my accuracy isn't anything near yours." Mark rushed out his words.

"Or maybe you won't be under attack anymore." Clint raised his hand to stop him when he started to respond. "Now hear us out. The Monarchs are searching for us. They are targeting Casey specifically. If we leave, then we potentially take that target off your backs and carry it with us. The rest of you guys will slip away unnoticed and live under their radar."

Mark nodded fidgeting with his watch on his right wrist. "That's a good point. I hadn't thought of that. But what if I play devil's advocate and that isn't what happens? What if they come after us even worse because you aren't here to protect us."

"I don't think they will split up their resources and pursue two objectives. There were too many that were taken down in the raid for them to have enough troops to target two at once. At least, that is my opinion. Pray on it. Let God lead you where He needs us to go. We are doing the same and waiting for an answer so we can keep everyone alive as long as possible." Clint held out his hand to Mark, who shook it, and then stuffed his hands back in his pockets, hunched over to guard his body from the wind, and walked away.

Ben opened the back door for Casey. "I can see it both ways. I believe that is why we need to get God's answer on this before we make a decision that could be detrimental to so many people."

"I agree." Clint slid behind the wheel.

Five

Clint pulled out of the grove of trees and steered toward the neighborhood they left only about a month ago. No one said anything. The nearly two-hour drive was a quiet one. Clint continually checked on Casey, who chose to ride in the backseat staring at the scenery that blurred past the windows with a blank look on her face, as if deep in thought.

Clint guided the car to the shoulder of the road as they entered the suburbs they had called home not so long ago. Casey flinched when the tires nicked the broken concrete curb. "Here's the plan. We're going to investigate first. If the Monarchs have completely overrun the area, we aren't even going to try anything. Chloe's uncle confirmed they moved into the houses after we left. But doesn't look like they found a way into the basements. The man that was in the lower level of your house must not have relayed that information to them in the short amount of time he was there."

An ankle holster on Clint's leg concealed a handgun. He also kept one in the back of his waistband. Casey's eyes bulged and she eyed the double holster slung around him with a gun on each side. Ben waited at the front of the car, and Clint directed her to stay down in the seat. He smiled at her before he took off with Ben in tow.

They were far enough away that the Monarchs wouldn't think anything about a car being on the side of the road. He had to hope they didn't have anyone scouring this far out

A mile down, he pulled one of the guns from the shoulder holster. Ben copied his action. Crouching in the tree line, they scarcely made out the houses that were reduced to a pile of rubble. Decomposing bodies strewn on the streets emitted such a horrendous stench, that bile in his stomach churned viciously. This must be the dumping ground for people they interrogated because none of the bodies of their friends that were there from the bombings would still be at this level of decomp. Those would have been reduced to just bones in a matter of ten days—give or take a couple—due to voracious appetites of insects that ate dead flesh. Clint held his breath as a Monarch with an assault rifle casually slung over his shoulder approached the trees.

The weapon flickered in his palm. He turned the center stone to the first setting and waited. The male looked over his shoulder to the street and then entered the timber line. With another glance over his shoulder, he relaxed. He hid his actions from the Monarchs patrolling further down. He pulled a cigarette from the pocket of his uniform and put his back to Ben and Clint. A flame flared as he held a lighter to the end, creating embers that flashed and burned when the crushed tobacco packed in the end of the paper caught and held the spark. He inhaled deeply with his eyes jammed tight. The smoke he exhaled curled around his face, and the cracked corners of his mouth ticked up into a sick satisfied smile. Clint directed a pulse his way.

The Monarch crumpled into a heap on the ground, the cigarette rolled into dry plants and minuscule flames flared, dancing as they consumed the withered fall leaves that had turned brown. Clint lurched to the fire, stamping out the dry crisp rotting vestiges of autumn before it alerted anyone of their location. They dragged him to an oak and made use of the ties he carried in his pockets to secure him.

He twitched as sharp steps sounded behind them. Clint turned and shot the weapon toward whoever was approaching. The pulse passed through Casey; blue static sparkled in her eyes.

Clint rushed to her. "What are you doing here? I told you to wait in the car."

"And we came here to help me work through this!" she hissed in a whisper. "I don't want you to treat me as if you have to look after me or as if I'll break. I'm struggling at the moment, but bear with me."

"You're right. I'm sorry."

Voices on the street drifted to their location. Clint steered her by the arm, yanking her into the bushes across from where they tied the Monarch. Ben maneuvered her back into him and pulled her into a squat.

"What the!" one of the Monarchs bellowed.

"What?" A grimy male who walked with authority wandered over, with no urgency in his movements. Grime smudged on his ill-fitted uniform, hiding the true colors of the camo fatigues, telling them appearance was not their priority or even a concern.

"Someone's here." The younger male indicated to the one tied.

The older sloven Monarch pulled his Ruger and fired two rounds into him. Casey turned her head to Ben as she deployed the shield. Clint held his hand up that possessed the weapon. He glanced at Casey and thought that maybe it was a mistake bringing her here.

"Pass the word, this is the punishment when you let the enemy get the upper hand. You need to be alert at all times. There is no leniency for this pathetic excuse of patrol work!" He rammed the gun back into the holster at the midsection of his uniform, which moved with the heaviness of the pistol sitting off-kilter on his looming frame, and marched off from the body.

"Yes sir!" the younger man scrambled after his superior, glancing around to his left only once.

Clint placed his hand on Casey's shoulder. "Are you okay?"

"Yes."

Ben stood and pulled Casey up with him. Clint narrowed his eyes at the Monarch that was murdered. He took his knife out of his pocket and pried the back off the radio. Numerous wires connected to circuit boards and crisscrossed through the depths of the radio. He wedged his knife under one of the circuit boards and pried it up, plucked it out of the radio, and crushed the square under his boot. "Tracker."

"Wait. What are you going to do with that?" Ben leered over Clint's shoulder.

"Possibly listen in and maybe turn the tables on them." He turned on the radio after turning down the volume. A squelch changed over to static that seeped from the speaker and then squawked again. Someone keyed up from another location. Nothing was said as open air leached through the speaker. They unkeyed.

Clint powered it off before clipping it to his back pocket. "Casey, keep the shield up and let's try to move to the other side into the woods to the south of us."

Casey nodded to Clint and gave a half a grin. He liked seeing the almost smile. She hadn't smiled since the incident. This gave him hope with her seeing what the enemy was capable of, killing one of their own. A young man who hadn't even started to live his life. Maybe she would get a glimpse of the evil and what they would do if they caught them.

Halfway across the road, a diesel engine sounded behind them. Clint laced his fingers together with his palms up. Ben put his foot in Clint's intertwined hands and was boosted over a privacy fence. He was ready to hoist her over to Ben, but there wasn't time. The truck roared toward them. Clint pulled Casey to him, covering her with his body. An energy pulse radiated from her causing his heart to hammer. Her fear permeated into him. He whispered, "Ben stay there. We have the shield."

The engine cut off and three men leaped out.

"I'm telling ya, someone was standing by that fence." The large overweight man who was soft all over didn't exactly exit the truck but more or less fell from it. Sweat ran down his red face as he bumbled toward them. Gasping for air, he was out of breath before his feet even made contact with the curb that ran down the length of the property separating the sidewalk from the street.

Clint arched his eyebrows to Casey, his arms around her. He held his palm up, weapon ready to fire. Diamond flecks dotted the shimmering shield.

A skinny rail-thin kid laughed. "Oh, what! Did aliens beam 'em up?"

"Don't laugh at me. I know what I saw, runt!"

"Ooh, I'm so scared. Do you think the aliens will take me also?" The kid backed up to Clint and Casey.

Clint tapped Casey on the shoulder and motioned to her to extend the shield to include the kid. Her eyes found his and she shook her head no. He put his finger to his lips. She walked two paces away as he stalked up behind the kid. The men still joked about aliens when there was a commotion down the street. With all their heads turned, Casey pitched the shield out and Clint nabbed the kid just as the weapon stunned him.

Clint urged Casey to go around the corner as he followed. The unconscious male was flipped over his shoulder as if he didn't weigh a thing. He was impressed that she sought for the areas with the least amount of foliage to walk so she was silent as she edged around the corner and out of sight.

"What the..." the sweaty man yelled when he turned back around and gawked at the empty vacant spot by the fence his cohort occupied only moments before.

The kid had vanished. They turned in every direction. "Where did he go?" They pointed their guns when a fourth man scrambled from the truck to the top section with a mounted turret. He swiveled in every direction, ready to fire on command. Clint monitored everything behind the corner of the fence.

"Dude, he's playing a trick on you. He probably ran and will show up later. Who cares?" The driver slipped behind the wheel and cranked over the engine.

The large sweaty man walked several paces up and down the fence line. The diesel roared to life, drowning out any noise around them. He shrugged and then cursed as he lumbered toward the truck. It took three tries before he was able to launch himself into the cab. The man still crewed the turret while the last one piled in. They motored down the road toward the commotion when the man in the passenger seat yelled for them to stop. He whipped his gun from his side and fired the entire clip into the fence. Clint covered Casey even though the shield was in position.

"In case he thinks he's funny and hiding," the man smirked and spit out the window before giving the order to continue.

Ben jogged up to Casey and Clint. "What was that? How did they not see you?"

"Not sure, you tell me. I wished we were invisible and...I don't know, we became concealed to them." Casey collapsed the shield.

The kid crumpled to the ground like a sack of potatoes, and the air whooshed out of his lungs when he landed.

"The interior of the shield also changed. All I saw were diamond sparkle things. It has never looked like that before." Clint stood over Ben who restrained the kid securing him to a broken slat in the fence with his own ties.

"Won't they, you know, punish him?" Casey looked at the kid.

"Probably worse." Clint signaled to Ben and they edged around the corner of the house leading Casey by the hands.

"He's just a kid," Casey argued.

Clint pulled up short and turned Casey to him. "Well, he would pull that trigger at any of us without hesitating. He's a Monarch."

"But he's so young." Casey tried to look past Clint. He stopped her. She didn't need to see these people as anything more than Monarchs, terrorists bent on evil and tearing down Christians.

"Casey, the Monarchs train their troops from a very young age. They hand them a knife and teach them to cut and thrust that blade into people. They don't teach them to shoot from a distance separating them from the experience, but more of in your face, taking in the horror of their victim's death. It hardens them; they wouldn't hesitate to handle any of us who aren't on their side the same way."

"Wow, that was harsh. True, but harsh." A man stepped out from behind a rusted-out vehicle and leveled his rifle at Ben, a red dot appeared on his chest.

Six

Casey put herself in front of Ben. He steered her out of the way. She fought to stay in front of him, dodging his grasp a second time.

"Move her out of the way." The man put his finger on the trigger.

Clint held up his camouflaged weapon, that they couldn't see so it would seem as if he were putting his hands up in surrender. Casey gazed behind her; they were ready to die for her, and in that instant, she would die for either one of them. She put her hand back for Clint to take. He tried to give her his left but she slapped it away. She arced an eyebrow. He frowned before he took her outstretched waiting hand with his right. Static charged through the weapon to her arm up and across her body to settle in her eyes.

"What is that?" The man looked around the sight of his rifle.

"Here. I'll give it to you." Casey reached forward. Ben leaped for her but Clint stopped him.

"Why would ya do that?"

"Look...here." Casey cast out her hands as static surged to the assault rifle the man held. The ammunition in the clip exploded, killing him instantly. Ben pulled her to him as Clint darted in front of her.

They turned and examined what was left of the man who tried to take Casey. Clint squinted at Ben and then down at Casey. She stared at the ground as the static subsided that was lingering in her fingers.

Ben spun her around. "What was that?"

She shrugged. "Not sure."

"You good?" Clint studied the weapon; it was charged and ready to fire on a setting that didn't exist before. Red glowing static surged over and around his hand traveling up his arm.

"I think so, a little tingling in the digits but...I'm okay." She wriggled her fingers, balled her hands into a fist, and then stretched them back out several times. Her heart rate slowed as the lingering static played over the tips of her fingers seemed to calm her.

"Come on. We better go. That explosion will no doubt bring curious people. I think we've seen enough of the neighborhood today." Clint clutched one of her biceps while Ben grabbed the other. They sprinted around several houses before a diesel engine had their attention.

How would taking another life affect her? It didn't get easier, but knowing what the Monarchs were, made the decision easier. The fact that he admitted what Clint said was true made her shudder. Clint leveled his weapon as they charged around the corner of a yellow faded house while Ben flung himself against her, hiding behind the brick chimney that barely adhered to the side, capable of collapsing at the first strong wind.

She deployed the shield, making them invisible. Clint held up his hand, weapon ready. Casey gripped him as hard as possible and only shook her head no. He narrowed his eyes at her, and she mouthed, "It's okay" and let his hand drop.

Men shouted and yelled; there was a single gunshot. She pictured the kid they left bound to the fence. There were no mistakes allowed in the Monarchs. She held onto Ben, her head buried in his chest. Listening to the rhythmic thumps under his ribcage calmed her. He held her tight with one hand behind her head and the other around her lower back, pulling her to him. His breath against her skin sent goosebumps down her arms.

Men yelled to secure the sector and to exterminate anyone out there except for her. Clint pulled them to the next house. They ran around several houses, darting in a zig-zag pattern.

After several near misses with their enemy, they skirted outside the zone. When they piled in the car, Casey retracted the shield and smiled. Clint didn't hesitate to flip the car around and race out of the neighborhood.

Casey sat with her head resting on the seat and breathed heavily. A stitch in her side from sprinting to the car annoyed her, but she pushed her hand against it. She ignored Clint's gaze through the rearview mirror.

His left eyebrow twitched yet he didn't say anything.

"I'm fine. You don't need to keep asking me if I'm okay. Just one thing."

"Sure, name it."

Ben turned in his seat and she straightened up. "Can we eat? I'm starving."

Clint laughed and nodded to her. Ben dispensed sandwiches and bottles of water. She put hers on the seat next to her, unable to believe how much running from someone who wanted to harm you ramped up her appetite. She tugged off the plaid jacket she wore. She couldn't cool down as the sun heated the interior of the car. She dabbed a napkin across her brow to sop up the moisture.

"Casey, what's wrong?" Ben turned in his seat.

"It's hot." She chugged half of her water.

Clint did a double take over the seat. "The temps are only in the forties."

"No, that's not right." Casey pulled at her collar and tipped forward in the seat.

"Babe, look." Ben signaled to the dash. Sure enough, forty-six degrees was displayed on the screen. Wind speed, direction of travel, along with numerous items she assumed detailed future weather including humidity and allergy levels also accompanied the readout.

Her mouth fell open. "How's that possible?"

"Was it when you harnessed my weapon?" Clint peeked over his shoulder at her.

"No, I was warm before I did that."

"Have you ever been warm when you healed anyone?" Ben's first two fingers compressed down on her pulse.

"No, but I've never activated the shield for that long before." She took a bite of her sandwich, washing it down with another swig of water. She fanned herself with her napkin. It did nothing to cool down the interior of the car. She raised her face to the open window. The fine small hairs that escaped the braid she twisted her hair into before they left tickled her skin on her face.

Casey swallowed the bite of sandwich. "Why did those men sound like they were from the US?"

"They attracted the good ole boys from the southern states to join the Monarchs. They chose people who had past run-ins with police agencies and who didn't agree with the government and the direction it was taking this country. Using social media apps where they flaunted their hatred of anyone in authority, made it easy to find loyal followers. The individuals who got a power trip hurting and killing others were made lieutenants over squadrons of the homegrown boys." Clint's eyes bore into hers through the mirror perched on the windshield.

"Wait, those men aided a terrorist group to take over and destroy half of this nation?" Casey balled her hands into fists.

"Sorry to say, but they aided the Monarchs' infiltration to overrun this country." Ben didn't look over the seat at her.

They rode several more miles in silence. Casey wasn't as apprehensive as she had been in the previous days, her neck muscles in knots of pain. Maybe Clint was right and she needed to see for herself what was going on. She smiled as she thought about where they were headed. It was starting to be home to her. The fact that the one Monarch didn't shoot when she put herself in between him and Ben made her hopeful that she was important enough they issued a do-not-kill order for her. She'd put herself in front of them in a heartbeat. The shield now was an invisible cloak given to them by their Heavenly Father.

They pulled into the driveway of their farmhouse, and Clint cut the engine. Doc was there to greet them. His silver hair stood out in several different directions as he rubbed sleep from his face before he took another drink of the coffee he never went anywhere without. Clint stretched, placing his hands behind his head after he got out of the car, his back popping a couple of times as he pushed his shoulder blades together. "Hey, Doc."

"We went on a food run, and there was a couple on the side of the road. We brought them back here and put them in the empty house at the far boundary of the clearing. They're really nice and grateful we found them."

Clint pinched his eyebrows between his fingers and thumb as his voice lowered. "You let random people follow you and lead them here? Doc, that's dangerous. What if they are in league with the Monarchs?"

"I think they're okay. They're really nice. Seems to me they are part of our eternal family. Just wanted you to know." Doc smiled as he ambled away.

Casey wasn't sure but thought that his limp had started to get worse. She wondered if she could heal that type of problem.

"What if they're with the Monarchs?" Casey balled her hands into fists. They barely escaped from their last location but still took losses. She didn't like strangers being a possible threat.

Ben applied a little pressure on her lower back with his hand and walked her into the house. "It's okay. I'll have a talk with them." He wiggled his finger with the ring on it in front of her face. She laughed and swatted at him.

"I say better sooner than later. We'll be right back. Ben, let's do this now." Clint slid the keys to the car across the table.

Ben kissed her on the cheek. "I'll be right back."

They left her in the kitchen peering through the window as they strolled through the yards, passing several houses before disappearing from sight. Her heart pounded into her throat when she couldn't see them. This was her nightmare, never seeing them again. She clutched at her sternum as she gulped air into her lungs. She shook the unease from her thoughts and turned on the water.

Suds danced under the faucet as hot water filled the sink when she added soap to clean their breakfast dishes and pans they used. Fifteen minutes later she finished, her fingertips pruned from the scalding sudsy liquid. A glance out of the kitchen window; Ben and Clint were nowhere around. What if something happened to them? She walked to the back porch. The day was warming up; the sun was almost overhead. Wildflowers at the border of the trees were in full bloom, the dew on their petals gone from the piercing rays of the sun that shone down through the trees, giving a hint of what lurked in the perimeter of the woods.

She sat back in a chair and propped her feet on the railing. A soft breeze sent the fragrances of the blooms into the early morning air and delivered several scents to her. Her hands rubbed up and down her arms as she shivered. Unsure what house they'd gone to, she scolded herself for not exploring the last couple of weeks. She didn't know who occupied what residence or where all the structures sat. Maybe it was time to take a tour of their community.

She hopped down to the car for her plaid top and jacket she had left behind before she started her adventure. A glance at her watch told her she had a couple of hours before dinner. There was plenty of sunlight still left in the day before it reached the other side of the grove on its way to setting. She curved around to the right, in the opposite direction Ben and Clint walked, and surveyed the land.

It looked like they lived in the last house to the east of the property. Woods blocked her view in that direction. A rabbit scurried and hopped away when she kicked through the undergrowth of the forest. A house next to the trees held Doc's car. No movement through the windows told her it was empty. Ben and Clint discussed that Doc had been treating a young girl who had bad allergies this time of year. He was probably with her.

There were at least seven cottages nestled together but far enough apart to allow small gardens for each yard.

Animals scampered through the underbrush as she continued. She wondered what all lived in the woods. Fresh foliage burst forth from the buds of new growth and saturated the air with the bouquet of nature coming to life from a winter hibernation. New pine needles had her reminiscing about Christmas. If they had been abandoned for years, there was no telling what wildlife had infringed on the farmhouses nestled in the trees. Something large scuttled to her right. She was startled, gazing into the shadowed trees, trying to make out shapes. Something large moved, dark enormous eyes tracked her. She backed up, her eyes on the animal.

The doe turned its head, her ears like satellite dishes listening and turning in several directions before she went back to eating from a bush. Casey smiled as her hand clutched her heart. She walked the perimeter of the wilderness taking her around the boundaries of the yards. This was a perfect serene cove. She hoped they got to stay.

Seven

Ben called out for Casey as he and Clint entered the house. The dishes previously piled in the sink were gone. He opened the cabinet doors to find them neatly stacked. He strolled to her room off the back of the kitchen. His soft knocks went unanswered.

"Is she in there?" Clint called out from behind him.

"No." Ben stood with the door open to her room. His heart pounded as he shut it behind him.

"Ben," Clint called from the kitchen.

"Do you see her?"

Clint pointed to the far line of the property.

"What's she doing out there?" Ben started for the back door.

Clint caught him by his elbow. "Stop."

"She's alone." Ben extracted his arm from his grasp.

"Look at her. She's smiling."

"She is?" Ben's heavy-soled boots clumped on the porch. Sure enough, she had a huge smile plastered on her face. She looked at peace studying everything around her. Her head turned in several directions as she skirted the edge of the property. He wanted to go to her and walk with her; she looked happy for the first time in weeks.

"We can keep an eye on her from here." Clint sank to the railing, hiking one of his legs up. It stretched the length of the weathered and worn rail while the other anchored him in place, his foot flat against the rotting boards of the deck. Any movement from him and the board would shift and rub against the board next to it.

Ben pitched forward, his hands planted firmly on the rail. Casey knelt; he stood ready to go to her. A purple flower twirled between her fingers when she straightened. Making it spin, she squinted at the petals before bringing the flower up to her nose.

"Do you think she'll be okay?" Ben saw Clint's mouth twitch and almost smile.

"She'll be just fine. She didn't struggle with the death today. I'm not sure she thinks about it as a life she took, but more of it as our lives that she kept safe. We're all she has here, and the fact that she absorbed the shield after Amanda's death makes me wonder if she would absorb our powers if we die. That has to be an enormous load to carry, knowing she may be everyone's last hope if something happens to one or both of us."

"I'm going to play devil's advocate; she kept us safe from the man in the closet also." Ben slumped against the post holding up the roof of the porch.

"True, but the underlying issue was not that she took a life but the thought that he was going to take one of ours. I think she's okay though. We'll keep an eye on her for the next couple of days for it to register that she was the one who took his life today. Don't bring it up though." Clint narrowed his eyes as she moved on.

"She won't hear it from me. I'm going to start dinner. Keep an eye on her, would ya?"

"I always do." Amanda told Ben about Clint's urge to defend her as part of his place in the prophecy. Being his best friend, he had no doubt Clint would do anything and everything to keep her shielded, even if he had to give his own life to do it.

Ben rummaged around in the refrigerator and came out with steaks. He combined the ingredients for his famous marinade to soak the meat in a dish from the cabinet, piercing it with a fork to draw in the flavors. With the spices and seasonings mixed and drizzled on the marbled slabs of beef, he set them back in the refrigerator and snagged produce for a salad. With the cutting board over the sink, he kept an eye on Clint as he prepared the vegetables. He'd be able to tell if something was off by his posture. Clint relaxed and reclined back against the column as he played sentry over their Key.

Ben thought back to the first day he laid eyes on her in the sphere and how she mesmerized him. His heart raced and he remembered avoiding reacting when the other two stood with him and she appeared in the phased-out field the sphere projected. How he had reached out ever so slowly and brushed his fingers at the image of her, and to his astonishment, found himself standing in her closet as she walked out of her room.

She left the house, and a furtive glance at the sphere and the wavering light behind him made him pause on what to do and how to return to his sister and friend. He wanted to explore and find out everything about her. He dashed down the hall looking for anything with her name to let them know who she was, when he found an envelope. He fell in love with her as he read her name on the torn dirty crinkled paper as if it had been caught in the sorting machine. Her house was immaculate yet lived in. Everything had its place but not as a sterile environment in which to be uncomfortable.

Her dog barreled through the small door on the back wall, startling him. A virus wiped out most dogs in his time, and he knelt as the huge animal approached, teeth bared. His growl made Ben's hair stand on end and his gut flip flop. The sun from the front windows glinted off the tag attached to his collar with Mason stamped in the metal in the shape of a silver bone.

He said the dog's name out loud, and Mason stopped his forward approach to Ben and tilted his head, first to the left then to the right so Ben said his name again. Mason sniffed the air and backed up. After several moments, his stump of a tail gave a spastic wag. Ben held his hand out and the dog sniffed him and then sat.

Ben stayed where he was for several minutes, letting the dog size him up when Mason finally trotted over and let Ben pet him. After that, Ben was able to continue his information gathering before heading back to the closet.

He stood in front of the wavering light, not sure how he was supposed to go home. He remembered that a mere touch of the image transported him to her, so maybe if he did the same to the wavering haze against the back wall, the reverse would happen.

With a dizzying jerk, he found himself in front of Clint and Amanda. The room spun and Clint steadied him by his elbow to help him sit when Amanda almost crushed him in a hug. They dispatched the information he found to Chloe's uncle. He still remembered the delicate scent of Casey's perfume she wore that day. He closed his eyes and smiled.

Ben stirred the finished salad and plunked the bowl back in the fridge. Clint's hulking form rose. Goosebumps sprang up on Ben's arms when Clint's back stiffened. Ben held his breath and waited for Clint to move when he settled back down. Ben relaxed and peeled potatoes for homemade fries.

His mind wandered back to their encounter with the Monarchs and wondered what was visible from the other side of the shield. Was invisibility really an option for them just by Casey willing it? He wished for a more proactive relic to help defend them. What could the ring do in battle to guard the other two? Rumors of the Monarchs performing lab experiments filtered around, but nothing was confirmed. They wouldn't put it past them to release another slew of airborne pathogens. Would he and Clint be lucky enough to survive another round? And with the deadly impact the last microbes had, what could they possibly create this time to even compare to that type of carnage they dealt with in the aftermath of bacteria and viruses released the first time.

Clint veered off the railing again, his spine straight. Something caught his attention. Ben fished his Glock from the top of the refrigerator and darted for the door.

Eight

The sun dipped low on the horizon as it started its descent in the west as Casey walked at the threshold of the woods. The property was larger than she thought, and she wondered if she missed dinner. The fistful of wildflowers had started to wilt in her hands. They were too fragile this early in the season for them to last any amount of time. She let the flowers drift to the ground one by one, marking her path.

Growling to her right startled her, making her drop the rest of the flowers and they landed in a large clump toppling over each other as they came to rest in the grass. She had made a full circle and was almost back at their house. She wobbled back and her breath hitched in her throat. Teeth snapped at her from a long snout that cleared a copse of trees. A wolf crept forward; foamy saliva dripped from his enormous canines as it angled its head one way and then the other to study her. Out of the corner of her eye, she saw Clint lurching off the porch of their farmhouse. She started to turn around when Clint's voice reached her, yelling at her not to turn her back on the animal.

Ben dashed out of the house toward her with his hand around the grip of a gun, his knuckles white. She was almost facing the house, her back to the wolf. She turned and met the ferocious animal that had narrowed the gap; per Clint's instructions, she didn't turn back. The wolf matched her step for step as it reared back on its hind legs ready to pounce, the immense muscles tensed and flexed in its rear legs.

Clint sprinted toward her as she slowly backed away. The wolf snarled at her and a second one appeared behind the first one. They snapped at each other as if telling the other they called dibs and got first bite. Her heart thundered as her hands trembled. Another set of eyes glittered in the dark shadows. There were three.

Her palms were sweaty as she took another tentative step back, feeling the uneven ground through the soles of her boots. She prayed she wouldn't stumble. That would only be seen as a sign she was the weaker one between them and be the equivalent of waving a green flag for them to leap.

Clint screamed and waved his arms as he ran while Ben did the same coming around to her left. She could barely see them out of the corners of her eyes. The wolves flinched. They didn't back down but only inched forward with carefully planned strides, taking them closer to their prize. Foam dripped from their mouths as they bared their teeth almost in a sinister smile.

The middle one lunged at her, snagging her arm she put up in front of her on instinct. Casey screamed as its teeth sunk into her skin. It barreled over her and threw her off-balance. She stumbled and rolled with the wolf that had her arm clamped in its jaws. Now on her back, her head inclined, she caught the sight of Clint dropping to the ground on one knee, the other bent so his foot planted on the firm soil that the grass had taken over, and taking aim.

As the wolf dragged her around, it wrenched back, knocking her off-balance, before viciously shaking its head. Her arm snapped with the first jerk, causing her to scream. It hauled her back toward the shrubs. The second wolf snapped its ferocious slobbering teeth at her other arm but only skimmed across her jacket as a shot rang out. It collapsed.

Clint's holler seemed far away as tears streaked down, and she clawed at the ground with her left hand, trying to grasp anything to stop from being pulled into the shadowy timber. Her nails tore against the hard, untilled soil as the wolf jerked her toward a third one. Its hind leg muscles flexed and tensed as it pulled her to impending death. If the third one got its jaws on her, she would be no match against them and they would pull her into the trees that much faster. Others from the houses stood wide-eyed while Hank held an ax and ran full speed toward her. Ben and Clint gained ground.

The third wolf lurked in the shadows, as the first one still tugged her into the murky depths of the trees, as if it waited for the security of the trees before it could sink its saliva-dripping iron jowls into her. Sweat dotted her forehead. The shield jetted out, tossing the wolf back.

It only angered it. It stalked toward her again, and terror caused the shield to drop. She heaved up her uninjured arm, holding her broken one to her body, trying to keep it out of its way, when its teeth sank in again as she screeched. The third one clamped its jaws around her foot and yanked back, dragging her away. She looked up as Ben and Clint disappeared when the wolves pulled her further. Their screams pierced the air and the wolves flinched but didn't loosen their jaws.

She shut her eyes and threw up the shield, tossing them to the side, and enveloped herself in the safety within, wanting to disappear. Someone crashed through the thick underbrush to her left when there was a discharge of a firearm and the third wolf collapsed. The first one sniffed the air, blood dripped from its canines. As more crashing in the underbrush neared them, it turned and disappeared.

Hank yelled as he crossed Ben and Clint, "Where is she?"

Ben and Clint ignored him as they sprinted to Casey. Clint reached her first and yanked off his shirt, ripping it in two. He then tied it around her arms as blood seeped through her open wounds. The shield retracted and Hank's eyes bulged as Casey appeared seemingly out of the blue. Clint cleaned her arms. All her energy was spent trying to escape the wolves. Her muscles twitched from the exertion as she shook.

She laid her head back on the soft moss that crept along the ground under the canopy of the large oaks, gasping for air. Ben gathered her in his arms after Clint tied the last knot and bolted back to the house. Hank stood bewildered as Casey clung to Ben. Clint reached the house first. He pulled a chair away from the table for Ben, who set Casey on it.

Tears streaked through the dirt on her face. Clint came back in with a first aid kit. "Casey, do we need this, or can you patch yourself up?"

"Hold on." She'd rather save the supplies than use them on herself. Blue flecks swirled behind her eyelids as warmth spread down her arms, which shook uncontrollably.

Clint unwrapped her left arm; foam and spit seeped from the wound. "Flush the rabies from your wound."

"Rabies!" Dark dots bounced through her vision and the room swayed.

"Whoa, calm down, breathe." Ben held her to the chair.

"Casey, I think they had rabies, so concentrate on that." Clint ran cool water over a washcloth, letting it soak into the coarse fibers. Wiping away the blood revealed the deep, jagged puncture marks the wolves' teeth made.

Casey grimaced and snappy nods shook her hair around her as heat coursed through her. The room swayed as panic set in. Would the healing relic rectify natural elements in nature such as rabies? Rapid breaths shook her as her lungs tightened. If she couldn't settle this, would they be able to find the medicine to help her deal with this?

She bent over as tremors rattled through her body. "What's wrong with me?"

"Casey you're coming down from an adrenaline dump. Let it work through your system. Worry about the bite and what was in it." Clint hooked his thumb around hers and wrapped his long fingers around the back of her hand.

Blue flooded the kitchen. Clear fluid flowed through the gashes from the wolf's teeth. When only blood flowed from her wounds did they mend.

"Oh, gross." Casey turned her cheek onto Ben's shoulder. He cupped the back of her head and held her as he dropped a kiss on her hair.

"I think that was you pushing the rabies out." Clint nodded his head in approval and gave her hand an abrupt squeeze. He picked up the shredded material and lobbed it in the trash that was by the back door.

Ben wiped the perspiration and dirt from her face with a damp washcloth he got from Clint, who flicked the first one in the trash along with his shirt. "We need to alert the others to stay inside until we can destroy the last wolf and burn the bodies."

"Yep. I'll be back." Clint bounded through the door.

Casey stood on wobbly legs. She ripped off her torn blood-soaked red, white, and blue plaid and threw it into the same trash can Clint utilized. Ben held out his hands to help her, but she waved him off and plastered on a fake smile. She trudged toward her room, ready for a shower. The heat from the water washed away the grime and blood along with the tears she refused to shed in front of the others. She cried enough and wanted to appear strong in front of Ben and Clint, not a weak person who felt like she was falling apart with every ordeal they faced.

Nine

Ben lounged against the wall at the end of the hallway to Casey's room. His heart still hammered at images of her with the wolves' jowls clamped on her arms as she was being pulled away from him. Wolves that large were unheard of. They would have to make sure they dealt with them, especially if they had rabies. How many more lived on the edges? Were there more that were undetected with the trees as their shelter?

Clint would make sure everyone realized how important it was to stay near the houses and not venture farther than that. Even if there were just a couple more than the three they dealt with, it would take little to no effort for the wolves to overcome them all. Here he thought their worst enemy were the Monarchs, led by Satan, but he let it slip his mind that he needed to factor in nature and how deadly it could be and that Satan would use anything in his arsenal to take out one of God's children doing His work.

Clint stalked through the back door and sank into a kitchen chair. "How is she?"

"She seems to be okay. I thought they were going to tear her apart." Ben sighed.

"Me too. I've never been so scared for someone." Clint took his gun out of his holster as he rose. He pulled a case from the back of the pantry and draped a towel on the table. Ben gave him his own.

Clint worked on cleaning the guns; he hadn't done the upkeep on them in a while. The shower turned off and Ben glimpsed down the hall as the light came on and seeped out from under the door.

With the two semi-automatic handguns they carried now cleaned and reloaded, Ben pulled the steaks from the fridge and offered them to Clint to grill. He started the oil for the homemade fried potatoes and set dishes on the table when Casey finally emerged from her room. She was checking out her arm that sported a couple of dark purplish points where the wolf's canines had sunk into her skin. She shook her head and smiled up at Ben. His heart sped up; she looked beautiful. His breath stuck in his throat. His hand held the tongs for the salad poised over the bowl in his other hand.

She took a couple of strides, took the bowl from him, and put it on the table. "So, what's for dinner?"

Ben shook himself out of his reverie. "Steaks—Clint's manning the grill—homemade fries, and salad. Is there anything else you want to go with dinner?"

"No, sounds delicious." She took the trash bag out of the trash can and walked to the back door.

"Wait. Where are you going?" Ben took two giant steps in her direction.

"Just going to toss these in the trash can. I don't want these bloody shirts in the kitchen. Clint's out there so I'm okay."

Ben stood rooted in place as she scurried out the door. The sizzling potatoes in the grease reminded him to keep an eye on the food. He absently stirred the potatoes in the grease, snagging the finished golden brown ones, and added the raw, uncooked chunks.

The smell of steaks cooking on the grill wafted in with Casey when she came back in. His stomach growled softly. Casey came up behind him and slung her arms around him, resting her head on his back. He patted her hands and relaxed.

Clint came in the back door with steaks grilled to perfection and arranged one on each of their plates. Casey set the basket of fries that had finished cooking on the table. With a hasty stir of the contents in the pan, Ben then sat with the other two.

Casey bowed her head and folded her hands in her lap when Clint bowed his. "Dear Heavenly Father, thank You for today. We were able to do more testing with the relics, and You have given us another way for the relics to be a sentinel watching over us. Thank You for the heavenly warriors You no doubt had assigned over us while in the enemy's territory. Thank You for helping with Casey when wolves attacked her on our own soil here in this sanctuary You've given us. Help keep the others hidden until we're able to eliminate the threat from the dangers of wildlife in this wooded tract. As always, Your will be done and help our hearts know Your will and not stray from what You need us to do for You. In Jesus's name, amen."

"Amen." Casey smiled at Clint.

Ben nodded. He let Clint and Casey take fries from the basket. He strolled back to scoop the rest from the grease and turned off the stove. He plopped down in his chair. He sat there staring at Casey.

"What?" Casey took a bite of a fry.

"We could have lost you today."

She chewed on the rest of the sliver of potato, taking her time to swallow. "Well, you didn't."

"Why didn't you use the shield sooner?" Clint threw back.

"To be honest, I didn't think about it at first. I was skeptical it would work against God's creations in animals. Fixated on being pulled into the trees, I didn't think about it as fast as I should have. With people, I have no problem using the shield like I did today. I guess my brain didn't imagine the relics worked against nature." Casey blew out a breath.

"Okay, I can understand that." Clint went back to his steak as he stabbed a huge chunk. The metal tines on the fork scraped across the plate much like fingernails on a chalkboard, before he crammed it in his mouth.

"Makes sense, but promise me if something nature or otherwise attacks you, don't hesitate to use the shield for yourself." Ben diverted his gaze to the uneaten food on the plate in front of him.

"Deal." Casey winked at Ben who smiled and cut into his steak.

Ten

They stalked through the neighborhood to do further testing on his weapon. It had taken them approximately a week to hunt down the remaining wolves; there had been eight more. Free of rabid animals and shrouded in the trees out of sight of prying eyes, they came to the old neighborhoods as much as possible to test the relics. With the added setting that Casey enabled on a previous trip, it really ramped up the weapon's ability, and he was capable of disabling guns as well as the people holding them.

The neighborhood was unusually quiet as they edged around the corner of a house. On their previous adventures to the enemy's zone, they were able to mark the patrolled areas so they didn't venture too far into the central square of territory, where they could be ambushed. They approached from the opposite side so they wouldn't give the Monarchs an easy target.

Movement to their right made them stop mid-stride. Clint held up his hand. Dry underbrush crunched from someone on their left, telling them a patrol was nearby. It was still early enough in the morning. The sun was announcing its arrival on the horizon with hues of pale pinks and purples. Their breath hung in the air with each exhale.

More crunching underfoot alerted them that several Monarchs were either already out on early patrols or still out from the night before. Something struck Clint in the torso as he stumbled back. He glanced down. A cylinder protruded from his jacket. His vision blurred as he plucked it from his skin.

"Monarchs! Shield!" Clint hissed as he tried to turn to protect Casey and Ben. There shouldn't have been so many this far out.

He had only half turned toward them and saw they had similar cylinders piercing their skin. Ben collapsed as his eyes drooped. He tried to struggle to his feet just before he dove for Casey. She went down hard as she pulled the dart from her neck. Her eyes shut before she slumped to the ground. The shield concealed them, dissolved, materialized, yet vanished again.

"Casey!" Clint's voice faded.

The rough ground played havoc with Clint's head as they hauled him through the autumn's fallen tributes from the branches overhead, his head bouncing along the hard, unforgiving ground. He tried to lift his head, but with the effects of the tranquilizer, every bit of him was heavy. The canopy of trees was a blur above him as he struggled to focus. Leaves floated down drifting on the wind that wafted through the boughs, dislodging the fall colors as they came to rest on the floor in the neck of the woods where they would decompose and fertilize the trees for the new growth the coming season.

He listened to the men's voices, at least six separate subjects that he could distinguish. The shield emerged, causing the men to drop him and the other two, but only lasted for the blink of an eye. The men cussed, elbowed each other, and then hauled them up again by their feet and continued to a building down the street as he raised his head off the ground.

Clint targeted the men dragging him and sent a pulse from the weapon molded to his hand to incapacitate them. The problem was that the weapon didn't fire. He concentrated and tried once more only to succumb to unconsciousness again.

The next time he came to, he had rope around his wrists and threaded through chains that clanged together across a concrete floor. He groaned as his arms were hoisted above him, and with another yank, his torso lifted from the floor, putting pressure on his shoulder and wrist joints. Another tug on the chains and only his toes grazed the ground *if* he pointed his feet down.

A glance next to him and he saw Ben was already in the same position. He didn't see Casey at first but then saw her dangling on the other side of his best friend. With his palms facing each other he couldn't use the weapon if he wanted to keep his opposing hand.

Clint's mind was still foggy from whatever was in the sedative they injected. It made him want to close his eyes and doze so he could clear his head when he woke again. He knew he couldn't do that. He had to consider a way out for everyone. Ben groaned and dragged his head up, taking in their surroundings. Clint had gone through extensive training in the military to include torture and chemical agents that could be used against him.

Casey still hadn't moved. Several men filed through the door of the building and left them with only a small, skinny, rail-thin man with more grease in his hair than a car engine required and a large bulbous man who he recognized as the one who took out the kid they had left restrained to the tree just a few weeks ago.

Crates adorned one corner next to the door. They were haphazardly thrown in an attempt to pile them as high as they could while still being lazy about it. Clint looked to his right and found nothing of interest. This looked to be a catchall for junk they didn't take the time to dispose of properly. It was a dump. Something was rotting in one of the crates and it reeked. He tried to keep from inhaling through his nose, but it didn't seem to help.

"Okay, so here's what's gonna happen. We know she can cure herself. So we're goin' to play a little game. Give her a reason to cure herself and if she doesn't, then you two take the brunt of our experiment, and you will only have her to blame for it." The leader sank onto a metal folding chair that had seen better days. The legs sat precariously at odd angles, and the one on the back left seemed to buckle a little as it took his weight.

With that, he gave a head nod to his minion, who pulled a large knife out from behind his back. Twirling it against his palm on his other hand, he licked off the drop of blood that appeared showing them how sharp it was. Casey's eyes widened as he approached her.

"Don't you dare touch her!" Ben thrashed around, making his chains ring out through the cavernous room.

The leader spat a sludge of brown tobacco on the floor and smiled. "I don't think you're in any sort of position to be demanding nothin'."

The greasy-haired man approached Casey. She tried to suck her belly in and hunched her back to get away from the knife that slowly cut through the thin fabric and into her abdomen. She hissed and gasped at the blood that trickled down her.

"Now alls you gotta do is heal yourself, and we won't slice up your bodyguards." The leader's smile was not friendly. "The boss wants to find out if the stories are true and if your little injury disappears, we have our answer. Then we have a little guinea pig to experiment on and see if we can transfer that ability over to our troops. We will be unstoppable.

Casey muttered, "Father."

"Oh, your daddy ain't gonna get you out of this one, girlie. Give her some incentive." The leader tipped back on the two rear legs of his chair.

The greasy-haired man strolled up to Ben, not hesitating to plunge in the knife. Ben's scream cut short and turned into a gurgle.

Casey's cry masked Ben's. Tears marred the dirt that had collected on them from being brought here.

"Now's the time to fix yourself, and we will take him to the hospital and see if they can save him. Time's a-ticking. What's it gonna be?" The leader spat on the floor again the second spit of sludge mixing with the first one.

Clint didn't want to aggravate the problem so he worked on trying to get his hands turned to free up the weapon. The issue was that they had bound his hands palms facing each other, and it was so tight, he couldn't twist or maneuver into a different position.

Blue floated over to Ben, who was now unconscious. Casey sniffled as she squinted, the blue brightening so much that it even had Clint narrowing his eyes, and he had seen her use the healing gift often.

"Eenie meenie miney moe, which one gets another poke?" The greasy-haired one indicated with the tip of his blade, swinging it between facing Ben and Clint when he narrowed his gaze and stopped in front of Ben. "Yo, check this out."

"Wait, she can heal someone other than herself?" The leader levered himself off the chair, which tipped precariously on the front two legs as he lumbered to his feet. "Well, that definitely changes things."

"The boss will want to know about this," the minion announced.

"Yeah, yeah. Now hush, I need to think." The leader paced several feet away from them and then paced back. Muttering to himself, he took several laps.

The other henchman grabbed his knife again and with no hesitation, he plunged it into Clint. Casey shook her head and yelled no as she threw out healing to him.

"Yo, she's doin' it again." Evil trickled over his skin as the other man just laughed before jogging over to his superior.

"Well, the boss has an intriguing suggestion. Can she pass it down to an offspring? Now, wouldn't that be an unstoppable army? Men who can keep fighting and regenerate themselves and others at the same time. It will take a while, but can you imagine the implications?" The leader went back to his phone, his thumbs clumsily trying to tap out a message.

The minion and the lead terrorist huddled by the door and had an animated conversation.

Ben turned his head to Casey. Her breath whooshed out of her at seeing Ben awake. "Casey, put the shield up and make us disappear. We can't let them imprison you to use your power as the face of an entire army."

The leader spun at hearing Ben talk and faced an empty space. "What the..."

"Where did they go?" the minion shouted

The minion then approached as far as the shield would let him. Tapping on the bubble of protection, he grinned. "This could come in handy." He then took his knife and ran it along the shell before attempting to shove it through. The knife couldn't penetrate their defense. Casey appeared to alter the shield just enough for the knife to get stuck. As long as the shield was in place, they had a chance to make it out of this alive.

Eleven

Casey sweated as she held up the shield. "Clint, can you use the weapon to get out of the chain? I'm not sure how long I can keep this up. We never tested endurance and what it would do to me."

Clint grunted, his chains clanking around as he contorted this way and that, trying to change the angle of his wrists.

She tried to tune out what their two enemies were doing on the outside and prayed she could keep the shield up as long as necessary, at least until one of them could work themselves free and liberate the other two.

The lumbering boss broke out his Ruger and started firing at the shield. Of course, it did nothing but send the bullets ricocheting all over. She didn't want to let bullets hang in the air like they had in the basement when she first tested the shield's abilities.

Clint struggled when Ben started shifting his hands and wriggling his wrists.

"Clint, are you making any progress?" Ben grunted when he swiveled his hand around.

"Maybe...hold on," Clint grumbled as they heard a pop.

"Did you just break your hand?" Casey cringed before involuntarily shivering at the thought.

Clint whooshed out a long slow, pained exhale as his left hand sat at an odd angle but still restrained. "Not on purpose. Man, that hurts."

Casey blew out a breath as she mended his bones. His hand shifted back to its normal position. Meanwhile, the two outside hammered away at the shield. As they were unable to penetrate the safety it gave the prisoners, Casey, Ben, and Clint had a respite from further torture while they worked on their escape.

"Father, we need you." Ben eyed Casey as moisture dotted her head and neck. She tried to smile at him but knew it came out more like a scowl.

"Hang on, my children."

They exchanged a look, having all heard the same thing.

Casey shook as they waited for their Father's timing. Closing her eyes, she let out a shaky breath and concentrated on the shield.

A boom of thunder echoed in the distance. The men's yells and screams of frustration at being on the other side of the shield filled the cavernous warehouse. They were loud enough to drown out the thunder that rumbled closer with each call of its impending arrival.

"I can't think with all that noise. If only the shield had a noise dampener." Ben chuckled, trying to make light of their situation even though it wasn't funny.

The deafening silence that filled the space brought all their heads up. Their gaze darting between the three of them would have made them laugh if they weren't in such a predicament.

"Casey, did you?" Clint arched his eyebrow.

"Not intentionally." Thunder drowned out her last word.

Lightning lit up the spaces between the bent sheets of metal that they considered a roof. Thunder so loud it shook the sides of the building made the men cower and raise their hands over their heads while the three of them looked on.

Bright white light lit the ceiling and coursed through the chains that held them, and turned the shield clear, letting their enemy see them. The metal links became white-hot, and each link stretched out so they were slowly lowered to the ground. Casey immediately fell over to her side as Ben tugged at the metal clamped at his feet.

With Clint's hands now free, he leveled the weapon toward the bindings at his feet when he remembered to change the setting. The weapon glowed and changed itself before Clint could adjust it. Frowning, he concentrated on the stun level, and it synchronized to the correct one. A smile erupted across his face as he once again willed the change with his mind. Red flowed from the weapon and disintegrated the chain at his feet as he balanced precariously to keep from falling over. He quickly unshackled his ankles.

Clint had Ben and Casey free in a matter of moments. The boss was yelling into his radio for backup and shouted that the prisoners were not to be allowed to escape. He ordered his team to kill the two men if they had to but to keep the girl alive for their leader.

"Casey, maintain the shield where it is while we head to the back door. Then, once we are outside, we can retract it back to us and make it invisible so they won't have a clue where we are." Clint snagged a knife off the floor. Their firearms were not in sight, and they couldn't take the time to search for them.

She nodded as they approached the door and only focused over her shoulder once, to confirm the shield's placement and the location of the two fools hammering on it with their hands, unable to stop them from leaving.

Once outside with the door closed, she pulled back the shield so it surrounded the three of them. "Let's get out of here."

Clint started off at a slow jog with Casey between him and Ben.

After several minutes, she saw Clint crouch down by a building and gesture for them to get down also. She inched forward and saw that their car was surrounded by six Monarchs.

"How far away are we? Can we walk?" Casey didn't want to get into a scuffle with the sentries who guarded their getaway. She placed her hand on her stomach and pulled it away. She was concerned with the amount of blood she saw. If she healed herself, would she stay awake in case Ben or Clint needed her healing ability or even the shield? She chose to leave her injuries as they were until they were clear. Lapsing into unconsciousness was not an option, especially with how drowsy she felt now. If she closed her wounds, the darkness that wanted to pull her under would win and the shield would drop, leaving the two men with her unguarded. That wasn't a chance she was willing to take. Her injuries could wait.

Clint skirted around the building and took them through the woodland section. "We have several miles we'll need to walk before we get close. I'm not sure if we will get there before nightfall."

"I'm good with that. We can take breaks now and again if any of us need to." Ben clasped his hand on Casey's shoulder and gave it a gentle squeeze. "Babe, you're feverish. Clint, do you think we are good to drop the shield? I'm concerned with how high her temp is."

Clint surveyed the parcel of land surrounding them and tipped his head, listening. "I think we're good for now. Casey, heal yourself."

Casey dropped the shield with a sigh and relished the cool breeze that was almost brisk, blowing across her skin causing it to pebble immediately. She just then realized that the breeze hadn't penetrated the shield. When she thought back to the other times they were hunkered down under it, she realized that no air seemed to have been dispersed in it either. If there was another attack with biological agents, could the shield be used to keep those small particles from getting in and infecting them? "I'm concerned it will drain me too much. What if one of you needs me again? I think the bleeding has slowed down."

"We'll be okay. Just take care of yourself, baby." Ben edged toward her.

Casey dropped her eyelids and willed the cut to close but not mend completely. She could worry about that later, after she rested.

They hustled over two more streets and entered another batch of timber. Nothing could be seen or heard. Her heart finally slowed and beat at a normal pace. She couldn't wait to get back to their new homes. She felt safe there.

Movement up ahead had her skidding to a stop as two Monarchs appeared from behind a fence and opened fire before she could get the shield up.

Ben surged to her side when more than one bullet punctured her thigh. Clint fired at the men with his relic and took them both out so they would never be a threat to anyone else.

"Casey, open your eyes." Ben ran his hands over her body. He held them up, showing the blood from her leg.

"She can't put up the shield if she isn't conscious." Clint scanned the area.

Ben earned a groan when he put pressure on her leg. "I know that."

"Ben, are you hit?" Clint did a cursory exam of both of them.

"I'm fine." Ben swung her up in his arms and followed Clint at a fast clip.

Twelve

Clint sighed as the last of the patrols dwindled down to nothing and nodded to Ben. His friend pulled Casey's unconscious form in, holding her tight as they stayed to the shadows and worked their way out of the neighborhood. They wouldn't come back. They'd had several successful missions coming out here to learn about their weapons and what they were capable of. It was invaluable, but after this, it wasn't worth it. The intelligence they were able to send back to the military—a headcount of the enemy and their weapons—gave them an edge.

Yes, they had all survived, but he wouldn't put her in danger again. They would find another way to neutralize the Monarchs than slowly dwindling their numbers by taking out the perimeter guards on patrols here and there.

Ben stumbled but quickly got his feet under him again so he didn't go down. He didn't say a word.

Clint couldn't count the times they made it to the Monarchs territory and wreaked havoc with them. They had never come across this kind of trouble the last few times they hunted in the neighborhoods. A few stragglers on the border of the territory that the Monarchs had claimed, was all they ever encountered.

It was like they had intel when they would be there and planned a detailed ambush. This was not the Monarchs' style. They went in guns blazing and didn't think about casualties, using the mentality that the more destruction they caused the better. This was organized and well-thought-out. It was as if they had inside information. The Monarchs now knew about the shield but wouldn't be able to describe it or know how to get around it.

They crossed over into a sparsely housed residential section. Discarded towels, sheets, and other bits of laundry dangled from trees in a backyard they crossed through. Clint stopped to tear several down and ripped them into strips. Ben set Casey on the ground and put pressure on the wound as Clint tied and covered them.

Her leg was a mess as they folded one towel a few times over before tying several strips of a torn one around that. They discovered a bullet wound in her shoulder, but it wasn't as bad as her leg. The miles they had to go would be hard. The temperatures plummeted. Their jackets were not thick enough to keep the cold from leaching in and chilling them. Their fingers were numb; soon it crept up their arms.

Clint had to help Ben stand when he tried a second time and almost faltered. He grabbed him by the elbow and waited until he was steady on his feet before releasing his hold. Sweat dripped and dotted his brow. In these temperatures, none of them should have been sweating.

Clint stopped and turned a full three-sixty degrees, taking in their surroundings when Ben stumbled for the third time. They would bed down for the night, but he wanted to be a little farther away from the Monarchs' territory before they attempted this. None of the houses were inhabited. This was one of the first overrun areas when the Monarchs first occupied this region. Getting past these residences before finding a place to stop for the night was a priority. Traversing several miles would be necessary to separate them from the Monarchs. He didn't want to be in proximity to their new lodgings.

Ben slowed down as they crossed over fields, his breath sawed in and out much louder than it had when they started out.

"Give her to me." Clint held out his arms.

"No, I got her." Ben rearranged Casey in his arms again as beads of perspiration dripped from his forehead, and a grimace marred his features.

"We can make better time if we take turns. Come on, give her to me." Clint edged closer.

Ben reluctantly passed Casey over to Clint, who shuffled her in his arms for a more secure hold and took off. They made good time as they crossed fields, wooded areas, and roads. Over an hour later, they came to a shack nestled in overgrowth that was still in Monarch territory. Clint passed Casey back over to Ben, who almost let her slip out of his arms, and keyed up his weapon. He didn't say anything about the cold that seeped from Casey's lifeless body. She lost too much blood, and he wouldn't be able to do anything for her unless she harnessed the relic's healing.

A yellow orb sailed out of Ben's ring, lighting the way as Clint pushed the door back on its unoiled hinges that screeched and groaned. They both stopped as the yellow light illuminated the interior.

"Ben?" Clint scanned the building and their surroundings.

"Don't ask me. Didn't know it could do that." Ben jostled Casey higher in his arms, tightening his grip.

"Well, that's new." Clint paced inside and nodded that the shack was clear.

They secured the door behind them, and yellow orbs lit the room. Clint loaded the fireplace and made sure the flue was open. The dry, brittle kindling ignited when Clint guided a pulse at it. Flames licked and soon embers were glowing as the heat overflowed from the fireplace into the shack. Crackles and pops exploded in the air as the blaze disturbed the silence in the deserted cabin.

Casey shook in Ben's arms. Clint chucked more logs on the fire. They thudded against each other before settling on the molten embers collecting at the base of the grate. Hypothermia set in as Casey's body temperature dropped. She wasn't able to keep herself warm, and he stole a glance at Ben, who was not aware of the level of her condition. The shack didn't have much. A small couch with critter-eaten cushions that sank into the broken frame sat under a window across from the front door. The small kitchen was to the right of that with three cupboards over the sink and a corner log stove next to that. There was a wardrobe-style closet diagonally from the fireplace and that was all that was left. Not that much more could have fit in the structure with how small it was.

"Ben, she needs to fix herself or—." Clint slumped to the floor catching his breath. Did he dare try to give her some of his blood? When Chloe first researched her, they found out her blood type happened to match his. It was an option that he would only try if he somehow found something to transfuse the blood to her safely.

"You don't think I don't know that. Wait. What do you mean or? Or what?" Ben snagged a cushion off an old chair and gently lifted Casey's head to stuff it under her. "Hon, you need to heal yourself."

Clint rose from the floor and opened the closet. Clothes hung limply from the hangers, with a layer of dust discoloring the part of the fabric held up by the hanger. The previous owner abandoned the items years ago in a rush to escape from the pending invasion of Monarchs. He passed a T-shirt, to Ben who tugged off his jacket and discarded the bloody one before hauling the fabric down over his head. He draped his jacket over Casey as she quivered on the floor. Clint didn't miss the entry wound on Ben's chest, noticing the gray tint to his skin.

"Ben, how bad is it? You said you were fine."

"I am fine," Ben spat out, not meeting his eyes. "We need to worry about Casey. She's our priority, not me. You know how important she is."

"I need to take a look at that." Clint raised a single brow.

Ben smoothed the hair from her face. "Not now, Clint, please. What did you mean about Casey?"

"She's going into shock from blood loss. If she stays unconscious, she can't repair herself. We may need to take a couple of measures to rouse her. Or help me find something so I can give her a blood transfusion." Clint draped his own jacket over her as he tugged on the borrowed clothing himself. He pulled blankets out of a cabinet and obscured the two windows. Two of the extra blankets he draped over

Casey. Then he sank to the floor by the fireplace, where he settled a few more logs in the hearth. Ben wouldn't like the news, but he wouldn't lie to his friend about how near death she was.

Casey's pallid skin was a clear sign she couldn't make it back on her own. Mending their wounds had sucked the energy from her, and this told him that she wouldn't regain consciousness on her own. He ran his hand over his muscles, the wound he suffered, now non-existent, only leaving the shrapnel scar from the war. He met Ben's eyes, telling him he thought the same way.

"Clint, what are we going to do? She also needs water. She's dehydrated." Ben stood with a grunt and moved the blanket away from the window, showing the dirty, smeared glass panes. The moon's rays didn't pierce the night from the canopy of trees that hid them.

"Casey, can you hear me?" Clint's hand landed on her shoulder, slightly shaking her. She didn't move, even her shivering had stopped. "Casey?"

Ben hovered by Clint and pressed his fingers to her neck. His eyes grew wide. Clint moved his hand out of the way and checked for a pulse himself on her cold clammy skin.

Nothing.

Clint flipped the blankets and jackets off her. He performed a sternum rub with no effect. He placed his ear to her chest. He held her head and scooted the cushion to the side before resting her head on the floor and tilting it back. His hands navigated to her sternum as he extended up on his knees leaning over her and started compressions.

"Clint?" Ben uttered, his skin a ghastly gray.

Clint counted to himself in rapid succession as he pumped the blood through her heart in a methodic fashion. Her ribs cracked under his palms as he depressed down to reach her heart.

Ben gulped in air. "Father, please don't let her go. We need her...I need her."

Clint locked eyes with Ben as he kept up compressions. He watched him knowing his anxiety kicked up a notch that they wouldn't be able to save her. That knowledge flooded every part of him. "Look around for anything we can use to give her some of my blood."

There was a lot of damage by the wound on her leg, but he wouldn't give up on her. He was supposed to watch over her and here he was manually pumping her heart with his own hands. Ben tore through the cabinets and drawers dumping everything on the ground. The clanging of utensils hitting the floor reverberated against the walls.

"Clint!" Ben scampered over, holding thin copper tubing and clamps.

"We need something to use as needles. And find something to rinse out the tubing. If at all possible, alcohol." Clint counted his compressions.

"I found some whiskey in the cabinet." Ben set the bottle next to Clint and wrung his hands.

"Ben, the dead cacti in the window. Some species have hollow needles." Clint nodded toward the small square of glass next to the cabinets.

Fatigue started to take over; she never gave up on him and Ben. She refused to wear herself down by taking care of herself and jeopardizing them. He wouldn't let her sacrifice be in vain. They needed her; she was the one who was supposed to live.

"Clint!" Ben lurched to his side, next to where he knelt.

Ben held a Medipac kit. The cracked corners of the case told him it may not even work. If the contents were compromised and exposed, it would be no different if he used the harsh, drastic cactus needles and copper tubing. But if it came to that, he prayed she'd be able to clean out her system if he pumped enough blood into her.

Sweat poured from Clint as his breaths became louder with each minute he pressed down to keep blood flowing through Casey's heart.

"Ben, I'm going to need you to take over while I try to do a blood transfusion. Do you remember what I taught you?"

"Yes." Ben fashioned his hands like Clint's and took over as Clint sat back and fetched the Medipac. "Clint, we can't lose her!"

He dislodged the lid and blew out his breath when he saw the transfusion kit was intact. The rest of the supplies had been rummaged through, and most consisted of incomplete packs. He sunk his teeth into the plastic pouch and ripped the top open. The sterile caps remained in place over each needle. He jerked them off, and inserted one needle into his arm, followed by one into Casey's. The pump was fragile in his large hands, but he delicately worked it, pulling blood from him and sending it to Casey.

Ben kept the uninterrupted perfect pace that Clint started several minutes before. "Come back to me." Ben choked.

Clint's fingers checked her carotid. The blood pumped through her veins with every compression Ben completed. There was nothing except Ben making her blood flow. Clint bowed his head and kneeled. "Father, we need You! Let Your will be done here. First Amanda and now Casey. We are the Chosen Ones, You led us to find the relics. You brought Casey to us. Please don't let this be the end of the road for us taking back this country for You. I understand this is a war, but we can't do this without her, You made her the Key for a reason. Please tell us how to save her." Clint continued pumping the small ball in his large grasp.

Ben's fatigue registered in his compressions. This was their only hope of getting Clint's blood flowing through her veins. Seconds turned into minutes. Clint's head swam and he got dizzy, he took that as a good sign his blood would be enough to keep Casey with them. He squished his fingers down harder than was necessary, panic setting in, but still no pulse. She was ice-cold and that meant it was too late. They didn't transfuse her in time. "Stop."

"Does she have a pulse?" Excitement coursed through Ben's voice.

"No, it's too late. You can stop." Clint's head dropped forward his chin resting on his chest.

"No!" Ben continued.

"Ben," Clint hauled himself up and over to his friend, pulling back on his arms. The needle wrenched from his vein; blood sprinkled on the thin, worn planks of flooring under them before soaking in, only leaving dark oblong splatters.

"You can't expect me to give up on her!" He easily withdrew his arms from Clint's hold.

"She's gone. We need to stop." Clint's back banged against the wall, and he sagged to the floor. He was supposed to be her protector, and look at her: she was gone. It was obvious they wouldn't be able to save her even if he gave her all his blood, which he would do in a heartbeat.

Gasping in large gulps of air, Ben stopped and bent over Casey to kiss her forehead. "Oh babe, I'm so sorry." A tear fell on her cheek as he straightened up. He pulled the blanket from behind him where Clint pitched it and draped it over her covering her face.

Clint looked at his best friend. He had failed him. The room swayed from the lack of blood that flowed through his veins, and he prayed he didn't put them both in danger of dying. He looked at Ben, who lay down next to Casey, and pulled her to him, folding his arms around her. He may have taken two more people Ben loved from him. Clint knew he wasn't in a good place. Black dotted his vision as the room seemed to roll, and he slumped to the floor. Ben called his name, but his open, fixed eyes only focused on the flames dancing along the logs in the fireplace.

An image of Amanda comforted him. Light from the fire reflected from his eyes just as drab gray ebbed around his field of vision before he succumbed to it.

BEN MUMBLED CLINT'S name as he lay on the floor with his arms around the woman who was his whole world.

His heart ached as he tried to catch his breath. The shack closed in on him. Clint lay near death, close enough to Casey, their hands intertwined. He couldn't believe he was alone. His lungs seized and he couldn't breathe. Now that his adrenaline wore off, the pain from the bullet seared through him. His hand clutching at his chest as each breath he took shuddered through his body. How was he supposed to transport his best friend to Doc and carry Casey's body back to bury her?

He couldn't leave them. What would the Monarchs do with her body if they got their hands on her? "Father, please take me home. I would have given my life for Casey. Take me instead of her. Father...I can't do this. I need You, You said to bring her here. I didn't know I would have so little time with her." His words caught and became garbled in his throat.

Ben's sobs escaped. "Casey, I love you so much." Cold seeped in through his skin even with lying so close to the fire. It was then he realized he probably wouldn't last the night. A sharp ache sucked the wind out of his lungs as his eyes drooped.

Thunder rumbled in the distance.

Thirteen

An hour before.

Ben's voice sounded far away. Her head pounded and she couldn't breathe. Coldness soaked into every joint. She restored Ben and Clint so she had no reserve energy for herself. Nothingness overtook her as Ben held her.

Pressure on her leg and shoulder annoyed her, but she didn't have the strength to protest. Something tightened around her leg; she wanted to pull away. Footsteps crunching over twigs sounded in the distance.

Black nothingness welcomed her.

Loud footsteps stomped around. Light brightened through her eyelids. Heat somewhere above her head warmed her, but she still had shivers traveling over her. Something heavy pressed down on her. Ben's voice intermingled with Clint's; she couldn't distinguish between them. Everything came to her in bits and pieces

The sound of feet scrambling across the floor sounded somewhere to her right. Someone whisked off whatever heavy items were on her earlier. Crushing blows against her rib cage made her want to scream. Cold leaked into her bones as pain compressed her ribs in a steady relentless pattern. Why wouldn't Ben and Clint stop someone from hurting her? With each press on her chest, she felt herself want to scream, but she had no control over her body.

Any warmth she felt seeped away from her as she blacked out.

Pain coursed and radiated from her heart as pressure on her ribs brought more discomfort. Even her eyelids twinged. *"Father, please take me home,"* she silently prayed.

"Not yet."

Not yet? What did that mean? Pinching in her arm annoyed her. Warmth flowed from that pinch and surged through her veins. Hope in that rushing fire now kindled something deep inside. Her heart warmed as love bled over and through her.

DISTANT ROLLING THUNDER woke Clint. He cracked open his eyes and took in the scene before him. Ben's arms lay limp. Casey had tumbled out of Ben's arms and lay motionless.

Clint crawled to Ben and shook his friend's shoulder. "Ben, come on."

Ben's body was cold to the touch. He felt for a pulse and held back his cry as he barely felt the faint push of blood through his veins. He studied a single perfect bullet hole in Ben's skin close to his heart. He was worse off than he let on. Ben's parents would be devastated by the loss of both their children.

Lightning lit up the gaps around the door. He looked up but only for a second when he felt for a pulse on Casey in a last-ditch effort, hoping something had changed. Thunder rattled the windows making him jump. Lightning arced across the roof and sent static scattering up and over the rafters as thunder sounded again so loud that Clint cupped his hands over his ringing ears.

Before he could sit up again, a strike of pure energy scorched its way across the ceiling and down into Casey. Her back arched and her arms flopped to her sides. A second arc struck and lifted her body from the worn planked floor. She opened her mouth in a silent scream.

Clint shielded his eyes as blue filled the space, escaping out of the gaps in the walls, doors, and windows. He could feel himself getting stronger, his body improving from the blood transfusion and his own exhaustion. It felt as if he had slept for three days.

The light subsided and Casey draped into a pile on the floor. He scrambled to her and held her as she opened her eyes. "What happened?"

"You and Ben were shot. You...you didn't make it." Clint gulped air into his lungs.

"Ben!" She swiveled around and dove for him. His pallid skin gave away his grave condition as a wail expelled from her, unlike anything he had ever heard before.

Clint squatted next to her by his best friend. He found a faint weak pulse on the side of his neck. Casey held her hands over him. Brilliant sapphire light jolted to Ben.

Clint rose to his feet and paced as Casey kept vigil over Ben. Twelve paces to one side and then twelve back toward the fireplace. Pulses of fearfulness and hope surged through him from Casey. Hearing no movement outside kept his faith that they were still undetected in the enemy's sector.

Several minutes passed and still nothing had changed in the interior of the shack they huddled in. Clint nervously took a glimpse at his watch. What was this doing to Casey, trying to heal Ben for this long?

A moan from Ben brought Clint back to Casey's side. Pink dotted his skin as the distressing gray receded. Casey slumped over Ben as he opened his eyes.

Fourteen

An energy pulse startled her, penetrating her heart. Her eyes popped open as the shield concealed them, love washing over her. Ben's eyes met hers. He sat up and almost knocked her off him to the floor. Clint's cat-like reflexes caught her before that happened.

Ben pulled her to her feet and slung his arms around her, squeezing with his massive, strong biceps and lifting her off her feet. "How are you...you're...how is this possible?"

"Ben, you're squishing me." Casey laughed.

"I'm so sorry. You...you weren't breathing...you died." His voice cracked.

"No, I didn't. I'm right here." Casey gaped; her jaw dropped open.

"You did. And Ben almost died," Clint muttered.

Snapping twigs at the back of the structure caused Ben to rush to the window.

She touched Clint's shoulder. Relief flooded his face as he wrapped her up in his arms in a fierce hug. "I thought I lost you two." A pulse shook her as she clutched at her heart.

"What was that?" She gulped air.

"What?" Clint held her. Blue surged up his arms, stealing her energy after his attempt to give his blood for her earlier.

Another pulse overpowered her, dismay, love, relief. "That, emotions just bowled through me."

"What emotions?" Clint hardly twitched an eyebrow.

"Dismay, relief, love." She turned toward Ben.

"Um, I think that was me." Clint let go of her arms and stood back.

Casey tried to catch her breath. "How did you do that?"

"I don't know. I was so relieved you two were okay. You do that all the time to me. Were you aware of that?" Clint peeked under the blanket covering the window to the night. The suffocating dark hid everything.

"I do?" Casey put her hands over her chest.

"Yes. Usually when you're dealing with something traumatic."

"Seconds before I came around something happened. I think the pulse woke me." She turned to Ben.

Ben pinched his lips together. "I think that one was me."

"I may hibernate for a week after this, but other than that, I feel pretty good." She started to chuckle at his concerned look but stopped, unsure what happened moments before she woke.

"You were gone. You didn't have a pulse." Clint scrutinized the blue that flowed from her to him as the color returned to his skin, even though she didn't touch him. His weapon charged and sent sparks and static up his arm as if it sensed his resurgence of life.

"That explains why He said that." Casey furrowed her brow as she thought back to the voice saying, 'Not yet.' She still had more work to do for God. They all did.

"Explains who said what?" Ben flinched when another twig snapped.

"When I was laying there, I asked God to take me home." Embarrassed with her confession, she hung her head. "I heard God tell me not yet."

"Um okay, and what did you mean when you said you lost both of us?" Ben turned toward Clint.

"Why are we here?" Casey bit the corner of her mouth, not giving Clint a chance to answer Ben's question. She thought they would have made it back home by now.

"We didn't want to run the chance that the Monarchs would follow us back to our friends so, we stayed here. We took a risk that they couldn't find us. But now I'm sorry to say that I think they have." Clint took a hurried glimpse through the window, where he barely moved the blanket aside.

"I'm sorry I didn't keep the shield up. When I was hit, I couldn't deploy it. I tried a few times but I couldn't control it. What do you think the Monarchs will do with the knowledge that I also have a shield?" Casey looked down at her bloody clothing. Clint gestured to the closet.

With the door open, she selected overalls and a top several sizes too large. Clint turned his back while Ben never took his eyes from the window he was in charge of, as she changed with the closet open only enough for her to fit behind the door. She traipsed over and plopped down on the floor, rolling up the pant legs that went well past her feet. Something rustled by the door as a branch snapped. Casey sprung to her feet.

"Wait, if I can't revive someone who's already dead...how am I still here?" Casey fanned herself with her hand. The shield that kept them shrouded boosted her core temperature.

"Maybe the compressions kept you going long enough for it to work while I gave you my blood. Are we good on the shield for now?" Clint turned from the door and his hand skimmed the back of his pants.

"Clint, quit dodging the question." Casey placed her hand over his that held the blanket.

Clint's voice was thick with emotion. "Ben, I'm not sure you also didn't die. You took one to your chest, remember, but you held on so you could help carry Casey here."

Ben didn't say anything and wouldn't look at her. She wanted to go to him, but if he thought a few moments ago that she was dead, she couldn't imagine the fear he went through. She knew how it would affect her if the roles were reversed. She only had a second of thinking Ben was gone before he was revived; Ben had a lot longer than that.

"Wait, you gave me your blood? Here? How?" Casey looked at the tubing on the floor and the scattered remains of the Medipac.

"We kind of had to make do with what we found. We have the same blood type. It was all I could think of to try. It was a hail Mary." Clint didn't look at her.

She touched his arm; he had barely turned from the window when she put her arms around his neck. He held her tight.

"You saved my life." Her eyes filled at her lower lashes but didn't spill over when she pulled away.

"I think God did that through His lightning. Not sure exactly what happened, but it was as if there was a conduit for the lightning to travel to you." Clint eyed his best friend.

"What?" Casey faced Ben.

Ben's muscles tensed. "I asked God to save you and to take me instead."

"But Clint said you were shot also and you were close to death. You were lying right there. I saw you. If you were already gone, then how could you ask God to take you instead of me? That isn't how this works." Intense anger and frustration filled her, making her temperature rise.

"I don't know. All I do know is that I couldn't live without you." Ben shifted and leaned against the wall.

"You saved us back there." Clint turned back to the window changing the subject. "Why wouldn't you save yourself?"

Casey studied the floor and then eyed Ben as his eyes locked on hers. "I couldn't lose either one of you."

"Are you able to keep the shield up?" Clint interrupted them.

"I should be able to." This may be the first time she was aware that Clint didn't have a handgun.

"I'm not sure if we'll be able to make a run for it since the lightning strike in the warehouse made the shield visible to Monarchs. They may not be able to touch us, but they can follow us anywhere. Casey, can you try and make us invisible? I know seeing the diamond glitter in the shield is the way we can tell its different settings." Clint seized his jacket off the floor and offered it to Casey.

She smiled and shook her head. "With the shield up, I won't need a jacket any time soon. Are the Monarchs outside?"

"Not sure, but who else could it be?" Ben settled to the side of the window next to the door. He swept back the curtain but only shook his head.

"Maybe I should have fixed myself, but I couldn't take the gamble I wouldn't be able to keep both of you alive." Casey studied Ben's rigid, tense muscled body as he stood by the back window, his biceps flexing with anger, or was it dread?

"You should have tried!" Ben huffed.

"I'm sorry, but I couldn't. That was one choice no one would be able to take from me. It was about time someone saved you instead of you two always looking out for everyone else." She took tentative steps to him and set her hand on his shoulder.

He turned to her and swept her off her feet as he folded his arms around her, pulling her to him and burying his nose in the crook of her neck. She draped her arms around him and let him embrace her. He trembled and his thought of losing her made her gasp as it pulsed through her and almost suffocated her. How could she love someone this fiercely that it caused a physical ache? She had hoped it was the same for him. She kissed his cheek and tightened her arms. He squeezed tighter, his breath on her neck, and that made goosebumps race across her skin.

Ben finally let the tips of her toes skim the floor but didn't release her from the death grip he had on her. He drew back, cupped her face in his hands, and kissed her. She pulled from the kiss; a blush flashed up and over her and across her cheeks. Ben smiled and ran the side of his finger along her face. She leaned into him, closing her eyes.

"Try to make us invisible, babe." Ben swept her hair back.

"Here goes." She tried to shift the properties to the shield. It held no glittery tale of being cloaked.

Clint frowned. "Did the lightning change it somehow?"

"I don't understand." Casey's shoulders slumped.

Then it shimmered.

They all held their breath. The reflective diamonds danced around. Casey beamed proudly as it hid them.

Fifteen

Clint held out his hand, weapon ready to go. The fireplace cast an amber glow through the room. The darting flames licking at the logs made shadows dance across the walls. He regarded Casey and Ben. She shrugged and he beckoned her to move behind the door. Ben seized the handle and nodded to Clint.

With a curt nod, Ben opened the door. Static coursed through the weapon around Clint's hand. He eased out of their line of sight as he moved past where Ben and Casey lingered. His footfalls thundered as he stomped off the porch prior to crunching through the underbrush, snapping twigs, which sent echoing cracks around them.

"Clint?" Ben stepped around him.

"No one's here." Clint threw his hands up in the air.

Casey didn't like it. It sounded as if several people walked around when she woke up, from the jolt God gave her through the lightning. She joined them at the front. The darkness from the trees that blocked out the moon and stars crept toward them. Turning back toward the open door, she saw that the only light came from the entryway as it was backlit by the fireplace.

"Are we alone?" Ben slunk to the side and snooped around the corner.

"I've got nothing over here," Clint backed up to the door.

Casey yawned as she moved inside. The shield retracted and her temperature dipped as the cool air washed over her flushed skin. She wasn't sure Clint and Ben were right that her heart stopped. Her relic didn't work on someone after they died; she tried before. How did the healing relic define dead? But if Ben kept her heart pumping while Clint gave her his blood, did that keep it active enough for her?

"Is there something wrong?" Ben rubbed her back.

"Trying to understand how I'm here." Casey sank to the floor in front of the fireplace to get closer.

Ben draped his jacket over her. "If you think of something, let us know. I thought for sure you were gone. We did compressions for a long time, longer than anyone else would."

She sagged back into him. The fire warmed her skin that faced the flames that leaped and shimmied across the crackling, popping logs that hissed from the release of any last bit of moisture that hid on the inside. Darkness crept toward her. The slim amount of adrenaline that it took to finish Ben and Clint's wounds completely finally took its toll.

SLOW, METHODIC BREATHS moved Casey's chest up and down. Ben was mesmerized by the fact that she was still with them. *Thank you, Father. I don't think I'd survive if I lost her too. She makes my heart beat easier by being in my life, and I thank You for that. You put the most amazing, beautiful*

woman in my world. Please give me the ability to protect this gift You've given me.

Ben brushed hair off the side of her face and held his breath when she flinched. He was sure he woke her up, but she settled back into her rhythmic breathing. He was so sure she would stop breathing again. Shaking his head, he could never erase the feeling of her broken bones as he did CPR.

"She's going to be fine, you know." Clint stretched out his legs as he rested under the window. His color had returned from its previous ashen skin tone he sported when he gave Casey his blood.

Ben sighed. "For now."

"We need to get home as early as possible so I can make some calls. I want to find out how much they know about Casey. Who wants her so bad, especially since they saw how she can use her gifts on others, not just herself." Clint clenched his jaw.

"I want to destroy them, even though I know I shouldn't. I thought they would have fallen apart and scrambled back to the dark corners that people like them hide in, once Polson fell." Ben rearranged his legs, which were falling asleep, without disturbing Casey.

"The feeling is mutual. I'll connect with my contacts in the military. Whether they can share with me what they know is the question. I thought Polson was their brainchild, but now I'm not so sure. The Monarchs are becoming too organized. The ambush on us today isn't their normal tactic." Clint yawned.

"Normal tactic?" Ben was curious about what Clint noticed during their torture.

"Monarchs charge in. They don't concern themselves with casualties or innocent bystanders. They're more of the charge in and obliterate everything and everyone type of mentality. Today was a careful, organized takedown. Someone's leading them, and my guess would be it's the one who wants Casey." Clint rose from the floor and gazed out the back window.

"Anything out there?" Ben tensed. The fact that there may be a new principal player in the Monarchs was disheartening. They wanted to shut them down, not help a new leader be appointed.

"No, still looks good to me. I still can't explain the sounds as if several people trampled in close proximity."

"I heard them too. Whatever happened here was God's will, and I can't help but wonder if it is leading to a new life for us." Ben pulled the blanket up over Casey's shivering form.

They were my avenging angels marching around the cabin, keeping the enemy at bay.

A wide smile from Clint told Ben he heard Him too.

"We need to regroup as the Chosen Ones and find out what it means that people witnessed the Relics in action. At least they know to keep it a secret, because if they let it slip, it not only put us in danger but also them." Clint read Ben's eyes. "We need to find the fourth and let God lead us."

Ben thought the same thing. Would they need to examine how to find a fourth for the Chosen Ones on the parchment? Amanda crossed Ben's mind and what they would have done to her if she had been with them today. A tremor hit Casey so he stretched over for the extra blanket heaped in a ball not far from where he and Casey sat. He took one end as Clint held the other and they covered her.

"I'll stoke the fire with more from the stack. We still have a few hours before sunrise." Clint stopped with his hand on the doorknob. "Or did you want to take the opportunity of heading out now?"

"Can we keep her warm enough if we travel?" Ben transferred Casey's head, propped against his thigh, to the pillow he found earlier.

"We can wrap her in blankets and create a sling so we can move faster with both of us carrying her between us. With how much she expended using the relic, she won't be conscious any time soon. I'm shocked she wasn't unconscious earlier. She's never stayed awake that long after using her powers. It took several minutes to bring you back from the brink." Clint slanted his head to the side.

Ben nodded. "Let's move. I don't like sitting here, waiting for them to find us. If they capture us again, I'm sure they won't put us down immediately and then have their way with Casey."

"Give me your belt." Clint pulled his own from the belt loops in his pants. He used the largest blanket they found. With the belts buckled at the farthest notch, he tied the ends of the blanket through the loop. He lit the end of a long piece of tinder from the fireplace. Flames sparked at the end of the stick. He held it under the knots of the blanket. The cloth flared up; Clint stamped it out with his boot. The fibers of the material scorched into a melted mass. He pulled the belt and the knot held. With the other knot also melted together, he spread out the blanket.

Ben removed the covers from Casey and spread them on the sling. He nodded to Clint, who grabbed Casey's knees while Ben seized her under her arms. They positioned her in the sling and flipped the sides over her, tucking the ends under. Ben panicked and checked for a pulse himself. He sighed and nodded when strong beats thrummed against his fingers. How long would she need to recuperate with this round?

Clint pulled a few of the small, palm-sized stones—so they wouldn't add too much weight—from around the fireplace and stacked them on the blankets tucked around Casey. "They aren't hot enough for the blanket to catch fire, but they will keep her warm." They slung the belts over their shoulders with Casey in the perfect sling between them and started for the door.

Ben couldn't take his eyes off Casey's small form nestled in the middle of the blankets. "If she slept for two days after my sister, how long will she need to recharge after this?"

Ben waited for Clint as he studied the sky and horizon, nodded, and set off into the dark. "I think it may be a while. She may not wake before we make it back." Clint checked the knife he made a sheath for and tied it around his leg for easy access since he didn't have his belt to secure it.

Ben trusted his friend, who could find his way out of any wilderness. He wanted Casey to be in her own bed in the morning, and if he and Clint made good time, his own bed also called his name. Today was a day they would need to deal with and talk through, but their mission was to make it home, and their best military brain was leading them.

Sixteen

Shocked at the near-weightless sling Casey snuggled into, Clint's hand instinctively swept across his lower back. He hated being unarmed as they trudged through the woods toward their cove. It had been a few decades since he went anywhere without a weapon. It was part of who he was when he enlisted in the military. He was exceptionally good with sniper rifles but would give his left arm for a good handgun in any fight.

If he judged it right, they still had about a three-hour walk back to their home, and that was as the crow flies. He was unsure what the terrain would be like once they traveled further away from the suburbs that the Monarchs inhabited. Since they only ever drove there, he was sure of the general direction to head but wasn't quite aware of all the dense woods and wildlife they would encounter. If they were lucky, the woods would keep them shrouded for much of the distance they would traverse.

With the belt slung over his shoulder and Ben walking on his left, the relic was still available to defend them if it came to that. His friend rarely took his eyes off Casey in the last hour as they struggled to find good footing on the uneven, rocky ground under their feet. The last thing either of them wanted was to easily twist an ankle and go down.

He had Ben send out the orb every so often for a visual of what stretched out ahead, but then immediately stow it to keep it from view. Unsure if the Monarchs were out this far looking for them, he didn't want to advertise where they were.

"Can we examine Casey? I don't like that I can't tell if she's breathing." Ben slowed.

"Of course. Hold on." Clint set her feet down on his side and cringed at how cold his fingers were against her warm neck, while Ben kept his side up. He knew it would take a bit for Ben to not panic when he thought about what happened.

She was warm and had a strong pulse. He nodded and tucked the blanket back around her, delaying the cold from seeping in past the layers. The stones didn't retain as much warmth as they did before but were still better than the air around them, so he left them.

"Is she okay?" Ben repositioned the belt on his shoulder.

"Yes, warm and has a strong pulse." Clint picked up Casey's feet on his end and nestled the belt over his shoulder.

Ben froze and didn't move. "Listen."

"Someone's coming this way." Clint held up his hand.

"Casey, if you can hear me, throw up the shield," Ben whispered.

The shield exploded from her, enveloping all three. It shimmered on the inside, telling Clint that she had them cloaked and whoever was near wouldn't be able to see them. "Father, let this part of the shield's ability stay masked from the enemy," Clint prayed.

"Amen," Ben muttered under his breath as heavy footfalls crashed through the underbrush to their right.

"Yes, this way. I saw them moving through the trees." The end of a rifle appeared through the brush first followed by a Monarch who held it sloppily in his hands swinging it left and right to clear the plants in front of him in a rookie move.

"Well. Where are they now?" The second Monarch staggered through and leaned against a tree, sucking in air as he tried to catch his breath. Something dripped from his unwashed oil-slicked hair that probably hadn't been shampooed in a couple of weeks.

They didn't move much less breathe. Clint held his hand up and eyed the two that stood less than a foot away. Their flashlights swept the clearing in front of them when rustling to their left made them charge past the three of them, crashing through the bushes toward the unknown sound.

Ben raised an eyebrow and sighed at Clint, who held his hands palms up and shrugged. "Thank you, Father."

"Amen." Clint checked the area in advance to starting off again, this time taking extra time to not disturb anything and leave a trail that could be tracked back to their homes.

Ben readjusted the sling so he walked almost directly behind Clint. That way, they were virtually single file with Casey suspended between them. With an alert scan around them, Clint changed their heading and took them further from the Monarchs, who crashed through the trees after them.

Clint wished he could take out those who tracked them so he would have more than just the knife, but he didn't want to take a long shot that there were more than the two in the vicinity. The shield dispersed and he scanned Casey, who remained unconscious. How did she put up the shield?

The next orb illuminated her first; his heart skipped at her flushed cheeks. The shield warmed her up. Maybe deploying it every so often would keep her from hypothermia. He and Ben at least had their almost intact jackets to keep their body temperatures halfway normal.

Their first priority when they got home would be to touch base with his contact in the military to check whether they had any intel on a new leader. They could catch up on much-needed sleep while waiting for the findings. Polson was a sniveling little weasel and about as low as they come, but something bothered him about this new leader. It was a gut feeling and something kept gnawing at the back of his mind. It had to do with the fact that his priority was Casey and whether or not a child would possess these powers through gestation.

They never researched if it was an option to pass it on through her family lineage if she went back. He shook his head; he didn't like the thought that the Monarchs would imprison her to try. What if she did pass it on? The parchment said God's Chosen Ones would be anointed to use the relics. The thought that the Monarchs may raise children to use it against them made him shiver.

Clint stopped to take in their surroundings. It had been almost two hours since they left the cabin. The road in front of them looked daunting. They would need to cross it, which would make them an easy target until they ducked into the cover of the trees on the other side. The sling dug into his skin, but they couldn't stop for long. They had to get home.

"Casey, we need the shield to make us invisible." Clint stopped and put her feet down when the shield didn't appear.

"Clint, what's wrong?" Ben knelt, resting Casey on the ground, and massaged his shoulder.

"I don't like being in the wide open while someone is waiting for us to cross so they can strike. This road used to be an old highway back in the day, separating the two counties where we now stand. It is like a line separating the Monarchs' monitored areas. Once we do cross, we'll have less exposure and risk of running into them." Clint held Casey's hand while his fingers felt for her pulse.

"Casey, we need you." Ben brushed the hair off her forehead and plucked the leaves that had landed on the blankets as they passed under the canopy of trees, flipping them off her.

Clint didn't like how cold she was, but her color looked good and she had a strong pulse. With how rundown she was, he was shocked when she deployed the shield earlier and hoped it would happen again.

"Casey, we need you to cloak us. Can you help us with that?" Clint surveyed the pavement in both directions, searching for any movement to alert him that the Monarchs monitored this stretch of road.

The shield sprang out. No diamond flecks shimmered in the barrier, advising him they weren't under the cloak of invisibility. "Casey, we need to be invisible."

Nothing changed and the shield only seemed to grow brighter. If the Monarchs were out there, it would only be a matter of time before they would detect them with the blinding white light the shield emitted. Clint and Ben covered their eyes as it shifted into a dull diamond-flecked bubble, making them invisible from prying eyes.

"Let's go." Clint hoisted Casey off the ground by the knot at her feet at the same time Ben took his side.

They didn't bother with the belts but sprinted across the road and into nearby trees before readjusting, and then slinging the belts over their shoulders. Casey moaned. Clint stopped after they made it well into the foliage and set Casey on the ground.

Ben put his hand on the side of her face. "Babe?"

"Where are we?" she mumbled.

"We still have about an hour to go before we make it back to the farmhouses." Clint took her pulse again. Her skin had significantly warmed with the use of the shield and the shivering stopped.

She slurred unintelligibly under her breath.

"Casey, a little longer and we'll be back at the house." Clint smiled at Ben. "We can remove the rocks. They aren't warm anymore and may only lower her core temp." They both took a few seconds to toss the rocks from the blankets.

Ben slung his belt over his shoulder as Clint did the same. Without the rocks, Casey was almost weightless, not hindering their pace in the least. The sun lit the horizon to their east. The rays would break through the canopy soon, and he wanted to be inside before that happened. Their prolonged absence would bother the ones who hadn't been informed they would be gone for any length of time. Doc would be a nervous wreck.

They were off a few degrees, so Clint made a sharp left in the trees as the sun shimmered on the horizon. The trees cleared out and the farmhouses sat straight ahead. They had come out exactly where Clint wanted to, and their house stood in front of them. He breathed a sigh of relief as they cleared the grove and everything seemed quiet and undisturbed.

Doc sat on their front porch, sipping on a steaming cup of coffee. Clint had no doubt he had been there for hours. His eyes checked them out from head to toe. Fretful concern spoiled his normal sunshiny features.

"What happened?" Doc surged from the chair and carefully sat his coffee mug on the porch and lurched to Casey still bundled in the blankets. He eyed their tattered jackets and the blood splattered down the front of their pants that had long since dried to a muted brown.

"We'll catch you up but we need to rest. We've been walking for the last several hours after escaping from the Monarchs, who captured us early yesterday morning. We need to get Casey to bed. She will more than likely be out for a couple of days. Can you help us settle her in?" Clint clasped Doc on the shoulder and moved past him into the house with his hand hooked around the knot at Casey's feet.

"The Monarchs had you?" Doc's voice rose an octave as he tried to keep up after holding the door open for them.

"Yes, we made it out of there and really need a bed." Clint released Casey to the floor and kneeled next to her feet as Ben went to her head. They carefully unwrapped her while trying not to jar her. Doc reached for her neck when the shield burst forth, knocking him back with his feet up in the air.

"Doc!" Clint grasped his hand and assisted him to his feet.

"Now, what in pray tell is that?" Doc waved his hand at the bubble.

"That is the shield." Clint waited a second for it to disappear.

Doc positioned his glasses so they perched just above his eyebrows and squinted while scrunching his nose. "Is that what it looks like?"

"Yes," Clint popped the door open on the refrigerator and flipped a water bottle to Ben, then opened one himself and drained it without taking a breath.

Ben scooped Casey up after draining his water and started toward her room.

"Can you make sure no one interrupts us unless the Monarchs show up?"

"Oh yes, of course. Is everyone okay?" Doc shuffled after Ben.

They looked horrible and probably scary as Clint glimpsed the blood caked all over them. "We're good, for now. Can you help Ben with Casey?"

"You got it." Worry dotted Doc's brow.

Clint frowned. She witnessed everything that happened to them. He trusted she would be okay. She never hesitated to be there for them even if it meant her own injury was left untended.

"Do I need to get my bag?" Doc ambled after Ben.

"No. Casey went through a lot yesterday and died because of it, but it all turned out OK in the end, after our escape." Clint turned toward the staircase.

"Died?" Doc snapped to attention.

"We got her back...it was bad. Ben almost didn't make it but, well, as you can see, he's still with us." Clint's heavy lead-filled legs lumbered upstairs toward the bathroom.

Ben said bye to Doc after they settled Casey in her room. The tumblers of the lock slipping in place filtered through before Clint turned his communicator off and hopped in the shower. Water washed all the visible signs of the terror of the last twenty-four hours from his body. Those images would haunt his mind for years to come. His weapon flashed as the anger built. "Father, take this from me. I can't let my anger boil over, or it'll put us in danger. Soothe Casey's spirit; she'll struggle with this. Help Ben be the light in her until You come back for Your children. Please give us rest on all sides today, and send Your heavenly warriors to put a hedge of protection around us. We need rest for at least today. In Jesus's name, amen."

Clint turned off the water and wrapped a towel around himself. His hand brushed over a shrapnel wound on his side from his time in the armed forces. He nodded at Ben, who waited for his turn, when he walked out of the bathroom. He looked worn out; they all did. Clint collapsed on the end of his bed after pulling on shorts. His eyes drooped. He turned on his communicator and fell back. His legs dangled off the end of the bed and he gave into the oblivion that swallowed him.

Seventeen

The yellowed flower wallpaper still peeled at the edges. They hadn't done any repairs to the house they'd moved into five months ago. She'd slept over forty-eight hours when they initially got back to the farmhouse. She still refused to talk about what all they went through. She told them she didn't want to endure the horror of their torture again. They left her alone and told her to come to them if she ever wanted to talk.

Some of the families started small gardens, which flourished in the unworked soil. They had plenty of vegetable plants blooming, and the fruit trees planted by the previous owners had gorgeous, mouthwatering fruit hanging from their branches. Those were bowing low from the heavy fruit, as they reached for the earth. Deer had encroached and they had to preserve the fruit trees and gardens from them. The venison they were able to store and also dry went a long way for their food reserves.

Food trips would be fewer and fewer with the produce they began to harvest themselves. Along the way, they added to their numbers with stragglers they found on the road during food runs. The new additions seemed to be a good fit, as if they had been a part of the group since the beginning. Now at almost twenty-five people, they considered they were secure for the first time in a while with news of Monarchs in the area.

"Morning, Beautiful." Ben added eggs to bacon grease as she stole a piece of bacon from the plate that was already piled high. He playfully swatted at her hand with a spatula.

"Did you want some breakfast with us?" The memory of Amanda's voice echoed through Casey's thoughts.

Her eyes glassed over, staring off into space. The image of Amanda leaning against her doorframe flashed through her mind, with a pair of atrocious fuzzy slippers covering her feet.

"So, what did you want to do today?" Ben's voice sounded far-off as he eased next to Casey and put his hand on her shoulder.

She remembered the day when Amanda asked if she wanted to eat with them. It was as if she were there only yesterday. The fuzzy slippers she wore all the time made Clint laugh at her. "I've missed you."

"Casey, who do you miss? We are right here." Clint called from behind her.

Casey shook her head and the vision of Amanda disappeared, "I'm sorry. What did you say?"

Ben set the spatula down and turned her toward him.

"I must have been daydreaming." Casey shrugged.

"Are you sure that's all it was?" Clint leaned his shoulder against the wall in the kitchen and crossed his ankles.

She turned and pulled plates out of the cabinets. "Yeah." She felt their eyes on her as she opened the silverware drawer by the sink. It hadn't been the first time she thought of Amanda as if she were still with them. It worried her that there might be a hint at an underlying problem when she zoned out like that and didn't hear Ben and Clint talking to her. There had never been mental illness in her family before, but of course, there never was until the first one.

Could it also have something to do with what happened? Did the way their Heavenly Father revived them open a link to something more?

There had been no reports about the Monarchs lately. Everyone settled into life in their little cove nestled in the middle of protective timberland. They didn't broach the subject of going back to the neighborhood since their narrow escape. Could this really be where they would spend their lives? They had a great community with neighbors they trusted. Several argued the need to relax the roving patrols, and when their nightly patrols ended a month ago, not even the holdouts spoke out. Someone ran past the window as Clint was propped against the doorframe that separated the kitchen from the living room.

Doc burst through the door. "I need you at my house, now. There's sort of a situation that you have to see to believe."

Clint and Ben followed Doc through the door. Casey went to the stove and removed the skillet from the burner and turned it off. She was the last to join everyone as they gathered around Doc's house, which they also utilized as an infirmary.

She edged past people and nudged Ben just inside the door as Doc pulled a clear case over. A gray object was in it.

"What's this?" Clint bent, to get a better look.

"I wouldn't get too close if I were you." Doc crept back.

The gray object suddenly charged at the side of the case. Clint dodged back, almost tripping over his feet.

"That is the second one we've seen around in the last couple of days," Doc explained

"Why didn't anyone tell us about this?" Clint put his hand up to the side of the container.

The object slammed into the case, trying to get the hand that Clint held out.

Ben pulled her closer. "That looks like a praying mantis."

"I thought they were bright green," someone stated behind them.

"No, there are several different varieties, and looking at this one, I would say it is the spiny bark praying mantis, but that ain't no bug. That's a robot." Ben tipped his head to the right at the bug that wanted to attack Clint.

"There's more." Doc invited them to follow him to his living room, which was a makeshift doctor's office.

Mark lay on a bed sweating with hives all over his body. Soon, convulsions shook the bed before Doc could inject him with something to sedate him. Doc capped the end of the syringe. "That is the second person to be 'stung' by one of those so-called bugs."

Casey placed her hand on Mark's head. Blue flowed over the welts on his body. He calmed before the hives shrunk, becoming nothing, and Mark opened his eyes.

"It's okay. I gave you something to help with the allergic reaction." Doc arched an eyebrow at Casey.

"I just wanted to check on you, but the injection was already reversing the symptoms." Casey smiled and rejoined Ben.

A knock sounded on the doorframe of the entry. "Clint, you have a minute?"

"I'll be back," Clint whispered to Doc as Casey and Ben followed him out.

"My uncle is waiting for some of his contacts to get back with him. I think they have information from an informant they have been working with." Chloe filled them in as Doc walked up behind her.

"I know there are more than just this one. We captured it when it attacked him. Mark said he saw one by the fruit trees the other day. So, who knows how many more are out there." Doc wiped his hand down his face before shifting his glasses back in place.

"What's causing the allergic reactions?" Casey hadn't dealt with healing medical issues, but she knew hives were an imminent warning that action needed to be taken to the body's reaction to something foreign invading its system.

Doc rubbed his hand through what hair he had left. "Best as I can tell, insect venom, most likely from fire ants."

Chloe stepped to the side so Doc could join their circle. "You can tell specifically the venom used just by the hives?"

"Oh goodness no, but that outcome was the same as when he was bit by fire ants a few years before Casey joined us. The same reaction time and results. Best guess is they are using fire ant venom in the darts those darn inventions are shooting."

"Thanks, Doc. We'll see what we can find out." Clint lifted his chin at Chloe. "I'll make a couple of calls to some people I know."

This new development only told Casey one thing. The Monarchs knew where they lived. She finally slept through the night. With the last run-in with the Monarchs, her nightmares came back worse than before. The stress of having to choose which to save and which to let go latched onto her like a plague. The images of them hanging, restrained from fighting back haunted her every time she closed her eyes. She woke up in a panic more times than not. On the rare occasion when the nightmares didn't rouse the others, she hopped in the shower as if to wash the images from her mind before crawling back in bed.

The water pipes knocked loudly through the walls, echoing down the empty hallways, whenever anyone turned on a tap anywhere in the house, so Ben and Clint woke every time she did. They never said anything but she felt they kept a closer eye on her on the days she fought her dreams by herself.

She couldn't count how many times Ben and Clint ran to her room as she woke up screaming, drenched from head to toe. Dread set in until both stood in front of her, and she saw with her own eyes that they were not only living but no worse for wear. Clint told her it was PTSD, but she didn't feel that was right. Then he explained, it not only afflicted soldiers, but also first responders, or anyone who had been in a traumatic situation. People react to intense ordeals differently. One may be able to handle something that would push another person over the brink. Pain and anguish flooded her thoughts with each plunge of the knife into the two men she loved and the one she wanted to marry someday. She had to save them. She wouldn't survive if they weren't here with her. How much worse would it be to go at it alone in this world she still didn't feel she belonged in?

Okay, enough daydreaming, they would have to move again and now this monstrosity, and the fact that there was likely more than one lurking, ruined that. She balled her hands into fists and fought the urge to scream out in defiance for the Monarchs to leave her country alone and let them live their lives without manipulating every aspect of it.

Concern pierced Ben's vibrant blue eyes when she gazed up at him, overwhelming her. He sat with her for hours during the endless nightmares that were more frequent than infrequent. Clint also talked her through several bad nights when she woke in a panic; it gave Ben a break. Casey squared her shoulders and straightened her spine. Her only option was to handle this, because God put her here for a reason. So, she had to have faith in Him that He would bring her through this.

"This means we need to move. Let's pack. Whoever's done first can pick fruit and divvy up containers between the houses. We have all those bushel crates in the old storage building on the property. We can use those to transport the produce. Chloe, let us know as soon as your uncle gets in touch with you. Doc, same with your friend, contact him and see what his take is on this." Clint turned toward the insect and moved his hand to his lower back, his fingers grazing over the holstered nine tucked into the waistband. No one hesitated when Clint gave directions. He had saved their lives more times than anyone knew. The new additions in their group took their cue from their friends and trusted

Clint when he asked them to do something. Clint ushered them out, taking the case with him.

Casey hooked her hand through Ben's elbow and walked back to the house with him. As they neared the door, he muttered something about breakfast burning and ran in. The corner of Casey's mouth twitched when he spied the skillet next to the stove and the burner turned off.

Ben chewed on the grisly end of a piece of bacon. Casey poured herself a glass of orange juice and held it up.

"Yes please." Ben smiled. Casey poured a second glass and offered it to him as Clint walked in.

"Do we really have to move again?" Ben chugged half his juice. His eyes found Casey's.

Clint placed the bug on the counter and pushed it back into the dark corner. Silver eyes illuminated and shone in the dark.

"Okay, that's beyond creepy." Ben threw a dish towel over it.

"I think we have to move again," Clint confirmed.

Casey could only nod, knowing she would never be able to let her guard down with thoughts of those shiny beady eyes.

"We should pack and load up, so we're ready to go." Clint didn't look at either of them before he marched away.

Ben arched his eyebrows at Casey and left to talk to Clint.

Eighteen

Clint paced up and down the hall. His best friend struggled to come up with a solution to the impending evil that had the potential to invade their lives at any moment. It was nothing new for Clint to feel the burden was his and his alone to bear.

A dark cloud swept over Clint, morphing his features into his military face; a determined intensity made Ben glad he wasn't the target. He worked through problems in life as a military operation. There was always a solution, but not usually apparent right away what that would be.

Over the last several years, Clint had kept their small group intact from the Monarchs who had infiltrated their country with the help from the president, the man who was supposed to give his all to make the country better. Their frustrations came to a boiling point on more than one occasion as they witnessed their freedoms taken away and innocents killed in the name of power.

Clint would wear down the floorboards until he came up with a plan to keep everyone out of harm's way. The frustration when someone died clouded Ben's thoughts. Clint's missions rarely turned out different than the way he meticulously planned them.

"Did you need a new pair of shoes for this one?" Ben scoffed.

Clint stopped and frowned at him. "What?"

"Your shoes. This is a tough one if Chloe's uncle doesn't have a place for us. I was wondering if you required a new pair before you wear those out?"

Clint looked down at his feet and gaffed at Ben as he loitered in front of his room for a second, before plopping down on the overstuffed chair that seemed out of place, compared to the rest of the furniture, releasing a cloud of minuscule particles of dust clogging the already stale air.

"Ben, we can't let it get to the point that we're losing more than we're saving." Clint leaned over, resting his arms on his knees and his hands clutched tightly together.

"I hear ya, brother. It's been hard, but let's focus on today, who are still here that need us, and leave the future up to God." Ben moseyed into his room. He hung his head; he missed his sister. His neck knotted at the memory. There would never be an easy day again, when he thought about her. His parents agonized over the death of their daughter. They all but demanded Ben join them on the West Coast and leave the rest of the country to work through this tragedy and not take their only surviving child away from them. The thought of Casey, living the life she did now because of him, tempted him to take them up on their offer. His parents were adamant she would be welcomed with open arms, he dashed their hopes of joining them when he told them he had to stay and fight. He tried to explain the relics and what they could do, which only panicked them more with the thought of Ben and the Chosen Ones taking on the Monarchs head-on.

Clint sighed from the other room, jarring Ben from his daydreams. Ben joined Clint in his doorway.

"We need Chloe to touch base with her uncle. The Monarchs could surround us here. We won't be able to escape if we give them enough time to get into position." Clint rose and his eyes bore through the ceiling, no doubt praying for wisdom from their Heavenly Father as he paced yet again.

Yep, he'd need a new pair of shoes soon. Ben lay back on his bed again, leaving Clint to his thoughts, his mind a blur of a different ending if they hadn't gotten away from the Monarchs as they tortured them. His heart galloped at the thought of failing Casey. No, not again. He couldn't go through suffering the loss of someone near and dear to him.

Nineteen

She sagged at the thought of packing again. Most of Amanda's things condensed into one rolling suitcase since she added hers to her wardrobe. Casey would gather the parchment, relic cases, and other personal items into a backpack so it would be ready to go. The boards creaked as she climbed upstairs toward where they had the relics hidden. She plopped down at the desk and pulled the parchment from the tube they'd found to keep it in.

The desk shook as something bounced around the back of it. She ran to the window but didn't notice anything hinting that the Monarchs had found them. Again, something moved in the desk. At the back of the roll-top, there was a faint glow from a couple of broken fragments of the sphere. They cast an eerie light against the back inside of the antique roll-top desk, bouncing around as if an earthquake disturbed them.

She inched her way to the door when the two pieces slammed into each other and flooded the room with light.

"Ben! Clint!" Casey shaded her eyes with her hands held in front of her face.

They advanced around her and stood in the room, hands around the grip of their weapons in their waistbands. Ben turned toward her, his hand palm up asking for an explanation. She pointed around them to the sphere fragments spread out on the desk. Clint stalked over and almost glared at the dormant ones.

"Two of them glowed and bounced around on the desk." She gripped Ben's arm.

Clint extended his hand and picked up the largest section that was once the two that gleamed now merged into one. "They aren't now."

"How many were there to the broken sphere?" Casey leaned her head back to Ben.

He raised his left eyebrow. "Seven."

"Clint, how many are on the desk." Casey's eyes still held Ben's

"Six," Clint answered.

"No, that isn't right, I remember seven." Ben walked around Casey.

"There are only six here. Did we misplace one during a move?" Clint put the shard back on the desk with the others.

Casey put her hands on her hips. "No, I counted seven a few minutes ago."

"Well, maybe we miscounted when the sphere first broke." Clint left the room.

Ben followed, not saying a word but only giving her a tender squeeze as he passed. Casey turned to the desk; no, there were seven. Did they not believe her? She shook her head. Was she now imagining things?

She waited a second before she blew out her breath and loaded the relics along with the paperwork in the bag and slung it over her shoulder. She didn't say anything as she passed Clint's room, where they huddled deep in conversation, and made her way to her room.

The rest of what she owned she folded and packed away, ready to leave this worn-down but peaceful home that she would miss.

She remembered the day when she gazed down at the sphere over Clint's monstrous arms to the relic shattered on the floor in the warehouse not so long ago. She counted the shards that day, it was seven. God's number. Ben was the one who tried to piece it back together for days. He would know and the fact that he stated the same number without thinking about it confirmed she was right. They were now dealing with only six shards left of the sphere.

Over the past couple of months, she really learned a lot about Ben and even Clint. Devoted disciples of Christ, they loved Him more than anything. They faithfully followed His teachings in the Bible, and she had never seen such blind faith and devotion before. They didn't leave anything to chance. They trusted in their Heavenly Father that He'd always be with them. Ready to be martyrs for Him, they knew it may come to that in this world. Ben would think about what she said and the number he worked with on the sphere. He would try to unravel what it meant and finally admit she was right and he couldn't ignore it anymore.

They practiced daily with the relics but didn't talk about the time when they were held by the Monarchs. She became proficient with the shield and seemed able to will it to do anything she demanded it to. Ben found that the ring had also become a signal and flared to alert them when the Monarchs were in the vicinity. They escaped an old farmhouse just in time before the Monarchs surrounded it as they kept an eye on them from a distance. Clint had unbelievable accuracy with his relic and found he was about as comfortable with it as with his gun that he still wore every day. He started sending out orbs to freeze the enemy, making it impossible for them to move. Of course, there was the explosive power she had when they came face to face with a few Monarchs, and she influenced the weapon and seemed to borrow its power from Clint to save their lives.

Ben expressed concern his relic wasn't weaponized with an active power and that he wouldn't be able to contribute to the war on the Monarchs like Casey and Clint.

Casey refused to learn how to shoot. She'd rather venture out and rely on the shield than shoot someone. Clint and Ben said they understood, but concern that she be separated from them and not be able to defend herself if the shield failed, flashed across their faces. The symbols on her skin grew brighter and more defined every time she studied the parchment, and they would dull down to shadowy markings after she put it away.

Clint took the time to coach her on more intense defensive moves, enhancing her fighting skills to make her more proficient in dodging punches. Any good hit would take her down no matter how much she trained. Men were inherently stronger than women so if she couldn't defend against an attacker enough to run from a situation, there was always a possibility that she would be taken. So, they wanted her to have more than one way to defend herself.

Now that the Monarchs had witnessed the healing ability and the shield when it didn't camouflage them, they wondered if they should show anyone else since Doc had witnessed it also. Now with the added people, they hesitated with whom to trust with that important information. They decided to use their invisibility with the shield to break into the Monarch's headquarters, after they located it, and take them down once and for all. No one would know they were coming.

As Casey used the last piece of tape, there was a commotion outside of the cottage they would be leaving soon. A scream pierced the air and the hair prickled across her neck. The shield projected and barred the door to her room. She took a deep breath, retracted the shield, and sprinted through the door as the other two made it downstairs, guns drawn.

Twenty

Brandon twitched on the ground as several large praying mantis robotic bugs clamped their jaws into him. They were protected by a tree bark-looking outer shell. Brandon bled from several wounds; his hands trembled from shock. Blood splattered over the metallic creatures. Brandon and his best friend Ed had joined the group during one of the last food runs.

They both barely missed being captured by the Monarchs when they were out wandering. For several years they'd been hopping from one place to another, trying to stay one step ahead. They blended in beautifully with the group and never hesitated to pitch in where needed.

They all stopped when Casey edged closer. The shield darted out as she also projected the blue health-giving aura. The shield knocked the robots back several feet as the aura surrounded Brandon. He looked down as the wounds in his torso regenerated. Several people gasped at finally seeing the relics' power. Brandon looked at Casey and smiled. Tears cleared a path through the blood spattered on his face, as his hands fiercely quivered. He recited the Lord's prayer.

"How many are there of these things?" Casey, her jaw open, was not sure she wanted to know how they were able to fabricate bug-like robots. The bark-style body could easily make them camouflage in the forest, but with the dusting of dirt, she had to ask herself if they moved underground. "Clint, the EM pulse!"

They were crawling up the side of the shield and using their front legs to punch tiny needle-like holes in the outer shell. Their shiny silver eyes pulsed as they forced their barbed legs further into the outer skin of the barrier.

"Clint!" Casey screamed.

A red pulse slammed into the bugs, and several slithered down the shield, landing on the ground unmoving.

"Again!" Ben grabbed an ax from one of the others in the group and went to work on dismantling the ones that were knocked down from Clint's pulse.

The rest of the machines shifted, seeming to vibrate. A small rumble moved along the ground as Clint shot a static orb toward them, which electrified and froze the bugs in place. With his relic, he blasted it again. The pulse from the weapon intermingled with the orb and electrocuted the machines. High-pitched robotic shrieks pierced the air, and several people dropped to the ground curling into the fetal position and covering their ears.

The critters collapsed as the shrieking stopped. Brandon's body no longer told the tale of being mauled by those abominations, and Clint hauled him to his feet. The blue aura trickled back to Casey. Everyone hoisted themselves from the grass and several dusted themselves off. Chloe ran up, motioning to Clint.

So many of them had blood dripping from their earlobes, and they shook their heads as if they were underwater. Several yawned as if trying to unplug them.

"My uncle said they're working on gene splicing to make an army to take us out. They want to overrun the United States, but their experiments are failing, killing the men they are trying to evolve after the military raided their headquarters. They're sending in these things instead, so they don't put their own men in the line of fire." Chloe fixated on the heap of components that littered the tall, overgrown grass.

Ben got her attention by waving his hand in front of her face. "What about a place for everybody to go?"

"Oh, sorry. He has a place. It isn't far but it's only a single farmhouse. There are several bunks in the basement to house most of the people, and the main level is littered with more cots. It will be tight until he can finish his other projects."

"So, we can leave and be gone before they send any more of...whatever those are?" Clint huffed.

"Yes, everyone's ready when you are." Chloe's eyes were glued to the ground.

"We're ready now. Tell everyone to load up; we leave in five." Clint marched to the house.

Brandon gaped at them. "What about Ed?"

"What's wrong with Ed?" Clint's jaw muscles clenched as he stopped at the top stair leading to the kitchen. The door was held open, straining against the rusted spring that tried to return to its normal position.

"The others took him." Brandon's shaky hand gestured to the trees behind the last house in the row. There was an opening to a tunnel as if something punched its way through from underneath them.

Clint pulled his firearm. "What others?"

"More of those things that attacked me. They took Ed while others focused on me. We're going after him, aren't we?" Brandon jogged to the mound.

"Brandon, how are we supposed to do that?" Ben kicked some of the dirt off the side into the crevice. It disappeared into the fissure as the recess swallowed it whole.

"You have to try!"

"Calm down. Casey, we'll need flashlights. Clint, grab some rope from the shed." Ben stood guard, gun in hand, over the shadowy bleakness that became gloomier the further down it went.

Casey ran back with flashlights as Clint met them at the entrance of the cavity. Would bullets even damage those things? Ben, how are we supposed to go in after that?"

"I think we have to—"

A scream that emanated from below ground interrupted Ben.

Clint tossed the end to Ben. "Tie that around something heavy enough to sustain our weights." The rest became lost in the suffocating blackness when he lowered it.

Ben secured the end; stepping one leg over, he pulled the rope behind one of his legs and up over the front of the opposite shoulder so that it sat diagonal across the front of his torso and then across his back around to the hand opposite from that shoulder. He backed up to the pit and started to descend controlling his speed by releasing a little of the rope through his hand at a time. "Give me a flashlight, Casey."

Casey didn't move. What was he doing? This was going to get someone harmed or worse. "Ben, you can't do this."

"Hon, never mind." Ben sent out orbs that followed him down.

Clint gently pried her fingers off the flashlights clutched in her white-knuckled hands as she stared at the man who was her whole world getting ready to descend into the insect's lair. Clint dropped them to free up her hands. "I'll be down in a minute after you clear the end."

"Wait, are you crazy?" Her eyes flashed as another scream reached them before it abruptly cut off.

"Casey, we need your shield." Clint held out his hand as Ben sunk into the dank cavern to a deadly danger that could lead to his demise before they even reached the bottom to help him.

Casey gulped in air at the thought of Ben never coming back, her heart racing. She surged to the edge in three short steps. "Okay. How do I do this?" Casey asked.

"Here." Clint rigged everything as Ben had and demonstrated to Casey how to hold it tighter if she wanted to slow down. "Do you understand?"

Casey nodded and gazed through the darkness below as yellow orbs floated in the shadowy tunnel. Ben was down there alone with no backup. She didn't hesitate and edged down over the lip. She controlled her descent as Clint showed her and soon found her feet on the bottom as three orbs splashed a blinding light over her.

"What are you doing down here?" Ben barked.

"Clint said you would need the shield. Where you go, I go." Casey unhooked the rope from around her body and tugged at it, to send the message to Clint that she was at the bottom. She reached out her hand and manipulated an orb to pan across from where they stood.

Clint descended next, meeting them at the bottom. The ground trembled under their feet as loose dirt sprinkled down on them from above. Ben circled to Casey. His ring shone, their eyes met and widened; something was coming. She made the shield an impenetrable solid wall to whatever approached their location. A thud shook the tunnel. She put her arms halfway out from her side to steady herself as she squatted. They found her shield. High, earsplitting shrieks made her skin crawl as she quaked while they stood, facing the side that the shield blocked. She flinched, covering the sides of her head to block out the racket. The shrieks ceased, at least for them on the other side of the shield wall she constructed as she willed the noise to be silent. Clint signaled with his head and readied a red pulse to disintegrate the small bots

After a bit, she allowed noise to penetrate but no sound came. Casey narrowed her eyes, concentrating, and changed the shield's density to show numerous robot carcasses lying in a crumbling pile on the ground. There were no signs of life in the autonomous objects that fell in front of them. Nothing, not even a spark, that they held life. Ben waved with his hand to drop the shield. Clint readied another pulse as the mound moved, swept Clint's legs out from under him, and dragged him down the tunnel. He tried to dig his fingers into the soil to keep them from dragging him away. The pulse discharged, right at her and Ben.

Another squadron of bugs barreled over those that had a hold of Clint and tore through the tunnel toward Casey and Ben. The redeployed shield cut off Clint's scream, and their ability to keep an eye on him, as the red pulse came into contact with the shield, electrifying it.

"Clint!" Ben ran to the shield.

"Ben!" Tears welled in Casey's eyes. Would Clint die because of her?

Muffled screams and yells reached them through the shield. "Ben, move behind me." Casey clenched her hands into fists, her face flushed as the veins stood out on her neck.

"Drop the shield!" Ben refused to move.

"Get behind me!"

Ben still didn't move. Casey's frustration ramped up as she tightened her fists even more, her nails digging into her skin. Another shield created and encapsulated Ben, depositing him behind her as he pounded on the inside of his bubble. She looked at her hands and then at Ben, who was still hammering away at the other shield. They would have to discuss this development later after they lived through this ordeal.

The shield swirled until it was almost a solid mass. Blue and diamond flecks thickened and danced through the shield, intermingling with the red EMP. Ben plummeted to the ground as his shield merged with the main one in the tunnel before she screamed and flung her hands out in front of her, propelling it down the passageway.

Bugs screamed as the shield slammed into them with a crushing blow that pulverized the scales in their hardened shells. Meanwhile, Clint's weapon's pulse electrocuted anything and everything in its path. The shield was past the third set when it pulverized some more bugs that stood over

Clint, who covered his face with his hands at the impending impact of the shield.

The shield passed over Clint as it encountered the fourth pile, slamming them into the tunnel wall. Casey gasped and breathed in a lungful of the freshly disturbed, earth-laden air, before deliberately releasing it in a single loud exhale in frustration. Sweat dotted her forehead as she slowed her breathing. Her heart raced as Ben sprinted to Clint. Casey clenched and unclenched her fists. Then she bent over, rested her hands on her thighs, nodded, and proceeded to where they stood.

Clint was on his feet with Ben's help, and they both gaped at Casey, mouths open.

"How did you do that?" Clint grimaced and looked at the deformed broken left leg he couldn't stand on.

"You said it. We're the Chosen Ones. I'm sick and tired of the Monarchs trying to take over my country! And I really, really hate bugs!" She positioned her hand on Clint's chest and concentrated on his leg as blue flooded through the tunnel, swirling around them. His muscles tensed when his leg stitched itself back together. As the blue subsided back into her, he had full weight on his leg again and hopped up and down a couple of times to test it out. She glared at Ben. "Next time I tell you to move behind me...go with it."

Casey maneuvered the orbs through the tunnels. They had to find Ed and get out of there. "Which way?"

"I think he's this way." Clint started to the right and stopped in front of Casey.

"What are you doing?" Ben bumped into Casey as she stopped to keep from running into Clint.

"Casey, turn around. There's nothing we can do for Ed." Clint's hulking body blocked her view.

"What do you mean, nothing we can do? Move out of the way." Casey tried to push past Clint, who shook his head at Ben. He put his hands around her, stopping her. She dipped to the right and gazed around Clint as he started to walk them back.

There was nothing left of Ed, if that was who she truly glimpsed in the tunnel. She turned her back and took in the emptiness of the shafts. She noisily breathed in and out as the bile rose and agitated her lunch. After several minutes, her head stopped spinning. She opened her eyes to Ben and Clint scrutinizing her. Ben pulled her along.

"Let's go. We have to get everyone out of here." Casey proceeded past Ben.

"I'll go first." Clint lugged himself up one hand over the other, using his feet to clinch and push up with each pull. The muscles in his arms strained, his veins becoming more prominent. As he crested the top, Ben looped the rope around Casey's waist and tied it off with a large knot.

"She's ready." Ben held the extra slack to keep her from swinging wildly as Clint hauled her up.

Ben followed and was through in a matter of minutes. They tugged up the rest of the rope as Brandon ran to them, his shoulders slumped when Ed didn't join them. "I'm sorry, Brandon. We couldn't save him." Ben looped the rope between his elbow and hand, winding it into a bundle as Clint strode to the house.

"Thanks for trying, I know how dangerous that was." Chloe helped Doc guide a dejected Brandon to his house so they could leave for their next destination.

Ben and Casey jogged to catch up to Clint who had already climbed the set of stairs to the back door. Ben nodded to Casey's room and she sprinted down the hall. She lugged on the backpack and grabbed the suitcase she had. Once in the kitchen, she thrust all the food into a tote before Ben and Clint reappeared. Clint tipped the plates with the cooked biscuits and bacon into a container and put several bottles of water in a bag.

They pulled out of the garage as the caravan of cars from all their friends were bumper to bumper behind them, ready for their next journey. Chloe ran up to their car as they sat at the entrance to their little haven they were now deserting. Her heart thumped at the thought of running again. The small houses looked so peaceful, nestled in the grove of trees that offered sanctuary to them for at least a short time. Clint lowered the window for Chloe to give him directions to their next destination. He nodded his appreciation as she sprinted back toward the end of the line of cars.

Clint punched the accelerator as the earth erupted behind the last car. They couldn't stop or all the cars would fall prey to the bugs that emerged from the ground. They rocketed through the trees and made it to the road in a matter of minutes. Casey squinted over the back of the headrest and counted the cars that trailed behind theirs. She only counted seven vehicles in the line; there should be eight. They were missing one. She wasn't sure who occupied it. Each car had between two to four people. Her heart fell at the thought of losing anyone. Several new faces adorned their group since they left the warehouses. So many new ones to keep track of, she couldn't even begin to count how many she didn't really know.

"I see the last car. It looks damaged but they're without a doubt back there." Ben let out a pent-up sigh.

They sped through the dark as their headlights punched through fog that seemed to come out of nowhere. Casey barely made out the car behind them much less the several that lagged behind that one. She bowed her head and breathed a prayer for them to make it to the new destination. Not ready to fail someone else, she noticed a fog creep and crawl across the road as if it were a living breathing entity with paws stalking toward them. It was almost mesmerizing, Ben glanced back and she glimpsed in his eyes that he saw it too. Was this part of the Monarchs?

Twenty-One

Clint concentrated, barely acknowledging Ben yelling his name. He saw it too. This was not from nature.

In front of them, several mantises appeared that were shifting across the road. Casey put up the shield, forming it as if it were a large plow attached to the front. Clint added his weapon as they drove at them. The outer wall of the shield solidified and moved the pile out of the way and to the sides of the road, electrifying the components of the small computer systems that made them run. "How many of them are there?"

"I don't know, Hon, but nice." Ben winked at Casey.

She gave an exaggerated wink back. "Thank you, sir."

Clint smirked through the rearview mirror. His forehead wrinkled and his eyebrow twitched for a mere second when he turned back in his seat, scanning the fog that still swirled and swarmed around their car. Clint tightened his hands on the steering wheel as the mist seemed to shift and sway in front of the headlights.

Their bumper finally cleared the mist, showing the open road ahead. They accelerated into the dark to the unknown. What would be waiting for them at the end? How secure would this new location be that Chloe's uncle had for them? Would they be able to fit into that one house? There were so many of them now. How would they handle the cramped quarters before finding something better?

Even though they drove for several hours, Clint was alert, eyes ever vigilant for anything that hinted at danger. They snacked on the food from their kitchen as they drove. The dry biscuits crumbled to their laps as they ate, the bacon cold and rubbery. The food was heavy and sat like a ton of bricks. The muscles in his jaw tensed with each passing mile. He reminded himself to relax or he would be a mass of taut sore knots when they got to their destination. As the moon cleared the clouds, Clint pulled down a driveway with no end in sight. The sporadic use of streetlights this far out in the country calmed him to a point.

Unfortunately, it not only kept them protected but it created cover for the Monarchs. He didn't like running, but would rather stay and meet the enemy head-on. With so many members who were unskilled in battle, running was the only option. He didn't want a replay of another session with the Monarchs with what they went through last time.

He was there for Casey and Ben as they worked through what they endured. There was now an unspoken bond between them even though they didn't talk about it. Casey struggled with her fears of being left alone. This took her closer to that fear than he ever wanted her to be. She laughed and put on a good front, but he was afraid she hid it from him and Ben so they wouldn't worry about her. She didn't want to be a burden and bottled up what scared her.

The wall she tore down for Ben was slowly rebuilt piece by piece but not to the unbreakable structure it was before. He had faith it wouldn't be fully reconstructed with her struggle and concern for this world that they fought for. She didn't have it up because she was afraid to let them in, but that if she did, they would then be taken from her.

Headlights illuminated the enormous house as Clint pulled around the back into a rundown, battered, and weather-beaten barn with enough room for ten cars. Everyone pulled in side by side, two rows of four, while Hank and Clint secured the doors behind the last vehicle. Everyone ran to Chloe's car. It was the last in line and the one the insects attacked. Deep gouges penetrated the metal down the passenger side, exposing the inner workings of the door, while the back looked as if a monstrous dog used it as a chew toy with the small darts loaded with poison. Clint sprinted to Chloe's side and scooped her out, sinking down on one knee, while Casey went around to the driver's side. Brandon sat behind the wheel; blood caked in his hair.

Casey pushed past several people to reach Brandon and smiled. "You again."

She placed her hand on his head as the blue aura coursed down her arms to her hands. The gash in his head vanished. Clint held Chloe to him until Casey finished with Brandon. Everyone whispered and murmured between themselves. Finally, they were able to see what he and Ben had seen for the past several months after the healing relic sensed Casey and surged into her, establishing her as the Key.

Doc ambled over to Clint with several towels from his car to put pressure on Chloe's wound.

"Casey will take care of it when she's done with Brandon." Clint tightened his arms around Chloe, whose small frame was engulfed in his massive arms.

"Twice in one day. How can I ever repay you?" Brandon smiled.

Casey edged around the car to Chloe, whose ghostly pale form clung to Clint. "What happened?"

"The robotic critters linked together and formed a larger one. They then swiped at the car and the barbed feet came through the door." Clint noted the pool of blood in Chloe's lap. Not only from her arm but also from her side. Doc held towels against the wound, but she already lost so much blood. The color drained from her natural beautiful olive skin told Clint she didn't have much time left.

"You're going to be okay." Casey nodded to Clint and bowed her head.

It angered Clint that the Monarchs kept messing with people who were dear to them. He didn't care what it took, but he would stop them if it was the last thing he did.

Everyone squinted and shielded their eyes with their hands as Casey revived Chloe. Color filled her ashen skin as the wounds mended. She smiled and pressed in on her side that was lacking the evidence of the gash from their escape. Clint kept hold of her to make sure she was steady.

"You're going to put me out of a job if you keep this up," Doc joked as he checked Chloe's vitals.

"Doc, I think we need you more than you think we do." Clint let Chloe down.

"Hank, any movement?" Ben inched closer to the door.

"I can't see a darn thing; it's dark as all get out. How can we tell if something is prowling or not?" Hank shook his head.

Ben's ring smoldered as an orb raced through a crack in the door and illuminated the backyard between the two buildings as it hovered in the sky.

"How did you do that?" Doc peered over his glasses.

Clint sauntered to the window with a perfect view of the backyard that showed nothing sinister lying in wait for any unsuspecting victims.

"Just something the relic does when we need it to." Ben smiled.

Doc beamed. "You definitely need to show us what you can do someday."

Everyone tried to crowd forward to where the orb went, and Clint held his hand up to stop them. He waited for Casey as she made her way to his side with Ben in tow.

"Looks clear. We go as a group. Everyone grab your belongings." Clint wondered if there would ever be a time when he wouldn't be in awe of how God took care of His children. Every time they turned around and implored something from God, He made it happen. There had been nothing mentioned in the prophecy about an orb from Ben's ring to light their way before they discovered it at the cabin.

"We stay close. Casey, use the shield and camouflage us, so if something or someone is out there, we'll be invisible to them. We'll just pray no one saw us drive in." Clint pulled one of the handles on the large rolling doors as Ben took the other.

The shield encircled them as it reflected the surrounding areas, hiding them from prying eyes. They moved as one across the yard toward the house. Everyone stayed clear of the boundary of the shield. If anyone ventured too far, someone quickly herded them back in. They weren't sure how the shield would react if someone, not a chosen one, crossed it from the inside.

The orb lit the way, guiding them. Once at the back of the house, Chloe opened the door with the hidden key her uncle told her where to find. With everyone inside, they secured the door and turned on the lights. Blackout curtains draped over every window and door. No light would escape to alert anyone that they hid in the secure structure. The orb melted back into Ben's ring as Chloe guided everyone downstairs. Ben and Casey unloaded the contents of the boxes for the kitchen.

Clint walked from room to room to make sure the windows were blocked with the darkening fabric and the front door was secure. The house was spotless. Clint's hair stood on end as he half expected someone to walk around the corner at any time. The house was too immaculate for being occupied only occasionally. Could they rely on the fact that the person who kept these houses ready to go for Chloe's uncle wouldn't turn them in?

Ben and Clint started back outside for the rest of their personal boxes; Casey caught up and Clint stopped with his hands on his hips.

"What are you doing? Stay in the house. We'll be right back." Clint frowned.

Casey smirked and deployed the shield around them. "Really?"

He chuckled. "Alright, you have a point."

Halfway back, movement on their right alerted them and they froze. Ben and Clint removed their guns from their holsters as Clint also held up his palm toward the movement, gun in his left hand. Ben straightened; his left hand positioned around the bottom of the grip he held in his right. Would they be running again so soon?

Bushes rustled again as they shook from the movement of something behind it. Clint continued, intentionally cracking a twig underfoot. The movement stopped.

Several seconds ticked by as they scanned every which way. With a mad jump into the grass, a deer leaped out of the brush to pluck a leaf off the nearest bush to the right of them. It chewed, flexing its jaw muscles as it devoured the foliage. It angled its head their way, sniffing the air as it moved closer. Ears twitching, they turned as the deer's wide eyes took in the yard.

Ben tucked his gun into the holster that clipped to the back of his jeans as Clint did the same as if they were of one mind. Granted, they grew up together, and they moved in one fluid motion as if reading each other's thoughts. The deer stiffened and it perked up at the sound of something on the other side. Ben turned toward the dilapidated outbuilding, hand against his holster yet again, but he didn't draw it out. Twigs crunched under the mass as another deer emerged from the opposite side.

The two deer stopped within feet of them, they had no clue they stood so close to humans. Clint fought the urge to have her lower the shield for their reaction to three people appearing out of nowhere. Casey kept the shield in place as the does made their way across the field to the other side and darted through the thicket.

They smiled at each other. Once inside, they hefted the last couple of boxes when Clint stopped in front of Casey at the door.

"Do we need to talk about what happened in the tunnels?"

"Nope." She didn't make eye contact.

"Um, you took out how many of those insects with one very angry burst?"

"It wasn't enough. Ed still died and we had to run." She edged around Clint and deployed the shield.

They had to jog to catch up. "Ben, you need to talk to her."

"I can hear you." She kept her back straight and marched toward the house.

"I know you can hear us, and I still say we need to talk." Clint touched her shoulder.

She rotated on her heels to face him. "Clint, I really am okay. They were machines, not humans. Something clicked in me that you'd be okay. I can't tell you how, but something told me in my heart the shield wouldn't affect you. I was mad, furious, that the Monarchs think they can treat us like they do. This is *my* country and I'm going to help take it back. The shield seemed to sense what I wanted or wished it to do. I didn't deploy it but it was more as if it erupted from in here." Casey moved the carton in her arms and pointed to herself.

Ben smiled. "I think she's okay."

"I want to say one thing." Clint narrowed his eyes.

"What now?" Casey distributed her weight from one leg to the other until her feet were planted firmly in place, energy coursing from her.

"I'm glad you are on our side." He smirked.

Clint turned, gazing at the dark behind them. The hairs on the back of his neck twitched. He cricked his neck forward as if it would help his eyes pierce through the haunting, shadowy blackness of the fields and trees.

Ben ran his fingers against his back. "Did you hear something?"

"No." Clint blew out his breath and came face to face with Ben when he turned.

"Soo...what are you looking at?"

"Nothing, a little edgy." Clint glanced over his shoulder on his way to the house.

Casey started up next. Clint secured the door behind them once he was inside. He stared out of the window for a second before covering it with the blackout curtain, shaking his head. He nodded to Ben who gave a chin lift in response and then returned to emptying the boxes. Footsteps from the basement got their attention when Chloe poked her head around the frame.

"I wanted to talk to you three." She bowed her head and averted her eyes.

"Is something wrong?" Clint stalked toward her.

"Um, well sorta. I know you were entertaining the idea of separating from the group. I don't want you guys to leave. I would want you to take me with you. I can help. I know what the prophecy says. I know all about the relics' abilities and what they can do. Amanda and I spent hours and hours scouring all the wording. I know what it originally said and can help keep track of the new text as it appears. Maybe that will give you an advantage compared to if I wasn't with you. I'm scared to be out here in this world without you guys to watch over us." Chloe swept the toe of her left shoe back and forth across the floor.

Clint's stomach rolled at the thought of the Monarchs getting their hands on Chloe, who was still so young and fragile in his mind. She was almost half his age. "If we take you with us, that would only be putting you at greater risk of our enemy getting a hold of you. Would you really want to take that chance?"

Chloe swallowed hard and took a couple of seconds before she answered. "I just can't imagine dealing with this world without you looking over us. You're our leader."

Clint agreed with her. He would always wonder how she was. "I couldn't in good conscience put you in greater danger by taking you with us."

"That makes this decision a little easier then. After what happened today, my uncle wants me to stay with him." She swiped at a tear.

"Can you blame him?" Clint shook his head as his hands fell to his side. It wouldn't be the same without her, but he, more than anyone, wanted her away from the fighting and frontlines. She was still a kid in so many ways, barely out of high school, but mature beyond her years with everything she lived through.

"I'm all that he has left, and he thinks I'll be safer with him than out here." She waved her arm around. "I was going to argue that you could protect me."

"We could protect you *if* we stayed together, but not apart. Your uncle is right to worry. We all know how much he loves you." Clint had known Chloe since the Monarchs' first attack. She ended up in the same grocery store he, Ben, and Amanda had taken shelter in when air dispersion systems discharged the pathogens that the Monarchs had created, causing a pandemic to sweep across the East Coast.

"With what happened when we questioned Polson and now today...he doesn't want me out here anymore. Honestly, I want to go if you split from the group. I'm scared all the time. Those things that we dealt with today was one of the deciding factors. The only reason I haven't left yet is because I want to help everyone." Chloe cried as she shook.

"You can still help us when you're with your uncle. You have a way you contact him, don't you? Well, what if we use that same way to contact you? You can still help us and not be out here with all this madness." Casey draped her arm around her.

Chloe hugged Casey and smiled. "I told him that I'd only go if I could keep in contact with you to feed you information from him. He wants my help to design better safe houses for everyone here and the other groups in hiding. Since I've been out here, I can give him firsthand knowledge of how it really is. Making me the point of contact will take some of the work off his desk so he can concentrate on other things that are a little higher priority. Instead of him setting up food pick-ups and deciding which group goes to what safehouses, I'll be making those decisions now while he coordinates where they are built and furnished."

"You need to go. I don't want anything to happen to you." Casey fiercely hugged her.

Chloe slipped Casey a small phone into the palm of her hand. It was no bigger than a deck of cards. "It's a UniSat so they can't trace it. My uncle has it connected to the satellite he took over years ago so no one can find it. I love you guys. I'll pray for you every day."

A brief hug from everyone and she angled for the door. Clint's heart pinched at the thought of never seeing her again face to face, which was more than just a possibility with the lives they lead.

Twenty-Two

"No! What are you doing? You can't go out there by yourself!" Long determined steps took Clint to the front door as he held it in place with his hand.

Casey drew back. She took in Chloe, whose eyes widened. They just agreed that Chloe would be safer than she was out here. Why would he want to stop that?

"My uncle has a car coming for me. You need the other vehicles. They're going to meet me at the end of the driveway. I'll lie low in the bushes until he arrives." Chloe looked back and forth between the three of them.

"I'll go with her. I can hide her." Casey grabbed her sweater from the back of the chair.

"Oh no, you aren't going either." Ben crossed his arms and squared up to her.

Casey shook her head. "We'll be fine. If the deer couldn't see us, who else is going to know we're out there?"

"How do you do that?" Chloe frowned at Casey and Ben.

"The relics." Casey quickly stated and then focused on Ben.

"But that was never part of the prophecy. I know. I studied it for days on end with Amanda."

"Not sure but we can do several things with each one." Casey shoved her arms into the sleeves of the sweater that was too big but warm, so she kept it. "Remember when you noticed the change in the prophecy when I absorbed the shield? I think they are still ever-changing as we need them."

"I'm going with you." Ben plopped down on a chair and stomped his feet into his boots.

"Ben we'll be fine. It'll be like we aren't even there." Casey giggled and winked at Chloe.

"Well, you have to go through me to leave this house, and that ain't happening." He mock-glared at Casey and wrinkled his nose.

"Sorry. I agree with Ben. You take one of us with you." Clint blocked the front door with his muscled body tense, ready to defend his stance. There was no way anyone would get by him if he didn't want them to.

"Fine, I guess I'll *let* you come." Casey winked at Ben.

With the lights off at the front of the house Casey projected the shield around them and skipped down to the grass. Ben's ring deployed a yellow orb as they crept out into the night with Chloe, who slung a backpack over her shoulder. All she owned in the world was contained in that one fabric bag. Images of her parents, a few articles of clothing, and that was about it. She looked so small under the huge pack. It only reminded Casey how young she was. She was glad and relieved she was going to be with her uncle. She'd be safer than if she was with them.

The night was quiet. Nothing stirred as they made their way down the long driveway. Their shoes crunched on the gravel under their feet. Crickets chirped, until their loud footsteps disrupted the hum while they passed, only to resume their songs in the night. Chloe's hiccupped cries were muffled under her hand, but she didn't say anything. They left her alone but would be there if she asked them to. Casey wasn't sure how long she'd known them, but she was attached to them. Casey thought she might have a hint of a crush on Clint and was glad he didn't come. Maybe that's why he stayed back at the house. Give Chloe a clean break and let her go to her uncle without having him there as she got in the car.

At the end of the driveway, they glanced both ways. The phone Chloe gave Casey vibrated. She tugged it from her pocket and read the screen. It stated less than three minutes. Fresh tears graced Chloe's lower lashes as she looked at the screen over her shoulder. Casey gave her a huge hug and held on. She couldn't imagine leaving; she was at a young, impressionable age. She suspected she would overcome this quickly. As Chloe would still be able to talk with them and help them out, Casey trusted that would help alleviate the pain of not physically being with them.

Headlights appeared to their left. Casey withdrew the shield. "Are you going to be okay?"

Chloe looked at Casey and nodded as she steeled herself and wiped away the last of the moisture. Ben gave her a one-armed hug as a car stopped. She squinted through the window and smiled. "It's okay. That's my uncle's best friend."

She quickly hugged Casey again and then ducked into the car, giving the driver a quick embrace before they rocketed down the road. The car kicked up dust as the tires propelled chunks of gravel from them as they hit at the right angle, making them fly off to the side of the road. The bright taillights pierced the murky gloom for a second before they were engulfed in the cloud of dust stirred up by the back wheels of the car. Would they ever see her again? Casey's heart ached for Chloe, but she was happy she'd be safer with her uncle than on the front lines.

Casey should have sat down and talked to her more than just discussing the parchment and relics and translating the text. Maybe gotten better acquainted with her. All she knew about her was what others had told her. She saved her twice and never took the time to talk to her, really talk to her. She told herself that wouldn't happen again. Ben put his arm around her, and she jerked. Caught up in her own thoughts, she forgot where she was. She raised the shield and put her arms around him. Ben launched the orb again that had returned to the ring while the sedan approached.

They were one as they walked back to the house. Clint opened the front door before they even got to the three rickety creaky stairs that led up to the porch.

"Did she safely escape without any notice?" Clint's gaze darted several times to the driveway before they made it inside.

"Yes, the driver was her uncle's best friend." Casey patted Clint's arm. He peered into the night, taking in their surroundings and noting nothing was amiss.

Ben put a hand on his shoulder as he stayed glued at the front door for several minutes before locking the door, blocking out their presence to the world.

Casey held out her hand for Ben. As soon as his fingers twined with hers, while he still had his hand on Clint's shoulder, they were enveloped in the shield.

"Casey, what are you doing?" Clint's gaze darted around the house.

"I'm not doing this." Casey flinched as static seemed to flow through her eardrums.

Ben cupped his head with his hands. "What was that?"

They were alarmed by a small scraping sound. Clint whipped his gun out and took point moving around Casey and Ben.

"I think it's over there." Ben pointed toward the corner where several boxes from the previous owners sat.

A large beetle scurried out from the lip of the box where the flaps were folded over, interlocking to keep it closed tight. The sound of scraping and scratching as its barbed legs found purchase on the corrugated paper was deafening.

"How can we hear that?" Casey felt nauseous.

"Now you can hear the enemy easier."

"Father?" Clint holstered his weapon.

"I have given you a gift to give you an edge over them. Use it."

Casey's food churned in her stomach as twigs snapped through the dry brittle ground cover as something moved outside. This extra sensory ability was going to mess with her vertigo if she couldn't find a way to keep it under control.

Clint moved the curtain to the side and spied out the window. "Deer. Three of them."

"I can't deal with this. My head is swimming and my stomach is doing somersaults." Casey inhaled deeply through her nose, trying to calm the queasy rumblings in her.

"It may just take time for your body to adjust to this new gift." Clint hooked his elbow around her neck and kissed her on her head.

"Close your eyes. Try and separate out the sounds." Ben put his hands on her shoulders. "Concentrate on the bug. Block everything else out."

Casey frowned. "I hear. Everything."

"Block it out. Then pick up one sound and pull that in to you."

Sure enough, scratching came from the corner and she no longer felt dizzy. Shifting her hearing, she was able to cut off the bug and reign in the sounds of the deer eating the leaves outside. She could almost picture them standing in front of her as they chewed. Cutting that one off she zeroed in on Ben's heartbeat. It soothed her hearing the thumps. She smiled. "I can hear your heart."

"Seriously?" Clint concentrated then smiled.

Ben squeezed her arms. "Did that help?"

"Yep, it did. I'll have to practice when it gets overwhelming. My stomach no longer wants to let the food I ate before revolt."

"Come on. Let's get you tucked in for the night." Ben put his hand on her lower back and guided her to her room.

Twenty-Three

Several months had passed since Chloe had joined her uncle. The absence of the robotic bugs was a relief. So far, they hadn't found them, although they did get word from Chloe that patrols were roving farther and farther from Monarch territory.

They had traveled close enough that they all hid and didn't go outside for several days while the enemy wreaked havoc in the neighboring areas. It was only a matter of time before they hit this one. Ready to move on, they were patient with their exploits outside of the house they hid in.

The stored fruits and vegetables had long ago been consumed. Unable to make food runs, they resorted to the canned foods they had scavenged from the previous houses and other outings. People were starting to grumble and ask how they were supposed to survive with no food.

Last night Chloe gave them a heads-up that the Monarchs were back and going house to house with their bugs leading the march. Even as she sat contemplating where they were supposed to go from there, they watched over the children who played in the fields. They were going stir-crazy and needed to expel all their pent-up energy and stretch their legs. They gave them one hour to work everything out of their systems before they hunkered down again. Ben, Clint, and Casey stood sentry over the children as they played, using their advanced hearing to track the Monarch's movements.

The idea was to have Casey hide the house behind the invisible cloak, then ride out the storm as the Monarchs moved through. If they could make the Monarchs think they were gone, then that could give them the advantage of staying for a while and leaving at a later date. Another group had just received details about their next location to move to when they were attacked out of the blue and had to move. They lost half of their group before they got away.

The rumble of thousands of small robotic legs sounded to the east. It was too soon. They weren't supposed to be in this area this fast. Clint and Ben whistled to get everyone's attention.

The Monarchs were coming and not everyone was in the house. She couldn't put the shield up if people were outside. She would have to drop it every time someone tried to come or go, since only the Chosen Ones were able to travel through the shield's walls. They lived in this farmhouse, crammed in a small space. Everyone was nervous and bickered over the smallest issues. Frost now coated the ground, and the Monarchs' robotic insects were sent out on daily roving patrols to handle their dirty work.

A couple more stragglers had joined their ever-growing family. They tested the maximum capacity with the basement full. Bunk beds let them house more people than the house was originally built to support. They had moved Doc, Hank, Mark, and several of the original group to the top story to make room for the additional people.

"Everyone inside!" Casey commanded Clint. Tunnels zigzagged along the field, pushing up the earth as robots tore under the ground toward the house.

When the previous houses were being scavenged, they were able to hear the chirping sounds the bugs made, even from a distance. The chirping was making her cringe.

Everyone donned their coats in the brisk morning air while their breath escaped in small sinewy wisps of steam. A side effect, in every aspect of the term, when she kept the shield up for any length of time, her body created a fever. She chucked her coat and long-sleeve sweatshirt to the ground, leaving her in a short-sleeve T-shirt and jeans. It had taken approximately a month before she was able to get a grip on their new hearing ability. She spent a lot of time in the bathroom heaving up her meals. She had a decline in her weight and worried Ben and Clint, but after those first few weeks, she sat down and forced herself to learn how to select a single sound, silencing everything else around her like she did that first night when it was quiet and no one was talking or moving around. It was hard to do at first because of all the activity of the residents. Ben and Clint took her out and would continually talk, then stop and start again so she could get used to the normal sounds that happen daily around them. She found she was able to single out a solitary bird's flapping wings out of all the other sounds around and concentrate on that alone and follow it where it soared.

That was why they knew the Monarchs were coming. They could hear the small beeps and scraping of the robotic scales that made up the bugs' exoskeleton as they moved.

With everyone finally in the house, she bowed her head, projecting the shield to surround the entire structure as well as the roof. If any part of the roof was exposed, it would make the house vulnerable. A kid sprinted across the field; she had believed everyone was already inside.

"What's going on?" he asked.

"We need you inside now!" Casey yelled as she released the shield giving her time to also remove the fingerless gloves she wore. As she flung them away, she looked at the ground. The soft earth had been disturbed with impressions from the human feet of the Monarchs' boots. Wait, where were they though?

She yelled for Clint and Ben; who had gone in to make sure everyone was secure. They charged out the door as robots climbed out of the earth behind her. One was huge and it was mean-looking. It made her skin crawl as its red eyes narrowed on her. Was this what Chloe and Brandon dealt with, the robot that attacked their car? Spotting the smaller mantises everywhere was becoming the norm, but this one was huge. She had no clue how they got it to work like the intricate smaller versions, but this seemed to move as if it were cognizant.

With the shield over the house, she tried not to let the critter behind her distract her. She indicated to Ben at the back of the house to make sure it extended far enough so that whoever was inside would be protected. He gave a chin lift; they were good to go. The shield shimmered as the creature batted at it.

Ben took his time to find the target, making sure his shots counted. This one was worse than the pocket-size mantises they encountered. The Monarchs, mad at being exposed, were not going to stop until they eliminated everyone who stood in the way of gaining access to her. The fact that their prize specimen eluded their capture for them to perform tests on irked them to no end. The bounty on her head had been raised to such an amount they kept it quiet so it didn't tempt anyone to turn her in. The new leader of the Monarchs was bent on getting to her and making her his, for unfathomable tests that made her skin crawl.

The robot charged at the shield with Casey as the main target. She stumbled back. Wait, did that thing snarl as it clawed at the shield? It was mechanical; how could it growl? It stopped pacing as it studied her. It started to dig. Several feet down, its head thumped into the shield. The insect scrambled out. It seemed to push ever so slightly into them. Casey screamed as she held her hands up in front of her and strengthened the shield so it became a blur of color. Ben's steady shooting filled the air as Clint moved into a different position. They didn't make a dent in its scaled outer layer as it attacked the shield again. Clint launched a static pulse, and the robot only shook its head, as if the pulse was more of an annoyance than a threat. The electromagnetic hit didn't even slow it down.

Its eyes never left Casey. It tracked back and forth in front of her, glowering through the shield before it pitched forward. Ben and Clint yelled for her to run as it pushed into the shield. One barb at a time from its spiny legs penetrated so that it scaled the side several inches off the ground. Maybe they could lure it away from the house to fight it far from the innocent lives of those who hid inside. Casey was hesitant to drop the shield and run and leave their friends susceptible to the smaller versions.

"Clint, if we leave the smaller ones can get to them inside."

"Can you expand the shield in all directions with one massive shove?" Clint seemed to be working out a solution to their situation.

"You know, I think I can. What are you thinking?"

Ben joined her.

"When I tell you to, expand it like you did to the one in the tunnels and project it out in all directions." Clint worked several red energy orbs across his fingers of both hands. She had never seen him create so many at once.

Ben had a wicked smile on his face. "Oh, I like where you are going with this."

"What? What am I missing?" Clint enthralled Casey as he manipulated with ease the numerous floating static globes.

The globes took off, racing out from them, growing in mass to wrap the inside of their protective dome. Casey raised an eyebrow as she smirked. She got it and gave a Clint-style chin lift.

"Now!" Clint's red static discharges slammed into the shield that she sent far and wide from them, disintegrating the smaller bots. He then discharged several successions of pulses from the weapon at the larger one, causing static to course over the metallic body and making its red eyes glow brighter.

Frozen in place, it emitted a growl. Casey retracted the shield and sprinted across the field. Ben and Clint didn't take long to join her as the large praying mantis tumbled forward when the static fizzled out. The force of its claws dug fresh dirt into mounds as it chased after them. A growl reached them as it pulled itself along the ground with its deadly talons chasing after them, forgetting about the people inside the house.

Thunderous strides shook the ground as it hunted them before silencing. Ben and Clint fired at it and yelled for Casey to make it to the trees as it took to the skies, unfolding circuited membraned wings from its back. The whine from the integrated circuits filled the air. She pumped her arms, sprinting for the largest pine. Maybe they could escape it in the woods and find a way to defeat it, but it didn't look promising. The shield didn't keep this one out like the smaller versions. At least they could buy time for the people in the house to flee or take refuge before it made it back to them. If this one defeated them, would it return after the attack and finish its preprogrammed orders?

Clint gaped at the weapon's stone that twirled in the middle, and red staticky sparks ran over and around his hand. He skirted around Casey and slid around a very large trunk. He targeted the robot as it circled above them. Ben and Casey sprinted past him as it crested the top of the small hill they had sprinted down, sheering off the highest limbs.

A red pulse made a direct hit that seemed to slow it down as it swiped at the damage that now existed on its scales, dropping it to the ground. Clint smiled and fired again; this time he went for the underbelly where the majority of the smaller, more sensitive components were held. There was an explosion of red as a huge gaping laceration opened on its abdomen, causing it to stagger forward as electric impulses tore through the mangled circuits. Furious, it screamed and swiped at the tree Clint was behind.

Ben yelled "Clint!" as the tree splintered into a million pieces.

Clint ran to the next one, and it staggered again. It slumped to the ground and twitched as it short-circuited; shudders rippled up and down its body. They emerged from the trees they hid behind to inspect the creation that the Monarchs had sent. This one was different than the mini mantis they encountered, the scales creating an outer shell that made it hard to penetrate, which would explain why the shots Ben took at it didn't do any damage. Or the EM pulse for that matter. The fluid that ran through the working mechanisms of its hydraulic system was blood red, giving them a sense that it was a living breathing organism.

"Okay, that's my favorite setting on this thing." Clint grinned; exhilaration flashed through his eyes. He was completely ecstatic with the weapon as if he was a kid with a toy.

"Is that the setting it let me use in the old neighborhood?" Casey turned his hand over.

"Yup." Clint beamed, his smile spread across his face, showing his dimples.

"Okay, we have to come up with a way I can contribute. The orb light so we can find our way in the dark and the truth part is not going to do anything to help me be a contributing factor in this war." Ben shifted from one foot to the other.

Casey's eyes burned with silver diamond flecks as her hair whipped around the back of her head. Ben almost tripped over a root that ran along the ground, buried by fallen needles from the surrounding pines. Casey floated an inch off the ground as the shield enveloped her.

"Casey. What's wrong?" Ben moved toward her.

"You can activate his ring."

Casey smiled as she held out her hand to him. He edged closer and stretched out his to her. She nodded and he grasped her hand as the shield pulled him into the air. His ring flared as gold flecks flowed over his body and swirled around him faster and faster until he was almost a blur.

Twenty-Four

"*Help your brother and sister in Christ fight for me.*"

The glowing subsided as their feet landed on the ground. Casey smiled as her hair cascaded down her back, settling in place again. Ben looked at his ring as Clint leered over his shoulder.

"Okay, what was that?" Clint eyed them both.

"God told me to activate his ring." Casey tried to catch her breath.

"And He told me to help my brother and sister in Christ fight for Him." Ben turned his hand over, and his ring flashed.

They were not sure what she did, but they would need to shed light on the newly created options before they went back.

"Ben, do you feel anything different with the ring?" Casey hunched over still out of breath.

"A static energy coursed through me when you had me in the shield." Ben smiled.

"Welcome to what I feel." Clint sat on a fallen trunk.

"What? Are you talking about the pulses you mentioned from you two back in the cabin?" Casey faced Clint.

"Yes, you give off pulses. They affected Amanda too. That's how we knew you were the Key and you couldn't go back to your time. When we discovered that your family would be killed by an explosion, you sent off pulses while you were in your room. Amanda and I both felt them that night." Only the left side of Clint's mouth spasmed as if to smile at the memory.

"You never told me that was how you realized she was the Key." Ben's ring brightened.

"You didn't need convincing to know she was." Clint stood and signaled to the ring.

Ben made a fist and straightened his arm from his body when a gold-flecked beam shot out and disintegrated the timber three feet away from Clint, showering splinters down on them.

"Whoa!" Casey stumbled back and fell into the wet slippery leaves.

Ben moved to her as the ring returned to its normal dullness, absent of the radiated yellow flecks. "Are you okay?" He hauled her out of the slimy mess that stuck to her pants.

She brushed the wet refuse of the trees away cringing, as she walked forward to join Clint at the demolished oak. "If that's not an active weapon to use in the fight against the Monarchs, I don't know what is."

"Unquestionably a step up from the man-made guns I've been using." Ben chuckled; his eyes glinted with mischief.

Clint clasped Ben's hand in a fierce handshake and nodded. "Glad to have more help against the one that graced us with its presence today. What's up with the plates on its back? I swear they seemed to be made out of the same material as the panels in the Kevlar vests we wore on combat missions."

"That would explain why my shots didn't do anything." Ben picked at the slivers and what was left of the trunk that took the brunt of the first display of his ring's new weaponized capability.

"Come on, let's go back. We'll have to move now that the Monarchs know we're here. I think we need to separate from everyone else." Clint started to jog toward the farmhouse.

Ben and Casey caught up to him as they reached the back porch. They entered to an eerie silence. Out of habit, he reached around his back, already forgetting he had another weapon in his ring.

"Hello?" Casey's voice echoed in the kitchen.

The basement door eased open, Hank was the first one through, followed shortly by the rest. "Is it gone?"

"It's taken care of. We need to move everyone. Sam, is the new safehouse ready?" Clint opened the refrigerator and selected three bottles of water, handing one to Casey and Ben before cracking open his.

Sam had been working with Chloe before she left, and he was kept as the point of contact for the building of their safe houses since he used to be an engineer before the Monarchs. If the other group hadn't needed the last place so quickly, they would have moved there. So, now they were left waiting on the next build site.

Ben saw Casey's jacket and gloves neatly stacked on one of the chairs; someone must have gone out when they charged away from the house and brought in her outer clothing.

"We still need a couple of weeks before everything is finalized; we need to add two more rooms for the last few that have become members of our little rag-tag group." Sam smiled and nodded toward the basement and the others. "Are we good for the night?"

"Yes, we should be fine. We're far enough away that if the Monarchs tracked the signal before we disabled it, they won't be here before tomorrow afternoon. It will take them a while to deploy an aerial drone to search for where they lost the signal." Clint's toss of his empty water bottle toward the trash can missed, sailing it over the rim.

"We're packed and ready to go when the house is finished. So, I'll tell everyone to hunker down for the night. I'll make a call about putting a bigger rush on finishing the two additional rooms." Sam shuffled away.

"Thanks, Sam." Clint put his hands against the refrigerator and dropped his head.

Hank closed the basement door behind Sam. "Are you going to go your own way when we move again?"

Clint raised his head. "We are discussing it."

Hank smoothed his hands down his shirt. "Is that a good idea? Who will protect us like you guys did today?"

"Hank, be honest to yourself and think about this for a minute. Would the Monarchs follow you if we weren't with you?" Ben calmly asked.

To Hank's credit, he took a minute to mull over the question. "No, I guess we wouldn't, would we?"

"We don't think so either. That's why we're seriously considering it. The creature followed us. It didn't attack the easy targets in the house, no offense meant when I say that," Clint reasoned.

"As long as you don't disappear in the night and leave without saying goodbye." Hank let himself through to the basement.

They trudged upstairs to the three bedrooms; Casey locked the door behind her. Ben didn't move for several minutes before he lumbered into his own room. This new weapon was a game-changer. Would it also evolve as the other relics had? Now, he didn't need to stay on the sidelines and let the other two take all the risks.

He fell back on his bed and squinted at the water-stained ceiling. This was an upgrade from the first creature. The new leader had to be controlling this part of developing the monstrosities they fought. They seemed to be quickly cranking out new improved versions. Ordinarily, Clint handled the military aspects of things. He would talk with him about the fact that they may have a spy in their midst and discuss his thoughts about whether the critters were tagged and tracked like the Monarch soldiers. If so on either count, they would need to handle the infiltrator as soon as possible. They also would need to cut off letting just anyone join. It only made it more dangerous to move that many people at a time. Maybe they would have Chloe connect with the northern sectors to see if there was anywhere they could send new recruits to, to help spread them out so they weren't such a large target.

The boards and walls creaked in the house, tormented by the wind transported in by a storm. He was dead to the world before the heaviness of exhaustion crept toward the bed and his tired, sore body.

Twenty-Five

A scream ripped Casey from sorting through the symbols on the parchment. She seemed to have a grasp on deciphering what the symbols meant and sent image sequences to Chloe as they changed. She tore down the stairs almost two at a time as her mind cleared from the newest projection of the prophecy that alerted big changes coming for the Key. She didn't see Clint or Ben; her heart hammered wildly. Again, there was a scream. She darted through the kitchen to the back door; it stood ajar as the sun streaked through the doorway blinding her. She blocked the sun out with her hand, squinting as she hurried through.

Doc knelt over a woman and child. Blood bathed them both. Casey rotated on her heels as the shield covered them. Still no sign of Ben or Clint.

"Casey!" Doc yelled.

Frantic, she ran over and placed her hands against each of them. She expected warmth to spread, but nothing happened. Confused she gawked at her hands. Where was the blue aura? Casey considered Doc's face. She stumbled up and away as it hit her. They were already dead; she couldn't help someone who was already gone.

"I'm sorry, Doc I can't...they're." She choked. "Ben!"

Casey scanned all around. A bullet embedded in the shield as both Doc and Casey jolted. Doc ambled to where the bullet hung in the air. Five more hit close to the first one, and he fell back. She hurried to help him up.

"Doc. Where is everyone?" Casey hissed as her voice broke.

"Inside. These two came out after a grocery run that we wanted to get in before we moved on; they had two strangers in the car. They're inside with the others. Jeannie said she thought she was being followed but didn't think anything about it when she didn't see anyone. After we carried the food into the house, Jeannie said she had forgotten Ashlyn's favorite toy in the car. She wanted to go with her mom when shots rang out. I got out here as Ben and Clint took off in the direction of the shooter." Doc never took his eyes off the two lying face down on the lawn.

"Doc, which way did they run?" Casey spun on her heels, back to where the bullets caught in the shield. He indicated up a hill into the timberline. "Go inside and lie low with everyone else. I'm going after Ben and Clint."

"No!" Doc grabbed Casey's arm. Shocked at his strength, she took a fleeting glance; his fingers had turned white from his grip. She calmly laid her hand on his and held it.

"I won't let them be taken from me, Doc. I won't lose them." She couldn't look at Jeannie and her daughter, imagining Ben and Clint facedown and being unable to help them.

Doc limped to the house as Casey pulled in the shield. Another shot rang out, but no bullets whizzed in her direction as a shield enveloped her and conformed to her body. She ran up the hill as another bullet whizzed past her head. She changed the density of the shield to camouflage her. Her feet found traction as she traversed the incline. A male voice screamed. She couldn't tell if it was Ben or Clint, and her heart pounded as her sweaty palms became slick. She couldn't lose them; she just couldn't.

Casey crested the apex of the hill. Figures stood over two people. Twigs broke under her feet as she forged forward. Ben and Clint turned pointing their guns at her, but then recognition dawned in their eyes that it was her. The shield vanished and she jumped into Ben's waiting arms. She buried her head against him and breathed in his scent, listening to his heart.

"What do you think you're doing running up on us like that?" Clint growled.

"How dare you run off without me!" Casey pulled away from Ben.

Ben held her and tugged her to him as she tried to go to Clint. "Calm down. We're all okay."

"No, we aren't. Jeannie and her daughter are...I couldn't save them." Casey frowned. "They were dead before I got to them. So no, we aren't all okay. What if something happened to either of you? Who would defend them? What am I supposed to do, absorb the relics of all the fallen Chosen Ones and bear that responsibility by myself, alone in this world that I don't belong in?"

"Casey, I didn't mean that, I...we didn't think about that. We just reacted. I'm sorry. You're right, we shouldn't keep you out of this. Please understand we both love you and it's a gut reaction to keep you out of harm's way." Clint examined the expanse of land bordering them.

Casey wondered if more Monarchs lurked in the shadows. "I love you both also." Casey took two steps to Clint and hugged him. "But do you also realize they won't hesitate to destroy you if you stand in the way of them capturing me? So, if I'm not with you, they won't waver in taking you out because I'm not here to cross through their line of fire."

Clint hugged her. "You're right. We need to stay together like the prophecy says as the Chosen Ones. Okay, let's find out what these two have on them."

Ben removed the guns, cleared them, rendering them safe, and then handed them to Casey. He slid the clips into his pocket. What was she supposed to do with them? She slipped one in her jacket pocket and the other in her waistband. Clint removed a radio from under one of the men. He turned up the volume. Static reverberated through the air before the radio squawked to life.

"Come in. Confirm you dispatched the two you chased. We need her unharmed. She could become a great asset to this team. Come in. Where are you idiots? Confirm you have eyes on the target. Casey is to be taken alive! Come in. What's your update? Stand by while we activate the locator and come for you. Stay where you are!" The droll of the annoyed person on the other end of the radio spiked jitters through her. Casey gasped; they still wanted her.

The previous radio they stole while they were in Monarch territory had been destroyed. Clint hadn't realized they put a self-destruct in each unit and were able to disable it from their end.

She shuddered at the memories of their last capture. Clint smashed the radio against a rock and then stomped the parts with his boot. "We have to move now!" He bolted past Casey toward the house.

Ben grasped Casey's hand and sprinted after Clint. She had to almost take two steps for every one of his. They scooted past Jeannie and her daughter; she couldn't bring herself to look at them. The rest froze, wide-eyed as they ran up the dilapidated planks into the kitchen.

"We have to move now. They know we're here." Clint put boxes on the table. Everyone kept bumping into one another as they were in a frantic rush to fill the boxes with what food they had in the pantry and the refrigerator. This was the food that Jeannie just brought back. Panicked voices reverberated off the walls as their thunderous footsteps on the boards echoed through the kitchen as they descended to the lower level. Ben and Clint took the stairs to the bedrooms two at a time to retrieve their boxes.

"Casey, get on the phone with Chloe, tell her what's going on here, and ask if her uncle has any suggestions for a place to go." Clint returned with the backpack that he offered to her.

Casey fished the phone out of her back pocket, and the gun dug into the skin in her waistband. She gave it to Ben as he passed on the way upstairs. He put his hand on her shoulder and gave her a quick peck on the cheek, goosebumps erupted down her arms. He still had it; she smiled.

A call to Chloe and she had directions to the next location for Clint. She sent prayers of luck to everyone. She said she would coordinate with the northern assembly for prayers and that she was shocked at the loss of family today. Clint took the directions from her as the rest made their way out of the house. Casey waited at the bottom for Ben, who emerged soon after. Hands empty, he winked and bounded down to her as they were the last to leave.

Cars filed out behind Clint. Casey sat in the front as Ben slipped in the back, and they departed to yet another new location. Would they lose anyone else on the way? She refused to let her mind wander to the hill where the enemy fell.

Several hours later, their caravan rounded a curve, and they found themselves at a rundown motel. This would be different but there were more than enough rooms for everyone. They pulled along the back of the building, to stash the cars.

They didn't unload everything but took food to each room. This would only be temporary housing. Chloe's uncle still had work to do on the additions to a place that had an underground bunker for everyone to shelter in place if needed, so this would be a brief solution until they figured things out. The two newest members took a room at the far end. No one had really met them yet; they were scared and seemed to already know each other.

There was a quiet knock on their door. Clint rose to answer.

Doc ambled in. "Someone needs to go back and bury Jeannie and her daughter. We can't leave them like that."

"Doc, I was getting ready to suggest that with Ben and Casey. I think it should be us that go. Casey can keep us in the shield if the Monarchs show up, and we can have them buried and back here before sunrise." Clint didn't look at Casey or Ben.

"Sounds good to me." Casey rose from the opposite chair from where Clint sat.

"Thanks. I didn't want to think about them being out there and the animals getting to them." Doc let himself out as Clint loaded the clips into the extra guns that Ben had taken earlier.

"Casey, you need to carry one." Clint clenched his jaw and towered over her.

"No, I can't." Casey crept back into a chair, causing her to trip.

"Clint, no!" Ben wrapped his arm around her.

"Casey, what if we're separated and can only protect one of us with the shield? You have to be able to shoot to have the other's back. You said yourself that you don't want to be here by yourself. Today showed me that I need to train you to use this to give you a fighting chance. If you're separated, you'll be able to defend yourself. Remember the drugs they injected in you? You couldn't raise the shield for us much less yourself until the sedatives wore off." Clint held out his hand with the barrel pointed away from her.

Casey's eyes bugged out as she stared at the menacing firearm capable of taking a life. She still thought of the first life she took and couldn't imagine doing that again.

"Casey, you need to take it." Ben nodded to her.

She jerked her head up and met his eyes. Tears blurred her vision. She blinked them back, refusing to let them fall. The pistol was a dark blur in Clint's outstretched hand. His eyes pleaded with her to take it. She reached her arm out. The gun was heavier than she thought it should be. Was it because of the damage it could inflict with a simple pull of the trigger?

"The safety is on. It's okay," Clint clarified.

Ben stepped behind her. "Here is how you check everything and use this. It will be a quick lesson, but we'll have a more in-depth one when we get back."

He showed her how to flip the safety off and how to hold it and keep it pointed away from anything she didn't want to shoot.

Clint also told her to only aim if she intended to use it to kill.

A quick nod of her head was all she could manage, too shaky to say anything. She didn't know why a gun bothered her except to say that the relics were a part of her. She was more comfortable with them than this lump of metal. What if she missed and didn't have time to take another shot if something happened? The relics could be made to be null and void so she had to shake herself out of the negative thinking that a gun was so much worse when it really wasn't.

She tucked it into her bag and slung the strap over her head and shoulder so it sat diagonally across her chest.

Ben followed Clint out as they moved to their car. She didn't say anything as she sagged into the back seat, knowing that she was now armed. She didn't like how it weighed on her; she wondered if that would ever change. Clint slightly grinned at her through the rearview mirror. He was worried about her—his eyes gave it away—but she had the shield, which was capable of killing people and creatures. She refused to think about the drugs they injected her with to disable her ability to deploy the shield. Couldn't they stay away from running headfirst at the Monarchs so they couldn't get the drop on them again? She traced the outline of the sidearm within the confines of the leather bag.

No one said anything as they started to drive back to where they had escaped from. She tipped her head back as the lights from the windows shrank behind them.

The car bumped over gravel and shook her from her sleep. There was a break in the tree line on the left, and Clint turned, the road vanishing behind them. The rocky, broken path they followed abused the suspension, jarring them inside. Casey latched onto the handle above the door with her right hand while her left hand splayed out on the seat next to her to give her support and stop her from being bounced around.

Clint slowed as they came to a bend in the road that pitched enough Casey was sure they would tip over. She blew out a sigh as they leveled back out. She didn't remember the road being this bad when they drove through before.

They had arrived back at the driveway to the house. She had slept the entire time; Ben and Clint didn't say a word but shared a look. Headlights lit the way, showing several large mounds of earth where the insects had pushed through. Clint pulled around the back of the house. Jeannie and Ashlyn lay crumpled on the grass. She sighed with relief that animals hadn't gotten to them.

Clint pulled into the barn as she put the shield up. The headlights lit the dark cavernous corners, showing several shovels and tools on the far wall.

"Okay, we need to make this quick. I say one spot and keep them together." Clint scanned their surroundings.

"I agree, we shouldn't separate them." Casey hopped out of the back seat.

Each with their chosen tool, Ben covered Jeannie and Ashlyn with a tarp while they went to work on their grave. Clint suggested a spot around the side where flowers had wilted from the low temperatures. Clint stepped on his shovel and removed the first mound of earth. Ben started just two feet to the left of him and they both dug for several minutes. They sat back and took a break; Casey distributed bottles of water from the back of the car. She dropped in and dug while they drank. She was more than capable of helping bury their friends. Granted, the amount she managed to dig out didn't compare to what the other two were able to accomplish.

When she started to slow down, Clint reached down his hand and in one swift motion nearly tossed her into Ben's arms, who was positioned at his left. He took over her spot. She accepted a bottle of water from Ben, who wiped a piece of dirt from her face as she lowered the shield, too overheated to keep it up. Within an hour, catching her breath while resting on the thick green carpet of grass, she only had glimpses of the tops of Clint and Ben's heads with each scoop of dirt they removed as they dug deeper than necessary. She stayed tuned in to their surroundings listening for anything that would let her know the insects were back.

Ben gave Clint a boost out of the grave. Clint held out his hand to help him up. "No, go and hand them to me so we don't drop them in."

Clint went to Jeannie and carefully placed them in the tarp to keep them next to each other. He gently lifted them and transported them to Ben who stretched up to take them. Within seconds, they were out of sight. Clint helped Ben out of the grave.

A shot rang out. Clint and Casey hit the ground as Ben crumpled backward.

Casey's scream for Ben pierced the night. The shield concealed her and Clint. They hadn't heard anyone approach while they dug. Even with their enhanced abilities, nothing alerted them that they were in danger. The shield held her and Clint in a capsule of safety; Ben's sightless eyes stared at nothing.

Twenty-Six

Her anguish was overpowering. Clint pulled her from Ben, her hands desperately grasping at his arm to let her go. Her back to him, he held and rocked her.

Casey frantically tried to get to Ben as she let out an ear-piercing wail. His body lay out of reach in the grave they just dug. Clint had to tighten his grip. She was a lot stronger than she looked, and he knew grief could give someone strength their body didn't normally have.

Clint and Casey crawled to the edge just as the ring sailed up and hovered over her before falling into her hand as she reached for it. Ben's broken neck told him he was beyond help. Her sobs tore through Clint's heart. No other shots rang out.

"Casey, we need to fill it in and get out of here." Clint pulled her to him as she tried to crawl into the grave.

"No, Clint. I have to try." Casey held her hands out to send the aura to Ben's body.

Nothing happened.

"Casey, it's too late, please." Clint shoveled a scoop of dirt and let it fall.

"No, how can you just give up like that?" Her gaze bore into him.

"Sweetie, he's gone. You saw the angle of his neck, and that doesn't include the hole in his forehead." Clint sent another scoop down.

Casey sprang to her feet and shouldered Clint as hard as she could to move him out of the way. He didn't budge. Her fists beat against him as he took the brunt of her attack without defending himself.

"How dare you give up on him! He's your best friend. You even said he's like a brother and Amanda was like a sister. He wouldn't give up on you, so we aren't giving up on him. Look what happened when I died. Help me get him out of there!"

"You can throw out your power now. Can you do that from here? If not, then there is your answer. You can't heal the dead." Clint held fast, knowing the fatal shot was more than enough to end Ben's life. It was beyond her relic's power.

Casey concentrated.

Nothing happened.

She closed her eyes and tried again.

Nothing.

Casey dashed for the side. Clint snagged her around her waist with one arm while the other went around her arms, locking her to him.

"No! No, no, no, no, no." Casey wept sagging in his arms. "I can't, Clint. I just can't do this without him!"

Clint took a knee and held her tight, not letting her move an inch.

"This isn't me giving up on him. It is knowing that we can't change what just happened. Burying him keeps the Monarchs from taking his body and using it. It's me upholding my promise to the prophecy to keep you safe and be your protector." Clint kissed the top of her head as her breaths sawed in and out.

"I need him. I can't breathe without him."

"I know, sweetie. I know." Clint couldn't stop the single sob that escaped.

He slowly let go after he lowered her to the grass and rose to his full height and snatched the shovel off the ground.

Clint let another load of soil drop.

Twenty-Seven

Casey couldn't breathe; black dots danced in front of her eyes. She was having a panic attack. She'd never had one before and didn't know how to stop it.

"Don't you dare let them win. You keep that shield up, or they'll kill me next. I have no doubt that there's a sniper in those trees somewhere, otherwise we would have heard if someone was nearby. Ben's ring also didn't alert us of any Monarch being in the vicinity. So don't you dare let them win! I can't keep an eye on you if I'm not here! This is the last thing we can do for Ben. This is the last way *I* can do something for him. Give him a burial," Clint growled.

Casey stood after she slowed her breathing; a waterfall of tears couldn't be stopped from falling. "I love him, Clint. I can't do this without him."

"I love him too. But there's nothing we can do to change this. Please help me. Then I'll take you away from here, but until we get this filled, we can't leave." He grabbed her close and put his lips to her forehead and held them there.

She numbly nodded her head and picked up a shovel. When she rubbed at her tears, she only managed to smear more dirt across her already stained skin.

The two of them finished as sweat seeped from their pores. They kept wiping their faces, using the sleeves of their shirts before it dripped in their eyes; the fabric was drenched.

A commotion to their right caught them off guard. Casey reinforced the shield she kept around them as they finished. An insect crawled along the ground as it rounded the side of the barn. She sucked in air and held it. It took a few strides forward, tilting his head toward her.

Ben's ring flickered as gold flecks gathered in a whirling mass of speckles above the stone. She blinked at Clint and gave a small pathetic smile. Her chin quivered. She made her hand into a fist and targeted the creature, that barreled down on her. A gold beam penetrated the shield into the thick scales on the back. The beam cut through the circuits. It landed in a heap on Casey's side. Clint nodded his head as another one moved to strike.

Clint looked at his relic after sliding his handgun back in his holster and changed it to the setting Casey initiated in the neighborhoods and aimed for the critters on his side. Red static circled his fist before pulsing forward, passing through the shield to the one by him. In a matter of minutes, there were too many of them crawling over every side of their protective dome.

"Casey, we have to get out of here. There are too many of them." Clint tamped down the soil on the grave one last time and then flung the shovel through the air. He hit several, which dislodged them and sent them flying.

"We need the EMP so we can get out of here, or they will be able to follow us, clinging to the shield."

"You're right. Let me know when you are ready." Clint rotated his hands around, creating several small red orbs that pulsed in and out with a red light.

Casey cautiously circled Clint and took in the enormous number of mantises that blocked out the world as they covered every inch of the shield. Clint threw out the red pulses. They hit and expanded with the shield, intermingling with the diamond flecks of the shield shredding through the insects. That only lasted a few seconds before they were replaced with others.

"Not bad for your first time with the ring, but we can't stay here. I say we try to make a run for it and once we are away from this main group, we then try to dislodge them from the shield." Clint's dimples popped as he tried to smile at her, but the smile didn't touch his eyes; she knew he was trying to suppress his pain and loss.

Casey understood why Amanda had a crush on him at one point in her life, but she didn't have that reaction when she looked at him. Ben was the only person she ever felt anything like that for and now he was gone. Pain lanced its way through her chest. Her hands shook as tears threatened to spill out. She would never be the same without him. Clint now lost two of his closest friends. How was he so calm?

"I know the ring doesn't fit very well, but I want you to wear it always since you can use it. I also want you to get used to using a firearm. I don't want to risk that they're able to sedate you like before and you lose the ability to use the ring." Clint surveyed their surroundings.

She didn't say a word, listening to the noises of the forest and nature's nightly calls. She would find a different way to carry the pistol. She didn't want it in her waistband like he carried his. She tugged off her jacket, dampness glistening on her brow. It was hot under the shield and she longed for the chilly night air.

Clint put his hand on her shoulder. "How are you holding up?"

"As well as you are. Hold on, I think I can give us a head start. I'm not sure what one of these would do if they got under the hood of our car." Pulling yellow sparks from the ring, she ran her hands along the inside of the shield, electrifying it in a bright citrine amber glow. With a yell, she sent the shield out pulverizing the bugs. None of them moved. They waited a few minutes to see if they would be replaced with more of them.

"Wow, not bad." Clint nodded at her.

She stomped off, angry that he refused to let her try and help Ben. Who knows, maybe they could have done something. Lightning brought her back; maybe it could have done the same for Ben. She rubbed at her chest, the ache a physical pain.

Clint picked up his tool and marched toward the barn. Once inside and out of sight of the sniper, she dropped the shield knowing Clint was almost there with her when he rounded the corner of the barn from the side where they buried Ben. She couldn't keep it up much longer. She was overheating and a headache started to take hold.

Casey pushed at the pain as it morphed into a stabbing ache. She turned the button off on her communicator as she waited in the passenger seat for Clint to join her. "Father, help me through this. I can't do this on my own. I need You now more than ever before. Please take this from me. I can't live without him!" Tears flowed freely.

A man dragged her out of the car and hurled her on the musty stale hay that rotted in the corner of the dilapidated barn. He jammed an injector into her neck and pulled the trigger before she could react. She tried to deploy the shield but failed.

He yanked her off the ground. "Sorry girlie, no armor for you to shelter behind."

Clint passed through the open door, dropping the shovel before tugging a handgun from his holster in a blur of movement.

The man pulled Casey between them. She trembled as she struggled to deploy the shield, her brow furrowed as she narrowed her eyes.

"Sorry, you can't defend yourself or him. You eradicated a lot of our pets out there tonight. Do you understand what making one of those entails and how long the process takes? The leader will not be happy you set us back." His hand snaked around her neck while the other one ran a knife across her abdomen, causing her to flinch.

The images of Ben and Clint restrained in chains flashed through her mind. She refused to let Clint go through that again. Her eyes locked with Clint's and she mouthed, "Sorry." Her hand reached into her bag and found the cold hard grip. Her thumb switched off the safety like he'd shown her. Clint nodded before stepping to the right.

She eased her hand from her bag as Clint took another step to the right, drawing the man's attention away from what she was doing. She tucked her arm next to her body and inched the firearm around her side. If she could pull the trigger fast enough, she might be able to take him out of the equation before he shoved the knife into her. The instant the barrel met resistance against the man's plump fleshy belly, she pulled the trigger several times.

The man stumbled back as red spread across his abdomen. His wide huge eyes realized what happened, but it was too late. He let the knife fall when his knees buckled. She surged to the front of the car.

Twenty-Eight

"Get in!" Clint was already diving into the driver's seat.

She barely got the door closed behind her before Clint threw it in reverse.

"I can't put up the shield. They can follow us." Casey trembled.

"What do you mean?"

"He injected me with something."

"Flush that out of your system first, and then worry about the other." Clint took a hard left out of the driveway.

Tears leaked from her downturned eyes. Clint knew there wasn't enough time for her to say goodbye and get any sort of closure. The Monarchs were taking everyone they loved from them. Yet he didn't want to be this person. The one that wanted to exact revenge. That wasn't his call—that was God's—for judgment to be delivered, but he would do everything in his power to save the people he still loved. Movement on their left caught Clint's eye.

"Get down!" He got out a second before the window behind them shattered. "Casey, we really need that shield."

"I know. I know!"

Clint swerved as another round took out the windshield from a sideways angle.

The shield emerged around them but blinked out.

"Try again, Casey."

An instantaneous blip shrouded the car, only to disappear again.

"I can't." Casey sagged against the seat.

"I have faith in you. Come on."

Another sprang forward, sending sparkles through their field of vision that told him they were finally concealed from sight. He smashed down on the accelerator and barreled down the road.

Her hiccuped sobs crushed his heart. How was he going to tell Ben's parents their last child was gone? His goal to take her away and leave the group was now of utmost importance. This was taking a toll on Casey, and he couldn't safeguard her like this.

"Stop the car." Clint gawked at her when she tried to swallow again. "Stop the car!"

The tires rumbled along the gravel as he pulled off to the shoulder. Casey barely cleared the open door when she started heaving. Everything she ate that day was now on the grassy embankment. She plopped to the ground as he came around the back of the car. Clint passed her water as he held her hair back. She gulped the liquid and rinsed her mouth, spitting on the ground. Clint wrapped his arms around her while his knees settled on the moist, dew-laden ground, soaking through his jeans.

Clint's warm hand flattened on her shoulder. "Father, help her through this, You're the only one who can calm her. Let her know You still love her, and she will always be Your child. Let her realize that You acknowledge she's fighting in Your name for all Your children on earth. Quiet her heart, from this, that this is life and death in this evil world that Satan has his hands on. Open Your arms for her to run too. Let her understand You're here for her and will never think less of her because of what happened. Father, carry her through this. In Jesus Christ's name, amen."

Clint kissed her head as she sighed. A light pierced through the sky, hovering over them. It was the largest star any of them had ever seen. It twinkled brilliantly, lighting the way to the car. "I think God's telling us we need to go." Clint hauled her off the ground.

The hair stood on the back of his neck; something was coming. The ring shimmered. They sprinted for the car, and a thunderous roar sounded in the trees as they dove into the seats. Clint punched the accelerator, which threw them back and locked the seatbelts they barely had time to click in place, and steered for the road. Their tires skidded on the payment as Clint spun the wheel to the left. Burned rubber marks on the road told where they left the gravel, and their tires finally found purchase on the asphalt. She scanned the wilderness behind them; nothing chased them. Casey sunk down in the seat as he reached over for her hand. "Are you good?"

"No. Are you?" Casey rolled her head back. "God already guided me through the first life I took. Please be patient with me on this one. He injected me again; I couldn't deploy the shield. You don't have to worry about me. I didn't like using a gun. Maybe I can resolve to carrying it, but the carnage of what it does shocks me. Before you gave me one, the Monarchs were a prime example of them being used for evil. They didn't hesitate to go to war against their own, triggering death and destruction as if it were a part of everyday life, just like breathing. You have to remember where I came from I wasn't subjected to anything like this. I worked in a bookstore. I had no life. I was a loner. This...this is more than I thought I could ever deal with, so be patient as I struggle with Ben...with everything."

He didn't interrupt her as she word-vomited her feelings and repulsion at using the handgun. He let her vent and clear her conscience. Clint studied her and their eyes met. He could feel her withdrawing. Her spine bowed as if she wanted to curl in on herself and shut everything and everyone out. "I think there's something else you aren't admitting."

"No, you're right. The fear of losing one of you is what wakes me at night. You worry that I'm struggling with the man's death that I caused in the old neighborhood, but that's not what wakes me. I have nightmares that you're injured or worse and I have to go on without you. That I will fail to keep you two safe and fighting for God. That in the end I'll have to absorb all the relics and truly be here alone. I thought being alone was a good thing before you brought me here. In fact, I wouldn't have it any other way. I didn't have any worries about not sharing my life. You showed me how great it is to have someone in my life, but the ache of loss, of the people you love, I don't think I will ever get over that. After Ben...you're all that's left. How will I deal when you are gone too?" Casey blew out a sigh as her head fell forward.

"Have you ever thought that God won't let you go through this alone? Who's to say that when it is His timing to take me home, someone else won't come along to help in this war?" Clint reached for her, his strong hand warm against her shoulder.

"I don't want anyone else I want Ben and Amanda back. We are supposed to be the Chosen Ones. And if it's true that there are replacements for you, then why haven't we found Amanda's replacement?" Casey frowned.

Clint held his breath. "We're going to get through this."

"Yeah..." Casey shook her head and gazed out the side window as the trees passed by in a blur.

Clint kept an eye on her as he kept vigilance over getting them back to the hotel.

"He said we destroyed so many insects that the leader is going to retaliate. That we set them back and asked if we had any idea how much time and components went into creating each one." Casey sighed.

"Did he say who the new leader is? My military contacts have nothing on him, except he is elusive and they can't track down anything on him. He's keeping his identity a secret even from his own men. The terror he instills is shocking, considering half the Monarchs have never talked to him or even seen him." Clint had spent hours trying to find anything out about the man who took over Polson's station.

"How do they even know he exists?" Casey sagged forward.

"Interesting point. According to rumor, only the leaders of the individual subgroups of Monarchs supposedly know him. They take their orders directly from him, but no one below the leaders has never seen him. Rumors have surfaced about a mutiny and groups leaving, but again, it's only a rumor, and nothing like that has been witnessed by the sections the military is able to keep tabs on." Clint pulled behind the structure.

Doc knocked on their door as Clint emerged from the bathroom, his hair still wet from a shower as Casey marched through the adjourning door with a towel soaking up the extra water from her hair.

"Did you finish it?" Doc ambled to the chair by the door.

"Yes." Casey sat in the chair in the corner flipped her head forward and absorbed the water with her towel.

"Thanks, I wouldn't have been able to sleep knowing they were still out there."

"More creatures arrived as we started to leave. Anything here we need to be worried about?" Clint brought out the extra ammunition and reloaded Casey's clip that had emptied when she defended herself and him. They didn't tell Doc about what Casey had to do. Clint wondered with their ever-evolving relics would it ever come down to them not needing to carry firearms? They were technically weapons themselves.

"Nope, everyone is in their quarters and already asleep. They're exhausted. And speaking of, I think I'm going to head to bed myself and try to sleep a couple of hours. Oh hey, where is Ben?" Doc gripped the side of the door.

"He didn't make it." Clint bowed his head as he slumped to the corner of the mattress.

"What?" Doc stumbled over to Clint.

"He's gone. Can we hold off telling anyone right away? I think we could all use a full night's sleep." Clint wiped at the wetness on his face.

Doc's sniffles followed him through the door.

"Casey, do you need anything?" Clint couldn't meet her eyes.

"No, I'm tired and I think I need to be alone before we tackle tomorrow and what the day holds." Casey clutched her satchel and hesitated. He recognized how the extra content bothered her. "And ... thanks. I...wanted to say thanks. I said some things back there—"

"No, there's nothing to apologize for." Clint crouched in front of her.

"Do you think you can find me a holster for this, but different than yours?" Casey shook her bag slightly.

"I can find you one."

"I think I'll feel better having the thing secure instead of loose in this bag. It's not convenient carrying this thing." She left and shuffled through the door to her room.

Clint gave a light tap on the wall and waited for Casey to acknowledge him.

"Yes?"

"Leave your communicator on, in case something happens."

"Okay, goodnight." Casey's muffled voice filtered through the thin plaster walls.

He put his hand on the wall. Tears coursed down his cheeks. He gulped down a sob. His friends were gone. If only he could have taken their place. Clint turned his back to the thin partition that separated him and the Key. He slid to the floor, pulling his legs to himself. His quiet sobs shook his body. "Father, help me. Help us."

Twenty-Nine

"Morning." Clint's voice filtered through the communicator.

"What time is it?"

"Almost nine. Now, come on. We need you to call Chloe and find out if she has anything new on her end." Clint tried to smile as he stood next to the door that connected them.

"Do we need to have a meeting and let everyone know about Ben first?" Casey kept her gaze on the floor.

"Doc and I already did that. I felt it would be easier on you if we had it handled."

"Okay." Casey latched the bathroom door behind her.

Her stomach growled as she drew on faded, threadbare jeans that had seen better days and a mustard yellow tank top. Her room didn't have any food. She knocked on the interior door separating them. Clint grinned as he opened it. "How are you feeling? I know, stupid question. Sorry, it's just so hard not to ask."

Casey ignored his comment. "What do we have to eat?"

Clint held up an apple and nodded to where their small fridge sat. The hard chair in the corner, which didn't seem to have any stuffing left in the seat or back, took the brunt of the impact when she sat on it with a thud. She bit into the crisp apple and had to use a napkin off the side table to catch the juice that started to drip down her chin.

"What's the plan for the day?" She relinquished the phone to Clint for him to call Chloe.

Tires on the gravel from an approaching car startled them, and they ran to the windows. A small gray car pulled in with a woman behind the wheel. She stepped from the car and scanned her surroundings. Something startled her and she vaulted back in and raced out of the parking lot. They didn't move but waited for whatever frightened her to show itself.

A low hum moved over the area and only grew louder.

"Casey, put up the shield." Clint guided her away from the door with his hand on her back.

Casey shielded them from end to end. All anyone would catch sight of from the road would be the timberline. The shield glittered on the inside, telling them the camouflage was working. It seemed to give off different appearances according to each situation they dealt with. She was glad the drugs they injected her with yesterday had worn off so she'd be able to keep them invisible.

Clint pointed to a caravan of vehicles that appeared in the distance. "I need to tell everyone the Monarchs are here and to stay inside, preferably in the bathtubs."

Clint had the door open and sprinted from room to room to give everyone orders to hide. At the last door, no one answered as he yelled through the door to take shelter. Clint raced back to Casey. Their only hope was to hunker down.

The cars slowed down and several occupants gestured in their direction. Casey prayed the illusion would work. She swiped her sleeve across her sweating brow and then held her hands up to project the shield. She backed away from the windows, placing herself between the two beds.

CLINT UNDERSTOOD SHE didn't want the distractions of what was going on to influence her ability to keep the shield up. She explained she would make it as though there was no motel and let the bullets through to the forest behind them. Two very large men exited the second car and pulled massive assault rifles from the backseat. They laughed as they cast sights on the illusion of trees that kept Casey's group undercover.

"I swear there was a motel here the other day," one of them hissed.

"Yeah well, where'd it go?" the other one drawled. "Did it mysteriously disappear in a poof of smoke?"

"It was here, I swears!" He hissed, dragging out the s in his words.

"Fine, let's see if I can magically hit this invisible motel." He spit, readjusted the assault rifle slung over his shoulder by a strap, let the stock rest on his thigh, and then took a clumsy aim.

Clint dove for the floor as bullets tore through. Plaster exploded around them as the bullets punched through the walls that were no match for the high-caliber rounds. It appeared as if the bullets disappeared into the grove that stood stalwart behind the structure they hunkered down in.

"There, proof there ain't nothing here. You need to lay off the drugs, man. They killin' yo brain cells." The man spoke with a thick southern drawl that dripped with dissension.

"No, maybe they hidin' it or somethin'." He reached his hand out, swiping at the air while getting closer to the shield.

Two more steps forward, he swiped again. Only inches away, the other man yelled at him to get in the car or they would leave without him.

"Wait, I think there's somethin' here." He reached out; his hand would come in contact with the shield if he kept moving forward.

"I said, let's go!" the other one bellowed.

"Look at this!" His hand only an inch from the shield wall, swept through the air in front of him, and he inched forward.

Clint took aim as he kneeled, ready for the gunfight that was about to ensue. He looked back at Casey, who shook as sweat dripped from her forehead. He realized this made her think about the life she took yesterday after they buried Ben and their friends.

A shot rang out as the other man fired into the air. "Now! Let's go!"

The man in front of them shrugged, stomped to the car, and dove into the backseat. The vehicles accelerated as the two men yelled at each other in the back of the car.

Clint jumped to his feet as the shield shimmered where he knelt in front of the window and trotted down to make sure no one was hurt. Everyone was uninjured, including the two newest members, who hugged Clint when he knocked on their door. He smiled and joined Casey, who stood out in the open area of his room.

When he turned around still rooted in place, Casey sucked in a breath at the hole in her side. As she met his gaze, her legs crumpled. Clint clambered across the bed and caught her before she landed on the ground. He applied pressure to her side with towels from the bathroom, wondering why they couldn't seem to catch a break.

"Is anyone injured? Do they need to be healed?" She winced. She clamped her hand over Clint's as she cried out from the pressure.

"No, everyone's fine. Why didn't you duck when I did?" Clint growled.

"I was afraid if I moved the shield would shift and show us." Her hands trembled.

"But you said you were going to make the shield show as if there wasn't a structure here and that only the trees behind us stood in its place."

Casey's skin was clammy. Clint wasn't sure if it was from the use of the shield or her injuries.

"I did but by the time I wanted to drop down, they were already out front, and I didn't want to take the chance that if I moved, the shield would shimmer or ripple showing it to them." Casey tried to pull her legs up as he pressed firmly against her injury.

"Casey!" Clint groaned as he pressed harder on her side. "You can't put yourself on the line like that."

The sparkling blue aura started at her heart and seeped down her body to her injuries. He nodded as the bleeding already indicated signs of slowing. He blew out a sigh. He would never get used to seeing her in that condition, even though she seemed to repair almost any injury she sustained.

She was what someone would consider to have clinically died. He remembered trying to keep her heart going as he struggled to come to terms with the fact that she was beyond their help in the cabin.

"Casey!" Doc's voice sounded from behind him.

"She'll be fine, Doc. Let her finish." Clint continued applying pressure as her fist clenched. She looked so pale and fragile, anger burned in his veins at the pain and ache the Monarchs put her through yet again. Blue light brightened for a fraction of a second before it started to retract back toward her heart. Doc squinted at them, peering through the aura.

Clint dropped his hands as the aura subsided and faded away. He offered her his hand and helped her sit.

"Ooh, gross. Now I need a shower." She stood and took in the pools of blood that came from her.

Clint lobbed the blood-soaked towels into the bathroom, then ripped the sheets from the bed, and heaved them on the towels. The phone in his pocket rang.

"Hello."

"Oh my gosh!" Chloe's voice screeched through the phone.

Clint smiled as her voice reached a high decibel and had to move the phone a few inches from his ear. "Chloe, take a breath for me. We are all fine. How did you know?"

"My uncle has his hidden satellite tasked over you. We saw the whole thing."

"Casey took one to her side but patched up herself. No one else was hurt. Where do we go now?"

Casey left them to clarify that and slipped from the room into hers to jump in the shower. She left her bloody clothes in a pile; there was no salvaging them. With her bloody bullet-riddled duds replaced, she snuck back to the other room as she ran a towel through her hair. Clint demonstrated to her how to put on a holster he was holding out for her, adjusting it so it didn't bother her. He walked into her room and reappeared with her bag and waited for her to retrieve the handgun to show her how to put it in the holster. As she donned her flannel, you couldn't tell she was now armed.

Clint finished his conversation. "You okay?"

"Yeah, thanks for the holster. It feels weird."

"Pretty soon you won't even realize it's there. I feel better knowing that you're armed. I appreciate that you didn't want to have to do this, but this is the world we live in. I don't think you really have a choice, since they have a drug that keeps you from deploying the shield. Did you want to talk about what happened yesterday?"

"No. What did Chloe say?" Casey changed the subject.

Clint hesitated handing her the phone, knowing she may not be ready to trust herself to have a conversation about Ben yet. He knew she loved him with all her heart. "We need to sit tight but keep watch in case they come back. I'll take the first patrol from your room while you lie down. Mark said he will take the one after mine. That way, if we need you to put up the shield, I can immediately alert you."

Casey yawned. "Wait, so I'm not allowed to stay up at all while you two look out for Monarchs?"

Clint crossed his arms. "Yep, you know how tired you get when you use your powers, and you need to rest in case someone needs you."

"I hate when you use common sense." Casey tried to smile.

Her trembling fingers picked up the ring from the nightstand. A bright yellow light engulfed her as the shield deployed and blue filtered from her. The ring's yellow orbs danced and pulsed around her. Then it slammed into her much like the bracelet had. The lights dimmed as symbols danced along her skin, adding to the designs already there. They littered her skin up and down both arms now. She slumped to the floor, the ring rolling several feet under the desk in the corner. She was right; she absorbed Ben's relic like she did Amanda's.

Clint kneeled at her side and scooped her up from the floor. His heart ached. The loss of Amanda took a toll on her. Took a toll on everyone, but now Ben, it could likely break her. He gently placed her on the bed. Quickly covering her with the comforter, tears dripped from his lower lashes. He couldn't let her see him weak. He had to be her protector; he had to be strong for her. Their Key. Now only his Key.

Thirty

They made sure everyone stayed inside for the day while they scouted the vicinity for unwanted visitors. They tracked several miles in every direction for any vantage point for someone to use to monitor them without their knowledge. Clint informed her he was satisfied, hours later, when they returned with no signs of anyone in the surrounding area.

With an early dinner, Clint suggested that they go to bed as Casey's eyes drooped. She should have slept more while they checked the region, but she told him she couldn't bring herself to leave them. Clint guided her to her room. As she sat on the bed, he removed her shoes. Covered with a blanket, she fell asleep.

"Casey, shield," Clint's whispered voice came through her communicator.

She sat up, wide-eyed, and put out her hands in front of her as the shield deployed. She was unsure how long she had been out. She shook her head to clear the fog as Clint burst through the adjoining door, gun held in front of him.

"Casey, over here." Clint directed her to a spot through the door.

She migrated to Clint's side. He motioned again to a spot in the trees at the curve in the road. Sure enough, there was a flashlight beam bouncing along the road as if someone was running. They stumbled, the flashlight skittered across the road, and the light spun in a circle before it came to rest. They scrambled to the light. It was a young woman who cried.

She was still some distance away, but they could hear her as if she were standing next to them. Was she sent to trick them out of hiding? Casey wasn't ready to let anyone know they were there just yet. She wanted to scream at the top of her lungs. How could she lose the one person she loved more than anything in life at the Monarchs' hand? Was this woman one of the ones that killed Ben?

"Where did it go? I stayed here last week!" She sobbed as she hiccupped through her next breath. She ran closer to the building.

Something about her tore at the true anguish that spilled from her lips.

"Clint, help her," Casey hissed.

"We can't. What if she's a plant?"

"Father, please help me!" The woman cried as she rubbed her hands up and down her arms and turned in circles in the middle of the road.

Casey started toward the door.

Clint held up his hand. "We can't."

Doc limped up to the shield, almost to the woman in the middle of the road.

Casey sought to create an entry in the shield so she would see Doc.

The woman screamed, "Where did you come from?"

"Quick, this way." His grandfatherly appearance convinced her to follow.

Once inside the shield, he guided her with both hands to Casey's room. Clint moved a chair away from the wall to the center of the room. The woman sat down hard as her legs gave out. Doc checked her vitals when headlights panned across the room.

"They found me!" she stuttered as she tried to stand.

"Quiet!" Clint hissed.

She gawked wide-eyed as the car slowed in front and panned a spotlight against the dark backdrop of night. She held onto Doc as she hyperventilated, gasping for air; her chin trembled. The light swung around again, making shadows dance on the walls. Men spilled out of the back as Clint urged Doc to take her into the bathroom. It didn't take much convincing for her to follow. They hunkered down in the bathtub as the men approached the shield.

"Come on, she isn't out here. Let's check farther down the road," someone yelled.

He trotted back to the van and stood on a step rail at the bottom of the door on the side as they drove down the road. His left hand clutched the rack on the roof of the car as they trolled past. His rifle was at the ready, primed to fire if they came across her. The spotlight searched for their target, who shook in the bathtub next to Doc.

Casey stowed the shield as the car pulled out of sight and around the next stand of trees. They turned to Doc, who talked softly to the woman cowering next to him.

"Who are you? How did you do that?" Her voice shook.

"Come on." Clint offered her his hand.

She hesitated, her hand hovering over his, just before she finally took it as she stepped out of the bathtub. Her legs gave out as she collapsed into Clint's arms. He swept her up and laid her on the second bed in the room.

"She's scared to death." Casey remembered that feeling when Ben took her not so long ago.

"Doc, what do you think?" Clint frowned at the unconscious woman.

"Help me roll her over." Doc edged up on the side of the bed.

"You want me to what?"

"Clint." Doc held her while Clint supported her legs. They rolled her toward them. "Casey, lift her blouse slightly."

"Doc, what are you doing?" Clint almost let go of her legs.

"Wait." Casey lifted the back, exposing scars, lots of scars; this woman had been beaten.

Clint and Doc placed her on her back as Clint whistled low.

"They were visible when we crouched in the tub. Someone did a number on this young lady." Doc's nostrils flared. "I think she needs our protection."

Clint only nodded, his demeanor changed, and he took a stance back at the door to the room. In that moment, Casey knew he made the painful decision that he'd die before he let the Monarchs seize this petrified young lady who had a strong enough will to escape from them.

The rising of the sun several hours later brought with it a frightened conscious young lady who had quite a story to tell.

"I tried to leave the triage center they were evacuating to board a plane home. We had gotten word that the Monarchs were close, and we didn't want to take a chance that we would be taken hostage." Gretchen pinched the bridge of her nose and closed her eyes.

Doc put his hand on her back. "Are you a nurse or doctor?"

"Oh goodness no, not even close. I work for Spiritual Redemption Ministries. I help bring God's word to areas where people have lost hope. We target the edges of conflict where we feel we are needed most to save people before it's too late." She beamed and her features softened as she spoke.

"I've heard of them. They do amazing work." Clint nodded for her to go ahead.

"There were three of us who were taken." She swallowed hard. "The other two were killed immediately when they found out who we were with. But I wasn't. Someone told them who my family was and their net worth. The Monarchs were practically salivating over those dollar signs. At first, they fed me and took halfway decent care of me, but that changed when they asked for double the ransom my parents paid and were told they wouldn't pay more. I think they knew they weren't going to get me back that way."

"That must have been hard." Casey's heart broke for her.

She lifted her chin. "I don't blame my parents at all. I heard them talking about how much they were able to get and said they wouldn't let me go if they could use me as a steady stream of currency."

"No one thought you would fault them for not continuing to send them money. If they couldn't keep their word, then they couldn't be trusted." Clint tucked his thumbs in his belt loops.

"I know. Anyway, the beatings started after the first time they were told no. I thought hearing others being tortured was scary, but not as bad as being walked down the hall to the room where they could care less how much pain they inflicted. You saw my back. The lashes were the worst." Her eyes became blank as if she were no longer in the room.

"One day they let a couple of us go outside. One girl ran. They shot her before she could get even a few feet away. They laughed. Can you believe that? It was like a game because they had gotten bored. No one else ran that day. Then the next week they did it again. I realized then that if I just kept my head down and did what they asked, as if they had broken me, then I might have a chance. The worst was when they would leave us out for hours. The hope that they forgot or that there was a chance that we would be able to escape was enough to get a few of them to snap."

Casey handed her a glass of water when her voice cracked.

She nodded and swallowed half before putting the glass down. "The next torture they liked to do was take us on errands around other people. If we talked to anyone, that innocent person was killed and they would tell everyone around us that it was our fault because we didn't know when to keep our mouths shut. I never spoke out of turn. I always watched and waited for the consequences of what the others did, and then I would file that bit of information away. They thought I was beaten down so they let me wander around by myself. After a couple of months and I still didn't run, they stopped worrying about me and put me to work cooking and tending to small wounds that their cohorts were dealing with. Yesterday, I made a break for it. I was a couple of miles away before they probably realized I was gone. I kept to the wooded areas and kept working my way west. If I could fumble along far enough west and find the territories not yet taken over by the Monarchs, I could get a message to my family."

Casey shuddered as she remembered being held for only a few hours. She couldn't fathom a few days, weeks, or months, much less years.

"I remembered the motel's location when they would take me on supply runs. They had the old phone systems that everyone stopped using decades ago, but this place was all about the vintage era and that was their selling point. People wanted the good old times and loved to show family how they used to live. That's when Doc appeared out of nowhere. I believed it had to be God sending someone to me. I thought they would take me back before I could find help." She gulped the rest of her water.

"Well, you are with us now, and we won't let them take you back. Clint and Casey will make sure of it, won't you?" Doc's proud smile almost blinded them.

"Wait, he called you Casey?" She pointed a shaking finger at her.

"Yes." Casey acknowledged. Her heart beat faster. Was she really a Monarch? Would they all be discovered by the next patrol that came through?

"They're looking for you. You have to be careful. They have orders to shoot on sight anyone with you, to recapture you. There was this crazy rumor going around that you're from the past and can heal people who'd been hurt." The woman shuffled back and yelped when she bumped into Clint.

Clint and Doc exchanged a look before glancing at Casey. "What do they say about her?"

"One of their spies told them her wounds and scars mended right in front of him. He got a message that you had some key they wanted, whatever that means. I mean, why do they want a key when they force their way into wherever they want to go? They don't need a key. Anyway, when he didn't hit his scheduled check-in, they activated his tracker to find you. You were already gone so they put him down as if he were an injured animal. The warehouse skirmish they have on an image sequence, with her doing what she did to you two!" She turned. "They want you and some other guy that was with you dead so they can take her. You have to keep her safe. She has the key to ending all this!"

Casey had a tightness in her chest as she realized the Monarchs probably didn't know Ben had died that night, taken out by their sniper. She took a second to compose herself.

"What do you mean I *have* the key?" It reminded Casey of when they first told her about the prophecy, and what it meant for the Chosen Ones. Did the Monarchs know something different than they did? Or did they find out about the prophecy?

"I keep having a dream about a key. The key is always changing but is one of the last hopes for America. I have never had dreams like this before yet they're so vivid that sometimes when I'm awake I feel as if they're real." She bowed her head.

"I'm sorry, we never asked your name." Casey sat next to her and held her hand.

"I'm Gretchen." She smiled and Casey saw the truth in her eyes. She nodded to Clint and sat on the other side of her and took her other hand. Citrine lights floated over Casey's hand, letting her know the truth relic was active in her.

"Gretchen, are you in league with the Monarchs?" Casey saw no ill will in her eyes.

"Oh, my gosh. No, they're evil. I prayed every day that my Heavenly Father would help me get away or that someone would come rescue me. I never gave up hope that He would send someone." A tear glistened in her eye but never spilled over when she smiled.

Casey stood and nudged into Clint's side as he stood by the door, his eyes ever vigilant on the roads.

"Wait, why did I say that?" Gretchen's eyes widened.

"I'm not the only one with powers. Ben's able to make people tell the truth, or he used to before; I now have it. We only did it to make sure you weren't with the Monarchs and leak our location." Casey smiled and squeezed her hand. "I can help you with the scars on your back."

Gretchen moved her eyes between Clint and Doc as if to ask if she should move. Doc nodded and sat on the other side of her. Casey ignored Clint, who kept watch. Blue filtered through her eyelids over to Gretchen through her hands, which shook as the skin smoothed out, erasing the scars from years of abuse at the hands of the Monarchs. Her eyes brightened as her skin returned to its pre-tortured state. The blue subsided, flowing back to Casey.

Gretchen straightened and ran to the bathroom and turned so her back was to the mirror, before pulling the hem of her blouse up. Her eyes widened to the point Casey wasn't sure they would ever go back. She smiled at her but didn't move from the bed. This was proof she could erase old injuries; she had never attempted anything like this before. Doc and Clint smiled at her, and she wondered if they knew why she did it.

Gretchen bounded out of the bathroom and almost crushed Casey's ribs. "It's true, all of it! Thank you. I can never repay you for this. I'd thought I would carry those scars for the rest of my life! Is that what that blue light is?"

"Yes, but you can't tell anyone. Please," Casey begged.

The roar of engines in the distance told them company was on the way. Clint drew his gun as Doc pulled Gretchen to the bathroom by her hand while Casey deployed the shield.

"Casey, stay down on the floor this time in case they shoot again." Clint indicated with his hand for her to lie all the way down on the floor.

"I told you the tracker showed she was around here!" A large, ruddy man flopped from the passenger seat and plodded forward.

They all three gaped toward Gretchen, who inched closer to Doc. Doc shook his head at Clint, positioning himself between the two of them.

"Doc, I need to." Clint changed the setting on his relic and aimed at Gretchen, whose wide eyes captured and reflected the sparks that raced around his hand. As she got ready to scream, he held his finger up to his mouth. "You'll be okay, but I have to give you a static shock to short-circuit the transmitter they injected in you. Where did they place it?"

Casey eyed the male as he swiped in front of him with his hand while the other held a small computer showing the dot from her tracker.

"I'm not sure where it is." Gretchen shook at the male outside the open door. "Do it, he is evil. He hurt me every opportunity he got."

Clint nodded as she let go of Doc, pushing back so she didn't touch him. A pulse of static coursed through her body.. She slumped against the back of the bathtub. Unconscious, Doc pulled her to him and held her as Clint jogged to the door.

The man shook the computer and slammed his fist on the display. "What happened to it?"

Another took the screen from him and tapped several icons on the device. He shook it and tapped the icons again. "It don't show her tracker no more."

"Come on, let's go back. I need a new trace applet. This one must be defective." Lumbering sloth-like steps took him back, where he had to take more than one attempt to haul himself up into the seat.

Casey lurched off the floor and into the bathroom where Gretchen was starting to stir. "I'm so sorry. I didn't know I had a tracker."

"It's okay. Can you tell where it is?" Clint wasn't sure if Casey would be able to manipulate the healing to pull it from her like she pulled the bullet from Chloe.

"No."

"They usually inject them in everyone so it is next to a good pulse point and they can keep track of their stats easier. Do you mind?" Clint held his hand out to take hers.

She cautiously put her hand in his and let him pull her to a standing position. His fingers searched along her left wrist to the right of where someone would take a pulse. Something moved under her skin. She grimaced as Clint maneuvered it around.

"Take it out!" Gretchen started to claw at herself.

"Shh, we can help with that. Doc, do you have anything to numb it before we cut it out?" Clint held her hand.

"Cut it out. I want it out of me!" She tried to pull her hand free.

Clint tightened his grip. "You're okay. I think the jolt I gave you shorted it out, which is why they left. They couldn't track you anymore."

Her wide fearful eyes met his. "Do you think?"

"Yes, we'll remove it. Just take a deep breath. Doc will be able to numb it so you won't feel it. Come on, let's sit down in the room. Casey, could your healing her old scars have healed the scar from the implant showing where they inserted the bio capsule?" Clint guided her to the bed she sat on previously.

"Yes," Casey mumbled in a soft voice.

Doc ambled back in. He unrolled a towel that hid a needle and a scalpel. She furiously nodded for him to cut it out. She looked away scrunching her eyes as he inserted the needle in several different places to numb the skin. Clint hooked his arm around her and held her steady for Doc, to use the scalpel. Casey had to look away as he removed the tracking device. Clint took it from him and ran across the street to the middle of the field across from them and crushed it under his boot.

"Casey, can you?" Doc held up Gretchen's hand to her.

"Sure." Casey took her hand and blue coursed through her fingers.

Gretchen's eyes bulged almost comically as her skin knitted back together. When Casey let go, she ran her fingers over the non-existent cut and smiled. "Now, I can fathom why they want you so bad. That is amazing."

"Not everyone with us knows what we can do. If you can keep our little secret, it will help keep us from developing into a national news phenomenon." Clint pulled his mouth into a thin line and raised his eyebrows.

"They won't hear it from me. I can never thank you enough for what you've done. You saved my life and took my scars from me. That would have been a daily reminder of what I endured for the last several years."

"Do you have anyone we can try and contact for you?" Casey sat at the end of her bed and blew out a sigh.

"As a matter of fact, I have family in the next state over that the Monarchs haven't taken over yet. Someone from there can come get me in the next day or so, if you let me stay until then?" Gretchen pleaded.

"Of course you can stay. We're targets and a risk, but you can stay until they arrive if you want to chance it." Clint moved the curtains to the side and checked out the window.

"They have a helicraft. If I can touch base with them, they can be here in less than a day. The Monarchs took me from an airport when I was trying to go home to my family.

I know they never stopped looking for me when they upped the amount of ransom." Gretchen stood.

"Casey, do you have that phone? We can have Chloe patch you through to them if you want." Clint took the phone Casey pulled out of her bag and held up for him.

With his back to Gretchen, he punched in Chloe's number, explained things to her, and then put her on the phone with Gretchen. She talked for several minutes before she hung up.

Her smile was contagious. "They're on their way and will be here in a few hours."

"She can have lunch with me before they get here." Doc ambled over, took her elbow, and walked her toward the door.

Casey reclined back on the bed and drifted off.

Thirty-One

"So, what do you think? Will she keep our secret?" Clint turned to Mark after he draped a blanket over Casey. He had Mark join them so they could discuss everything.

"I think so. Look at what the Monarchs put her through, and she didn't hesitate for you to shock her so they couldn't find her. I think we're good, and who knows... If her family has enough money to own their own helicraft, she may become a great ally to have on our side if she loves our Father like she seems to." Mark perched on the chair at the end of the bed that Casey slept on. Clint had filled him in on what happened.

"Agreed. I think God put us here to help her so she wouldn't be their prisoner again. She had no clue they tracked her. Hopefully, they didn't insert more than the one tracker in her. Let's pray her family arrives before they come back." Clint moved the curtains aside and examined the skies.

He had no clue of Casey's ability to obliterate old scars. He only thought it was new wounds or to save someone's life. Clint's hand absentmindedly grazed over his ugly scar. Shrapnel tore through him when he was overseas during one of his deployments, and it was a dreadful reminder of how deadly that certain mission was. Every time he took his shirt off, he was reminded of his friends who died over there in a mission that had gone wrong from the word go. He had her to thank for taking care of the fresh stab wound, which would have turned into yet another blemish to remind him of the previous encounter with the Monarchs.

"Want something to drink or eat? I'm going to make a sandwich." Mark stood and started for the door to head to his room.

"I'll make something later when you relieve me." Clint turned his back and kept watch through Casey's door.

"Sounds good." Mark let the bottom of his shoes drag against the concrete sidewalk with each step he took.

Clint absentmindedly rubbed at his scar while watching over Casey's sleeping form. He saw what it did. Even though she regenerated Gretchen's skin, he would put her at risk if he asked her to remove his own. He would never be selfish enough to ask for such a personal favor from her. It was something he expected to live with for the rest of his life. Looking at Casey, his mind wandered to before the time of his scars, when life was easier. He thought of Amanda but shook his head to clear it.

"That scar shouldn't make you feel guilty that you lived, and they didn't. That scar is a testament to the power of God over every situation. You survived because that was part of His plan. He still had plans for you. Look at the prophecy. You were needed here as a chosen one." The memory of Amanda telling him that after the world changed stirred in his thoughts.

He let out a deep sigh. "I don't blame myself anymore," Clint mumbled and pursed his lips as he talked to himself.

A few hours later, the sun crawled down toward the horizon. They had maybe an hour or so of daylight left when there was a shimmer of an object in the sky. Clint had made something to eat and joined Mark at the door as they took chairs from Casey's room and enjoyed the warm breeze for this time of year. Gretchen smiled as she sipped water.

"Is that them?" Clint rose from the chair his hand grazed over the holster in his waistband.

"Yes, that's my parents." Gretchen's infectious smile lit up her whole face.

"Do they have enough room to land?" Mark rose from his chair as the helicraft hovered toward them.

"My dad can land that thing on a dime." She never took her eyes off her escape from this horrible Midwest Monarch-ridden wasteland of monsters of all different types.

The helicraft landed in the parking lot, and her parents ran to her. She cried as they swept her into their arms. Her father pulled away and marched over to Clint and Mark and held out his hand to shake each of theirs. "I can't thank you enough for saving my daughter. I don't care what it is, if you ever need anything, don't hesitate to ask." He gifted Clint a small phone like the one Chloe gave Casey and a business card.

"Thank you, sir. I'm glad we were in the right place at the right time." Clint grasped his hand in a firm handshake.

"It was God's timing. And I'm serious, anything, anytime you call, and I'll provide what you need. Be careful. It won't be easy out here fighting these soldiers for Satan. At least you picked the winning side. He is risen!" He backed toward where his family waited.

"He is risen indeed!" Clint exclaimed back.

Gretchen's father smiled and trotted back to the helicraft. It took off smoothly as she waved from the small windows on the side while her mother's arms surrounded her. Clint smiled and waved back. He could count them as brothers and sisters in Christ and have faith in them to not inform the Monarchs where they were.

Clint typed a quick message to Chloe's uncle, giving him their new friend's contact information and a little about what they'd just gone through. If he did indeed have the resources to help fund their fight, then maybe he could collaborate with Chloe's uncle, and together, they would be able to get whatever they needed. He also made a note to Gretchen's father to expect contact from Chloe's uncle.

Thirty-Two

Casey woke with a start. She didn't remember falling asleep much less taking her shoes off. She turned over to Clint watching her as he sat in the open door. "How long was I asleep?"

"Long enough to miss Gretchen leave and her parents' offer to help in any way they can." Clint smiled and held up the small phone that matched hers.

"Wait. What?" Casey sat up and stifled a yawn behind her hand as she stretched her back.

"They flew a helicraft here to pick her up." Clint stood and offered her his chair.

"A heli what?" Casey frowned.

"An expensive type of helicopter that flies like a plane," Clint answered as she stood next to him.

"Can we be sure of their loyalty?" She sunk into the chair he vacated.

"Yes, they are brothers and sisters from our extended eternal family." Clint smiled and his dimples appeared.

"Great!" Casey smiled back and then stared across the field. It was quiet. Crickets chirped around them, and a loon somewhere farther away called to its mate. Frog croaks added the choir practice as if getting ready for a production.

Clint pulled a chair from their room and sat it next to them on the concrete sidewalk, which had seen better days, careful not to put a chair leg on a cracked crumbling spot. He handed Casey a bottle of water. "Did you want something to eat?"

"I'm starved. I'll make something in a minute, but thanks." She twisted off the lid of the bottle and gulped the icy cold water. It chilled her as it coursed through her body.

Clint stood and stretched. "I'm going to crash for a couple of hours so I can take an overnight watch."

"What time did you want to change duty?" Mark asked from her left and took over the chair Clint vacated.

"Zero three hundred." Clint's hand went to his side.

Casey frowned as Clint absently scratched the skin at his side. When Clint shut the door, she turned to Mark, who averted his eyes and took in the fields across from them.

"I know you heard about Ben. I'm so sorry I couldn't save him."

"Casey, Ben dying was no more your fault than it was mine. The Monarchs are evil and bent on destroying this country. Did Ben and Clint tell you about the first rush of virus that eradicated so many of us?" She shook her head no. "There was no pandemic. They lied but put such panic in the people that everyone rushed out for the so-called vaccine. That was supposed to be the magic cure the politicians shoveled down everyone's throats, even going as far as penalizing anyone who refused, and used scare tactics of having news stations exaggerate the death toll. What they didn't know was that the vaccine was designed by the Monarchs, and that was what started killing everyone. Then our scientists had to find a cure for the poison that they were pumping into our veins. No one, and I mean no one, did their own research. They all flocked to the health stations to get their free inoculations. That should have been a clue. Nothing the government does is free. They have always had their own agenda."

Mark's anger stirred something in Casey. "Who did you lose?"

He hung his head. "My twin boys. They were seven."

"Oh Mark, that's horrible." There was nothing more she could say. The loss of Ben caused such an ache, worse than anything, and it reminded her of when her family was left behind. But children, she couldn't imagine that pain.

"What is there to eat around here? Something simple? I'm too tired to make much."

"I think everyone has something to make sandwiches." Mark went to rise from the chair.

"No, let me." Casey approached the door to Clint's room.

She quietly walked through her room to the open door. The room was an inky abyss. Before she knew what was happening, an orb was sent out, lighting the small nook where they put the food. A few short moments later, she pulled a side table out to the concrete sidewalk directly in front of her room by the chairs, and they made sandwiches.

The sun penetrated the canopy as clouds dotted the sky. Goosebumps traveled down Casey's arms when the wisps of hair around the nape of her neck tickled her skin as the breeze caught them. Mark twirled the end of the bread bag until it was sealed enough to fold the end under. Casey slung the brown plaid quilted jacket that she took off the chair by the door around her.

The sun no longer hovered over the trees but streamed through them as rays of light pierced through the areas of limbs thinner than others, illuminating the field across from them. A shuffling sound coming from the dead twigs startled her. Should she warn Clint? Mark quirked an eyebrow at her when she stood and leaned against a support beam for the overhang shading the sidewalk.

Two deer poked their heads out of the line of brush. The buck was twice the size of the doe and ventured out first. Mark smiled at their cautious approach to the field. Casey studied him as he watched the wildlife. She didn't really know him, but the fact that he didn't grill her about Ben's death and didn't hesitate to take a shift to keep everyone safe, told her all she needed to know about him. He was one of the good ones.

She pictured Ben's eyes and how they took her breath away. She imagined him in his favorite dark blue polo he wore as it stretched over his biceps and pecs when he would relax on the sofa at night, kicking his feet out, and crossing them at his ankles. The black boots were severely worn on the back heels. She had noticed that the soles pulled away from where the glue held them to the material part of the boots. She wanted to surprise him with a new pair. There was no need for that now. What were Clint and she supposed to do with only the two of them left? Tears threatened to fall. She couldn't break down. They didn't have time for that. They would stay strong for the group until they moved again.

The thought of leaving Ben's grave bothered her. She knew he wasn't here anymore; he was with his sister in heaven but that didn't stop her from wanting to see him again more than anything.

They desired to boost morale. Even something small like new shoes and outfits would help. Chloe had connections to work on getting everyone new footwear and threads. They were worn and weathered from the life they lived, doling out punishment on their footwear as they hid from the monsters and terrorists that hunted them.

She looked down as her fingers brushed over her own tattered hem. She didn't think about anything for herself but wanted to take care of the people with her. The thin material of the plaid only made her smile; it was Amanda's favorite jacket, and she wore it all the time.

Clint moseyed through the door, yawning and stretching his arms over his head. He rubbed his hand over his face, which looked recently splashed with water. How long had she sat there lost in her own thoughts? She took the food from the table back to his room. Mark left from his rotation while she and Clint sat in silence. Neither one spoke; they were both hurting.

Several minutes passed as the deer grazed on the bushes that had taken over the field and dotted the landscape. Another doe galloped across. Their ears perked up and twitched every which direction, alert. Casey listened; she didn't hear anything. A second later, she noticed the hum of an engine. She deployed the shield as the buck, wide-eyed, popped his white tail up, letting the others know there was danger, and bolted across the road that curved and into the undergrowth of brush around the edge of the trees.

Clint's hand was warm when he swiped it across her back. She jolted and the shield glimmered on the inside, telling them the invisible setting hid them from outsiders. Her hands shook as she grasped his. "I'm going to tell everyone to hunker down."

Headlights pierced the night as diesel engines rumbled in the distance. A second set of headlights appeared behind the first set. Then a third. Something was up.

Casey raised her chin toward the seven large, military-grade vehicles that sat on the road with their massive engines idling. "We don't need to do that this time. With that artillery they have, this building will collapse on everyone inside, whether they're hunkered down or not. Not a single projectile will get through this time."

"Let them see what I can do."

Clint gave her a chin lift and activated his weapon before disappearing through the door.

A click to Casey's left startled her as Clint shifted his rifle in his hands. She was so intent on watching the vehicles, that she never noticed he had retrieved his weapon. He held up a holster and waited for her to put it on before passing her the handgun she had practiced with the other day. As she shifted it into the holster, his hand on her shoulder gave a nimble squeeze. He smiled and gave a curt nod. She gave a single stiff-necked nod back, trying to mimic his action.

"What are they doing?" Clint dropped to his knees to kneel in the doorway and peered through his scope, the rifle braced against a table.

"How many are there?" Casey stood proud yet angry. They took away the only person she had ever been in love with; she was fighting back no matter what.

"There are now nine vehicles and the windows are too tinted to get a visual of how many are inside. They're probably looking for Gretchen. One of the men also mentioned a motel built here, so more than likely, someone backed his story and they launched a squadron to investigate." Clint's right eye returned to the scope when the first vehicle in line started to inch forward.

"How dense can you make the shield? We may find out in the next couple of minutes what kind of assault it can withstand." Clint grimaced.

Casey's eyes flecked with diamonds and her hair whipped around the back of her head. She stood and walked to the open door as the first truck pulled in front. She cleared the shield's opacity so that they would see what they were up against. The loud reverberating diesel engine rumbled as five large men unloaded from the interior of the truck. A wide array of weapons slung over their torsos. "Don't you worry about the shield. They are only getting through over my dead body."

Clint studied her before lowering to gaze through his sight.

"Clint, when the last one gets in line, how about you disable their trucks." Casey didn't look at him but narrowed her eyes to the terrorists that stood in front of her. Her feet left the ground, her hair flowed around behind her. She refused to let a single bullet through this time. Let's see what they brought and how they would react to God's shield.

"They will have no way to retreat. We don't want them with no place to go." Clint rose and went to Casey at the door, taking in the fact that her feet didn't meet the ground.

"They won't be retreating. They're here to claim me. I'm their prize. How about we give them that prize, though not in the way they expect it?" Casey smirked over her shoulder at Clint.

"Okay, that's an ominous look. What do you have in mind?" Clint switched his weapon to the second setting and waited for the last one to join the others, so two rows of machines blocked both directions of the two-lane road.

"Father, help us today. Show us what You want us to do with these men who are bent on evil. Let us follow You and not our own will today. Let us hear You and know in our hearts it's Your will. Is it Your will to go up against them today and will You give us victory? In Jesus Christ's name, amen." Casey lifted her head.

Clint glowered at the growing number of men spilling out of the vehicles across the road. "Amen."

"Go against them. I will be with you."

The red pulse emerged and spanned the width of the vehicles. It increased as Casey concentrated on it, and she separated her hands as the red pulse spread out with the movement so it enveloped all nine vehicles at once. The deafening quiet that followed the disabled diesel trucks as the engines failed coursed through the air. She winked at Clint. His weapon never traversed that much ground and disabled so much at a single time. His weapon had delivered small compact pulses.

Several seconds passed as the men were startled by the revelation that their crippled trucks lay in operable heaps and that they were in trouble. The men tried to yell over each other as they scrambled to the other side of their vehicles and took aim at the diamond-speckled shield with their prize standing inside, out of reach. Their fear of her and the shield permeated from their hushed murmurs between each other. Maybe they were not as invincible as they seemed to be, and that would play in their demise.

Shots rang out as Casey's head drooped, and she raised her arms. The shield became a solid opaque wall. The bullets didn't lodge in the shield like they had in the past but were deflected, ricocheting back at the men who fired them. Bullets ripped holes in the dead vehicles, through the doors to the other side.

The men screamed and dropped to the ground. Several of them were taken down by their cohorts' friendly fire that ricocheted off the shield. Three men scaled the vehicles to get to the high-caliber turrets and took aim.

"Casey?" Clint called to her.

She strengthened the shield. Moisture trickled down her neck and dripped from her downcast forehead. Her skin flushed red as if she spent hours in the sun. The high-caliber reports pierced the evening. Animals scurried across the fields, fleeing from the deadly men. Again, the shield deflected the large rounds back at the men who fired them. More and more men littered the street between the mangled trucks ripped apart from the shrapnel of the lethal rounds.

Irreparable hunks of metal gave a vague resemblance of the vehicles they once were. Not a single tire remained inflated. Instead, they crushed those men who tried to hunker down under the hunks of bent metal when the bullets tore through the soft rubber sidewalls. With only a couple left, they must have thought it was all or nothing as two of them hauled rocket launchers to their shoulders. Clint scrambled, diving for the floor and calling her to join him.

The unmistakable roar and rumble from the rockets as they launched out of the tubes with a swooshing sound—almost instantaneously—made her flinch. Her ears rang as they exploded against the shield in a fireball. The fire roared along the shield, mapping the entire shape of the dome. The men's mouths sagged open. Citrine sparks glittered in her eyes as Clint moved behind her.

A yellow beam skyrocketed to the line of dead trucks in front of them. It struck it in the side, catapulting it over the men and into the field.

Casey winked at Clint as she stood on her tiptoes and peeked over her shoulder. "Clint, I need your weapon."

He scrambled, joining her on her right. The men took aim with their rifles.

"Do you really think that will work this time?" Casey tipped her head to the side toward the men that took aim.

The men looked down at their squadron, dead all around them. They pitched their guns and backed away with their shaky hands held away from their sides. Casey held out her hand and Clint took it. She turned his hand over and moved the stone in the center, and diamond flecks arced down from the shield to it as if small lightning bolts energized the weapon. Static danced over his hands and up his arms.

"Send a pulse at them," Casey sneered.

The pulse journeyed through the shield, and Casey maneuvered it with her hands and expanded it to include the trucks, bodies, and weapons that littered the street. Crackling static sizzled in the air as vehicles burst into white incendiary blurs. A blaze roared over the remains of the squadron as the metal turned into red smoldering embers in the melted steel, which resembled lava. Thunder rumbled overhead as the asphalt started to melt. The last two men took off into the field, running from their comrades who no longer fought at their side as the white-hot inferno consumed them. Lightning crackled and snapped through the air and arced down, hitting the last two surviving Monarchs in this squadron.

Clint flinched and ducked down as static danced through the air. Casey retracted the shield. Rain poured down on them. Metal sizzled in the hot molten piles left on the road and sent up plumes of steam. Soon, the downpour extinguished the last of the fires. Clint let out a long shrill whistle, something they discussed and practiced after the last attack on the motel. That way, everyone knew it was safe to come out.

Doors opened and their group dotted the front walkway under the overhang that protected them from the rain. Doc hooted as he joined the three of them.

"What happened?" Doc held the back of the chair for support.

"Casey," Clint answered.

"Wait. How did you melt cars?" Doc looked over the top of the glasses that were perched on the end of his nose.

"I set up the shield to cover everyone. They took themselves out. Well, more or less." Casey pulled off her light jacket, her skin flushed red as if she spent hours out in the sun. She swiped at her brow.

"So, everyone is tired with the late hour. Can I tell them they can relax without worrying?"

"Sure, the Monarchs are unable to pierce the shield no matter the weapon." Clint hoisted his rifle from the table on the way to his room.

Doc limped down the walkway and waved at the others to indicate that they were okay for the night. They all retreated to their place after several minutes of gawking at the remaining wreckage of the Monarchs squadron. The rain let up to a slow sprinkle as lightning tore across the sky.

"How did you know how to do that with my weapon?" Clint collapsed with a thud into a chair.

"Have you ever noticed the symbols on my arms glow in different patterns?" Casey draped her jacket over the back of her chair before dropping to the seat.

"I haven't paid attention."

Casey pointed to several that were still glowing faintly. "Those talk about the weapons. The prophecy is writing itself in the symbols of my skin. Like I'm an instruction manual. I never put two and two together until tonight when I was hovering, waiting for them to make the first move."

Clint gently turned over her arm as the last of the glowing symbols winked out to the faded hemp color the rest of them were. "You look overheated and your skin is warm. I thought that mainly happened when you had to use the healing relic along with the shield."

"Maybe the combination of the weapons together does it. I'm fine. I'm starting to think my core temperature increases during use. It's already dropping." She clasped Clint's hand.

"You mean you were hotter than this? I don't think that's good." Clint walked through to his room. Rejoining her, he cracked open a water for her.

"What are you doing?" Clint tried to pull his hand away as a blue spark zapped his palm when she grabbed it after taking the water.

"Hang on." She hooked her thumb around his, wrapping her fingers around the back of his hand as if she were going to arm wrestle him. Blue flecks skipped and shimmered down her arms to Clint.

He grimaced and flinched as a spasm rippled through his side. His eyes grew wide, which told her he figured out what she was doing. "You don't have to do this."

"Yes, I do." Casey let go of Clint's hand and tried to give him one of the chin lifts he was frequently using while the corner of her mouth twitched.

"Why did you do that?" Clint exposed his side and ran his hand up and down. The mottled shrapnel damage on his side marring his six-pack vanished.

"Because I wanted to." She walked around him and pitched the empty water bottle she drained in one go.

"Casey, you shouldn't have," Clint stammered.

"How often does someone do something for you? In the couple of years that I've known you, I've never seen you once ask for anything. You're a champion for these people and are ready to die for them. You are not only my friend but also my protector. I'm aware of what you told Amanda and Ben. You were there for me through so many nights when nightmares would haunt me. I can never repay the love and kindness you have shown me. It was time you're shown that love and how much you mean to people."

"That isn't why I do what I do." Clint huffed as he rubbed his hand over his unscarred side.

"I know that." Casey put her hand on his arm. "Clint, you are one of the sweetest, most genuine people I've ever met. Anyone is lucky to have you in their life. And the fact that God has you as my own appointed protector, you take that job seriously. You put yourself out there for me all the time. I wanted to tell you how grateful I am that you are here with us."

"I'm not sure what to say." Clint shook his head.

"There's nothing to say. If God didn't want me to erase old scars I wouldn't have that ability, now, would I?" She smiled up at him as she struggled to keep her now heavy eyelids open. She shook her head.

Casey meandered into their room for another bottle and sauntered back to the front door. Her eyelids sagged as she cracked open the seal and took a drink. "I'm tired, so I'm going to sleep for a bit. Warn me if we need the shield again." Casey tapped her communicator.

"Are you okay?" Clint steadied her with a grip on her elbow.

She smiled. "I promise." She nodded to the sky as lightning coursed through the dark clouds. "It's past my bedtime. The street lamps are on."

Clint's chuckle drowned out as Casey bolted the door behind her and drained the last of the water. She left her shoes at the end of the bed and smiled as she listened as Clint paced on the front walk. Exhaustion drifted in before her head sank into the lopsided, misshapen pillow.

Thirty-Three

It had been several months since Chloe left them; she messaged every day to ask how everyone was. She seemed to be in good spirits, and they kept her up to date on their progress. They moved immediately after the Monarchs attacked the hotel that left them with an obliterated squadron, sent to capture her. Cameras found in the melted aftermath of the vehicles alerted the Monarchs of Clint, who was now added to their so-called shopping list.

They had moved an additional three times since the incident with Gretchen. No one seemed to bother unpacking since the last location where they stayed for less than a day when the insects appeared. Chloe's uncle was almost ready with hopefully new permanent houses for them if not for the fact the Monarchs kept finding them. Several times, Clint spent an hour or more on the phone with her. She figured it was her crush and an attempt to talk to him, when one day he sprung the news the military wanted him back. The Monarchs had targeted more than their little ragtag group. Robotic insects were now attacking civilians and cities with refugee camps.

The death toll rose from those creatures, and the military required Clint's input and asked him to reenlist and engage in battle for the government to regain control of the country.

They offered him a large jump in pay and a nice advancement in rank to go with it.

"Clint, you need to go if your heart is pushing you to. What's God telling you?" Casey's heart ached and a knot formed in her stomach at the thought of being alone, but he was a soldier and he was used to fighting on the front lines; that was what he was good at.

"She's right, buddy. Where's God telling you to go?" Doc perched his glasses higher on his nose.

"No, we have to stay together. We're what's left of the bloodlines for the relics. We can't separate now since we're both targets. With Casey's improved abilities using the shield and being able to manipulate the pulses from my weapon, we are bound by the relics." Clint crossed his hands behind his head.

The military asked for Clint to head up the special team due to his military background, his relic's power, and what he learned about the Monarchs. He declined even though he was the right person for the job but offered to pass any information along to the person in charge. He was military through and through, and it was who he was, but he was a Christian soldier first and forever for his Heavenly Father and he refused to leave them. He was prouder of that than the honor of his military service from his enlisted time, that he usually didn't talk about.

The US military was unmatched in its relentless pursuit of getting America back to where it once was. Soldiers, strong and proud of their country, were unyielding in their pursuit of obliterating the Monarchs from America once and for all.

"This is where I'm needed. This is where God needs me, and I won't leave you, no matter how much you want me to go." Clint smirked and narrowed his eyes at Doc.

"Oh, stop it! We love you and we would hate for you to go back to the military and not have you beside us." Doc stood.

This was a decision Clint had to make himself, and he made it. Did he love the military? Yes, he was proud of his years of service, but it didn't have the same draw it had years ago. His place was here. She recognized the gleam in his eyes that there was nothing to keep him away from what God had for him, especially when they had learned that the world had agreed to go to a one-world currency. They were excited by this news, which was one of the signs that God was coming back soon for His children.

"Trust me, this is where I want to be because this is where God put me for a reason." Clint crossed his arms, leaning against the railing in the stall as they assembled in secret.

"Good enough for me. Let's take a headcount. This last attack the other day, our numbers took a hit, and we need to reorganize so we can determine how to move everyone." Doc frowned.

The new farm was set and ready to go, but it seemed that the Monarchs found them faster and faster with every move, and they came to only one conclusion. They had a mole in their midst, and it became vital to the lives of everyone to separate from that operative. The Monarchs were smart. They sent in unassuming people with no fighting skills. They knew they couldn't get past Clint to get to Casey because they always had her room at the farthest point away from the rest of the group as soon as the attacks started up after the motel. Clint was taking his job as protector of the key seriously and smothering her with his security.

They added some stragglers during their food runs so it was hard to tell who to count on besides their initial core group who started this together. They would have to stick with who they knew and trusted. It was hard to be that way, but it was perilous for them to continue to bring in just anyone who asked for help. They only put innocents in harm's way by bringing in so many people. Maybe if they stuck with referrals by trusted people, they'd be able to help more and stop putting lives in danger with the spies that worked with the Monarchs giving up their location.

They would need to discuss at length the possibility of separating themselves from those who came in after they left the warehouses. Maybe they would tackle that conversation with Doc first before their talk with him and the others in their trusted unit tonight. They'd want their opinion on what they thought of the heated conversations in separating into two factions. Could they establish a second location far enough away to keep their site secret yet introduce it as a way to keep everyone alive by living in smaller sets?

Clint and Casey talked about it over the last couple of days while the others slept. Tonight, they would try and present it to their trusted and closest friends.

"Looks like we lost a total of six out of this last attack." Casey shook her head she didn't like that people died on their watch.

"Six?" Doc dropped his mouth open.

"Yes. We have to find a way to weed out the spies, and I'm sorry to say, either leave them behind or—" Casey couldn't finish her statement.

"Kill them," Clint finished for her. She was aware her struggle with the day-to-day decisions they had to make when it concerned death bothered him.

"Can't we leave them behind with no way to follow us?" Doc backed up; his instincts were to save everyone he could because of his oath when he became a doctor. It was an always-occurring internal battle.

"This is war. If we don't fight back, we will lose more." Clint glared.

Doc let a sigh escape. "I wish it was different."

"It isn't. They don't hesitate to end one of us, and the person who's leaking our locations is as guilty as if they pulled the trigger themselves. We can't keep losing people, or there will be no one left to fight for." Clint kicked at a pile of dirt as he clenched his fist.

"Okay, first talk to the core tonight to discuss the option of separating ourselves from those who were not with us when I, um, became a member. They have been with us long enough that I think we can trust them. We'll have to present it just as we discussed." Casey looked around as a shadow passed by one of the slats that was askew on the back side.

Clint looked down as a smile played at the corners of his mouth, and he put his arm around her and gently squeezed. This was the first time they congregated during the day, but they were out of options to meet in secret with the turn of events. It was important to work everything out immediately and not wait for the cover of night.

"Okay Doc, head around and quietly inform everyone we want to suggest this to out of the original few, and we can decide from there." Clint proceeded through the rolling doors toward the house, his footsteps sluggish as if walking to a firing squad.

They had a huge feast planned for that night to try and boost morale. It had taken a severe hit after the last couple of moves they had to deal with.

People laughed and joked with each other. Small groups split and formed around the main spread of food. Chloe's uncle sent so many perishables, they had to find a way to consume them before they went bad so the feast was used twofold. One, to not let perfectly good food go to waste, and second, to bring everyone together in a family setting.

Everyone had really gone out of their way to make tonight special and put on the back burner the dreary world they now lived in, if only for a few hours.

Clint clamped his hand onto Casey's, drawing her from her reverie. "What's going on in that head of yours?"

"Just thinking about who is a danger to us. Everyone seems to be so happy and joyous. I can't picture one being the monster that they undoubtedly are. If Ben were still here he could help figure this out, instead of you feeling like it is all your responsibility." Casey nervously bounced from one leg to the other.

"Do you still want to meet tonight?" he whispered.

Casey nodded her gaze on the ground. "Yes, with the food everyone devoured today, their stomachs should be full enough. They will doze through our meeting, and we can pull this off without being noticed."

"They're aware and will meet after everyone else has fallen asleep." Doc ambled over to the dessert side of the spread and indulged himself with another piece of cake.

Everyone packed up the leftover food and loaded it into the once bare refrigerator that now held several days of food for everyone. Casey nodded to Clint. She wished they didn't have to separate. Several had become very dear friends. They talked about using the ring's powers on every new person, yet they would remember being questioned. She wasn't sure whether that was a way to earn their loyalty or destroy it. After this, they would be hesitant to bring anyone in since it was too hard with the world the way it was. Maybe it was time for them to go their own way. The Monarchs wanted them, not the others. They would be casualties, only seen as obstacles standing between them and the Chosen Ones.

Thirty-Four

Everyone snuck out of the house one by one after the others had gone to bed. The original core crowd consisted of only eight people now. The mood was a solemn one; no one liked the idea of splitting up as some of them had become more than friends, family even. Each had their own ideas of who to depend on and who not to.

Doc was quiet. Everyone stopped and looked at him as he cleared his throat. "I think Clint has the right idea. I didn't like saying goodbye to six of our own the other day. I'm tired of failing those closest in our family, who have been with us since the beginning. Rick was one of those we lost. Casey has her limits. She doesn't have an endless supply of energy to take care of all of us all the time."

Everyone murmured between each other, talking over others who tried to speak their mind. It was easy with their growing size to not realize someone was missing. Christy cried. She was going to marry Rick, and hearing his name caused the hurt to resurface. Red blotches dotted her face as she tried to hide her pain. Doc stood next to her and held her. He was like a father to so many.

"Please, we need to get to the bottom of who the leak is first. Then, I don't see why we can't keep us all together." This came from Mark, who was friendly to another member from the latest few to join them.

"We also want that. But in the meantime, to give you a fighting shot, until we're able to sort out who the Monarchs dispatched to destroy us from the inside, we need to break into smaller groups. The final decision would be majority rule. We don't want to dictate who can and can't join and make that decision for every person. Hence this meeting." Casey hoped what they suggested sunk in. She didn't want to fail anyone else, but she didn't want them to feel that they took over telling them what they could and couldn't do.

"I agree with Clint. We can't continue to suffer the loss of those that we love. And I'm not saying our loving someone is more important than anyone else. But we have to figure something out, and after this last bunch we took in, all we've been doing is running, and I'm tired. I want to be secure if only for a few months. This jumping up in the middle of the night because the Monarchs have found us again every couple of weeks or so is killing us a little inside. The positive perk of your new abilities to hear them coming and the early alert the ring sounds out I think is the only reason so many of us are still here. We can't keep our heads on straight and we're so scared. They're wearing us out. I vote to leave so we can weed out the spy that has found their way into our family and friends." Christy's nasal voice hitched as she wiped the tears with the back of her hand.

Everyone nodded in agreement. The monthly moves wore them down, and everyone was getting short and snippy with everyone else.

Mark looked at Clint. "You have always fought and put your lives on the line for us. I may miss some of the newest people, but we have to give them a chance to live. If they aren't traitors, we will be reunited and be a big family again someday. I say we give this to God and go out on our own and maybe live to spread his word and get a few more adopted into our eternal family."

"Okay, let's take a vote." Clint climbed up on the taller hay bale and nodded. "Who wants to divide into two sets?"

Everyone agreed; it was unanimous and everyone smiled and hugged one another. "Okay, that means we have to keep this quiet and not tell anyone else what we're doing. We need a second site ready to go, fast, so we can end this as soon as possible. This is the second longest we've been out and haven't had to move in the past few months so I'm expecting an attack at any moment."

"Clint, we already have another one almost ready. We decided this time to finish a couple so we had more options to hop faster when they find us. I guess God was already stirring our hearts to have more than one place ready to go." Doc smiled.

"Great news. We'll have you busy yourselves with packing things and loading all the newest members in the first van. Sam will drive them to the designation for them and give them the impression the second van will leave a little while after them, so both vans aren't spotted on the road together. They will expect you to follow, when in reality, you will head out to the one that was ready to go for you. It will be hard on them, and they won't understand why we're doing this, but I also have a note detailing what's going on and how to keep everyone safeguarded. I'm going to slip that into Sam's belongings so he can find it when they reach their destination." Clint shook his head.

Several praised God for the insight to have more than one location ready, and they agreed to tell them that, so they didn't wonder and feel abandoned. Everyone gathered in a circle to pray. Bowing their heads Doc's voice filled the air. "Our Heavenly Father, we thank You for this great family You have given us. You are our God and King, and we are here for You. May You keep us sheltered and help us find the one that the Monarchs directed to destroy Your people. May You give us the wisdom to open our eyes and let us know in our hearts who it is without any doubt or tampering by Satan. We thank You, Father, for Your love and sending Your son to die for us. We're not worthy of that gift and can only give You our lives and live for You. Thank You, Father, for all that You have given us and all that You have stored for us in heaven, in Your son Jesus's name, amen."

Everyone said amen and hugged before stealthily making their way back to the house in clusters of two or three. A set of eyes appeared through the slots on the side, and Casey clung to Clint's arm. He tipped his head to the side of the door, waiting for everyone to make it back to the house. Careless clumsy boots crunched through the shrubs, carrying someone quickly away from them through the shadows around to the front. Stealth was not in their ability to move through the dark of night.

Clint looked at Casey, his nostrils flared as his lips thinned to a small line. Someone heard their plans, and now they were in the house with everyone else. How could they discover who it was?

They quickly and quietly entered through the back. Clint pointed to the couch down the short hallway from the kitchen. Someone lay on their back shrouded with a blanket with their head turned toward the back of the couch. A snore reached them in the kitchen, as goosebumps erupted on Casey's arms. They made their way to the stairs that would take them up to their beds. As they reached the bottom, Clint squeezed Casey's arm. On the floor under the shoed feet of the person who curled on the couch a leaf came to rest on the solid hardwood floors that begged to be swept.

Clint motioned for her to move up, and they did without so much as a sound. They gathered in Casey's room, which was at the far end of the hallway. Clint locked the door. The latch didn't make a sound when it fell into place.

"Okay, we need out of here. I think we found our leak. Should we confront this person? Or do we keep to how we have it planned and agreed to tonight? This changes things." Clint plopped down on the end of the bed. The springs groaned under him.

"I'm now wondering if maybe we also leave. Who's to say we don't have more than one mole? We need to guard our initial bunch; we've never had an issue before, except for James. I say we go back to the original group." Casey edged over to the door and listened. She could've sworn she heard something.

"I don't disagree. There are other individuals out there for people who need help that we can send them to. I think this just confirms we need to go out on our own. Since we're the targets that the Monarchs want, we're only putting the lives of everyone else on the line by staying with them." Clint stood to the side so his shadow wouldn't be seen out the window.

"I know what you're saying makes sense, but the thought of everyone who was in the barn tonight being on their own without us protecting them rubs me the wrong way." She nodded to the door again. She put a finger to her lips, then toward the door. Clint strolled across the room as they shared a look when floorboards creaked. Someone made their way to the room, and she wasn't sure if that someone was friend or foe.

"We'll talk when we go for a walk in the woods. There, we don't have to worry about anyone eavesdropping." Clint pulled his firearm from his waistband and gestured for her to stand behind the door and open it.

Casey took a deep breath and nodded to Clint, ready to yank open the door.

No one was there. Crushed leaves littered the floor of the hallway. Clint whispered, "Lock the door tonight, or do you want me to sleep on the floor? I don't like you being in here by yourself."

"I'll be fine. You're right across the way if I need anything, and they will have to pass your room to get to mine." Casey clutched the doorknob, her fingertips turning white.

Casey secured the door only after Clint skulked off, keeping an eye on the dark space until he was safely inside and she heard the snick of his own lock. She put her gun on the nightstand, just in case.

"I'm tempted to go down and have a little conversation." Casey sat on the side of the bed furthest from the door and nervously toed off her shoes.

"Case, we can't. We have to think about the others. What if there's more than one, and they call for an attack when their partner is outed?" Clint sighed as she heard the bed springs in his room through their communicator.

She let her head fall forward, her shoulders slumped. Oh, how she missed Ben. "I just want this to end. Where does this all lead to?" She put her arms around her knees as she brought her legs up to her body, when a board rubbed against a nail outside her room.

She moved to the door and listened, firearm in hand. Another creak and her hand migrated silently to the doorknob. When a board on the other side of their door scraped against the nail again, she opened it. Clint paused with his toothbrush hanging out of his mouth. Casey laughed and shut the door. With the gun back on the nightstand, she flipped off the light, allowing just the moonlight to drift through the threadbare curtains that hung at an odd angle across the boarded-up window. All the nervousness melted away as she reached for the pillow under her head and crumpled it to make a fluffier mass to lay her head on. A small sliver of moonlight that highlighted the coarse planked floor directly underneath the curtains was the last thing she saw as she let sleep drag her under.

Thirty-Five

The sun streamed through the bottom of the curtains. Clint smiled. Casey seemed to be sound asleep if her soft snores coming through his communicator were any indication. He only slipped on his jeans before shoving the holster into the back of his waistband and then he eased the door open. He finagled the lock on her door so he could check on her. Her hair swept across the pillow behind her head. Clint fastened the door behind him soundlessly before he watched the living room for any signs of movement. The couch was empty; nature's fall colors still littered the floor where they had fallen the night before.

He squatted to view more of the living room from his position. Satisfied when no one was there, he rose and his left knee popped. He tugged the T-shirt over his head. He had flipped it across his shoulder before he left his room. An abrupt nod to himself, and he descended to the lower part of the house. A couple of women in the kitchen heated up parts of the dinner for a makeshift breakfast. Fruit piled high in bowls, and croissants overflowed to the table as they put jams and jellies out for anyone's liking.

Clint smiled at the women. "Anyone else up this early?"

"That one kid with the weird hair," one of them replied.

"Now, that isn't nice. Maybe he is finding himself?" the other scolded.

"But I don't get it." She held up a plate to Clint, who chose a croissant and ate it on the way out the back door.

Casey moseyed out. "Morning."

"Sorry, did I wake you?" Clint felt guilty that his moving around woke her.

"Nope, was halfway to the conscious world when you jimmied the lock on my door." She narrowed her eyes at him but couldn't mask the smirk on her lips.

"We need to determine where he went. He has to be the one from last night. I hope he hasn't told the Monarchs where we are yet. Maybe we can get everyone on their way before they show up," Clint said with a large bite of half the bread chipmunked into his cheek.

"I agree we go our own way." Casey nodded when Clint met her eyes. "It may be the only way to keep them safe. We can tell them that we're heading somewhere else. Let the person who infiltrated our group offer to stay."

"What if we have more than one plant?" Clint swallowed the bite.

"Do you think there's a possibility that there is more than one?" Casey shook her head.

One was bad enough. He couldn't imagine the Monarchs sending two of them.

"I'm throwing out possibilities. We've taken in quite a few over the last couple of months." Clint maneuvered the door to the side, trying to keep it on the rails it rolled across.

"I'm going to feel horrible if the newest group that we separated from gets in trouble because we did this and the infiltrator follows them. They will be compromised." Casey took in the space as Clint secured the door behind them.

An amber orb floated above them and illuminated the harrowing farm tools in a yellowish amber haze. There was no pulse alerting them that the Monarchs were in close proximity.

"Looks like he isn't in here," Clint claimed after the orb floated back to Casey.

Lit only by the rising sun through the narrow slats between boards and through the large gap in the roof that looked as though it may collapse at any moment, Clint wrinkled his nose at the mildewed bales of hay that still bothered him, even though he had been exposed to the microscopic spores of mold for over a month. As he sneezed, he doubted his body would ever get accustomed to it. Casey's sneeze a little later told him she had the same issues.

"Bless you. It'll be hard enough on the new people to find out they aren't included anymore. Let's hope there isn't more than one Monarch so they can live their lives. Doc won't be okay with us leaving." Clint hoisted himself to a splintered railing that creaked.

"Doc will want to argue. Are the vans ready to go? If we can move everyone out today, maybe the Monarchs will be thrown off and lose some momentum trying to apprehend us." Casey stretched her neck from side to side.

"Yes, the vans are ready to go. I think you're right though; we offer to stay behind, and if anyone volunteers to stay with us, it is who we are searching for. With a bit of luck, he'll be the only one to jump on board. I don't want people to remain to only muck up our plan. Who knows how many may offer to stay while there's only one who we're looking for?" Clint puckered his brow as the railing groaned again.

"We'll pray that God will keep who we want with us and keep both parties sequestered from the Monarchs. Like Mark said, maybe they can be reunited shortly and be one large family." Casey bowed her head.

Clint hopped off the railing. "Father, let the Monarchs' emissary offer to stay with us so we know that he is the only danger. Let the division work out and keep them both undetected as we lower the numbers to be less noticeable out there. Keep Your heavenly warriors as a hedge of protection around both groups. Thank You for Your love and protection through these trying times. Give them peace on all sides for a while like You did for Israel; they need a break. Your children cry out to You for help as they're worn out from the struggles in this life. Let Your will be done, Father. In Jesus Christ's name, amen." Clint glanced up as the door opened.

"What's going on?" Doc slinked into the shadowy gloom.

"Talking about the groups separating. We're going to tell the second group when the vans are loaded up and ready to go. We're also wondering if the mole will offer to stay with us, and we prayed that God would let that happen so we know everyone will be taken care of." Clint smiled. He didn't want to tell Doc the complete separation included him and Casey from everyone also.

"You have a good point. I think we need to keep the danger away from them. I don't think they'll be as much of a target if we leave." Doc's calloused hands wrung together, twisting his gnarled fingers.

"Good, we need to split up. When are we looking at the vans leaving? Someone was lurking around during our meeting last night. We want to keep it a secret that we know who it is until we load up and see if he is just curious or worse, someone with ill intent." Clint relaxed as Doc accepted his explanation of what the plans were.

"We're hoping this afternoon. Sam isn't aware we aren't going. He will struggle with this. We can keep in touch. Chloe sent me an extra phone that I'll give them to make sure they don't have any trouble." Casey stopped as a shadow moved across the back wall.

Clint couldn't tell if it was a large animal or someone walking around. He crept forward and tried to get a view through a gap in one of the boards. A shadow ran past. He removed his nine from his jeans before the shadow moved more than a foot. He repositioned himself so he could keep an eye on more of the remote woods. A deer stopped right next to the gap he was by. Clint smiled before tugging his shirt back in place over the waistband at the back. A rabbit darted through, startling the deer, and it took off.

"Who was it?" Casey stood on her tiptoes to see over the bail of mildewed hay.

Clint chuckled. "A deer and a rabbit."

"Sounds like the start of a bad joke." She smiled.

A tremor along the ground got their attention. They hurried out as the ground under their feet rumbled while a roar reached them. Here they came again. They yelled for everyone to go into the house. Casey slipped off her jacket when the last person lurched through the doorway. She held up her hands and the shield engulfed the house only seconds before the first insect erupted from the ground, spilling from the soil along with others, as if pushed up like an ant hill between the house and the tree line. Then one of the large beastly mantises sent more of the smaller ones several feet into the air where their wings unfolded and took them to the top part of the shield.

It shook itself, as if a wet dog, sending dirt flying in every direction. It narrowed its eyes at Clint. He directed his weapon, and it speckled red at the mantis. It reared back and moved to the side. Did it recognize the relic as being something dangerous for its survival? Clint adjusted his aim and again, it skittered to the side.

"Are you seeing this?" Casey's jaw was open.

"Is it moving out of the way of my aim?" Clint stepped to the left and trained his weapon at it when it did the same thing again.

"That thing recognizes our relics!" Casey ducked under Clint's hand and walked several paces to her left. Its beady eyes followed her. As soon as she tried again, it weaved out of the way. "Okay, that can't be good." Casey raised her eyebrows at him.

Clint rotated the stone. Static flowed over Clint's fingers and hand as he worked to manipulate the sparks into an orb about the size of a baseball by rounding it with his hands. He spun it in the air and lobbed it between his palms as if it were a real baseball. The creatures marched between Casey and Clint's positions. Casey nodded at Clint, like a catcher giving the pitcher a sign of what she wanted him to throw, and directed the ring again. The mantis darted close to Clint, who delivered a static orb through the shield, exploding in a mass of sparks on the metallic scales. Its high-pitched screech pierced the air. Casey and Clint clamped their hands over their ears.

It zigzagged several times before it scampered away as electricity charred the metal plates, sending a fireball back up through the opening in the ground seconds later. Casey shuffled forward as the smaller mantises dropped lifelessly around them.

"Nice." Clint walked through the shield. He turned back to Casey and shrugged.

Casey withdrew the shield and held his arm to balance herself as she took in the mysterious fissure. He steadied her by her hand as she inclined even farther over the gaping chasm. She straightened and shook her head. It was gone.

"Okay, let's load everyone up." Clint ran to the house.

Casey walked in the back door as Clint called for everyone to load up into the vans on the side of the house. Casey went to collect the parchment satchel and relics that they didn't wear on a daily basis since she'd absorbed their abilities.

Clint pulled one van up to the back doors as Sam steered the other one parallel to them. The original few had already discussed staying back in the house, busying themselves with things to do so the second crowd would all load into the van together. That plan seemed to be working. They stood with boxes in hand to go out to their van, loading them into the back before settling into the seats.

"We need a couple more rooms for the last few we took in." Doc was making small talk, knowing they would have more than enough room.

"They can use ours." Clint made sure no one else could eavesdrop on their conversation. He was still hesitant to leave them if they truly were in danger. Once the first van left, they would say their goodbyes to their friends, knowing they set off for a different place.

"Where are you going to stay?" Doc squinted over his glasses.

"We aren't going this time. Come on, let's go. Everyone pack up." Clint turned toward the window to keep a watchful eye. Unfortunately, a couple who were en route to the line at the van heard this, murmured remarks of frustration, and dismay traveled like a riptide through the people still leaving the house.

"You'll be safer if we aren't around. The Monarchs are after us and the relics. We have to leave. It gives you a better chance at survival," Casey explained quickly.

"But what if you need help?" Doc was as stubborn as ever. He didn't want any of the flock to leave.

"Doc, you know how much of a danger we pose to you every time the Monarchs are around?" Casey lowered her voice to make sure no one could overhear them.

"Don't tell us where you are. We can't give away any information we don't have, if either of us are captured." Clint whispered the last part.

Sam leaped in the van with the newest additions. He would make a great leader for them. He was smart and capable of running a farm. He was an engineer before the Monarchs invaded so his work history was perfect for being able to figure out how to run the large equipment. He prayed he found Clint's letter soon so they could settle on how they wanted to handle things, instead of waiting around for the others to join them. Sam would have his work cut out for him when he learned his van load was the only one going to their site.

"Wait, what are you saying? You won't even be able to come to us where we are?" Doc grumbled.

"We'll keep in touch with Doc, but other than that, you won't know where we are and vice versa."

"When did you decide this?" Doc gaped at Clint. He assessed both of their faces, and his expression changed to one of heartache that the two of them didn't intend to join them either.

"Just now, with the fact that we had to eliminate another one of those creatures. One wrong move and it would have had access to everyone. No one would have survived if pitted against it. If we aren't with you, you won't have to worry about those. In only a matter of minutes, they'll send more so we need to have everyone moved out and on their way." Clint placed his hand on Doc's shoulder.

"But you said you would have as in past tense. So, did you disable it? And if you did, doesn't that mean they won't send more right away?" Doc ambled after Clint.

"Yes, but we can't take the chance of any of you getting harmed, or worse, because of us." Clint secured the doors on the first van as Sam cranked over the engine.

"I can stay with you and help," a small voice called out.

Clint looked at Xander and gave him a chin lift. Walking up to the first van in line, he shook hands with Sam and nodded to indicate that he should go ahead and head out. "Look out for them, Sam." He anticipated they would be okay since they were doing this for their own good, not letting them stay in large numbers. There would be a lot of questions asked when they realized no one else was coming. They made sure the new place was fully stocked with supplies, but deep down he had his doubts about whether this was the right decision.

The van rolled down the driveway when Doc hopped into the second van for everyone to load into, and Clint motioned for him to lean down. "Xander seems anxious to stay with us. He may be who we've been wondering about." Clint didn't tell him about the leaf falling from his shoe the other night.

"He's such a young kid. Do you think he's really helping the Monarchs?" Doc scowled.

"Well, we came up with the possibility that if the Monarchs planted someone in our midst, that person would offer to stay behind. The Monarchs want us more than they want you." Clint smiled and looked back at Casey and shuddered. He tried to hide the fear, but it was there; the images of her hanging next to Ben and what happened afterward was still all too real.

"Watch your backs." Doc shook Clint's hand and waited for everyone to say their goodbyes to those staying behind and then drove away. He had faith it wasn't their final goodbye. He also knew Casey had grown rather fond of them.

Xander walked up to Clint. "So, what do we do now?"

"We also leave." Clint charged up the creaky weatherworn wooden planks that were in shambles to the back door and disappeared into the kitchen.

"Clint, is that you?" Casey called from the den. He had Casey enter the house before them to tuck away the relics and parchment before Doc got behind the wheel. She had them brought down earlier when they decided it was time to go. That was a convenient thing about their communication devices; they kept tabs on what someone else stated and didn't need to worry about conflicting storylines.

"Yep. Are we about ready?" Clint sighed.

"Yes, everything is in this backpack, and you have food and supplies in yours."

"What about mine?" Xander asked behind Clint, an eagerness in his voice that made Clint want to lash out and ask how he could treat his own country like this.

"Well, pack up what you want to take, and we'll wait for you in the kitchen." Clint didn't turn around as he answered. He didn't trust himself to stay reigned in and not expose what their real intentions were.

Thirty-Six

Xander was in such a hurry, he scampered upstairs, almost using his hands, to the linen closet where he kept his clothes. Clint reunited with her in the den and slung his backpack over his shoulder while Casey did the same. They silently proceeded out the door, to hide in the undergrowth and kneeled out of sight, still able to watch the back of the farmhouse.

Xander stumbled out of the kitchen door with his backpack dragging across the ground by a single strap. He looked around, eyes wide; he ran his hands through his hair. Casey's hand clutched her heart. She regretted leaving this young man by himself. What if he was not their mole? What if he was one of their brothers in Christ? Casey looked at Clint with questioning eyes. He looked so small and weak, she started to straighten, but Clint held her.

Xander ran into the house and screamed as doors slammed. His rants filtered out of the back door. Now, she didn't feel so bad about leaving him behind. The words this young man spat out were not words any of their Christian brothers would use. Xander ran back out and ripped open his backpack and used a small radio. He stomped around as he waved his hands in a temper tantrum to whomever he spoke with on the radio.

The ground behind him erupted when several of the insects leaped out and attacked him. Casey covered her mouth to stifle her cry as she buried her forehead against Clint. His hands held her head as he shushed her.

"At least we know." Clint crept back from the trees as they stayed out of sight.

Casey followed as he left.

"Do you think everyone's all right with Xander gone? Or is there more than one mole?" Casey didn't like the thought of their friends being a target. Now that they divided from the newest additions, it was still as if it was a burden forced on her to make sure they were taken care of. How would she take it if suddenly the people she had grown attached to left them stranded with no way to contact them or anyone else without exposing everyone?

"That we won't know with absolute certainty. All we can do is pray for their safety and that the Monarchs keep their focus on us." Clint slowed down. He unfolded a map to look for their location and smiled. He then set out to the North. She had no clue how he did that.

After a couple of hours in the wooded area, they came to a small gravel road. Clint hooked a right; they made good time as the gravel under their feet hid their trail perfectly.

Casey started to slow down and already emptied one bottle of water, drenched, her clothes clinging to her body.

"Can we take a break or how much farther is it?" Casey's limp hair dripped. The humidity was high and the rain the day before didn't help.

"Casey, can you handle another forty-five minutes?" Clint did a double-take when he looked at her. She overheated quickly with the shield absorbed into her; one of the side effects was her face flushed bright red. Too much time outside and heat exhaustion would set in.

"Yes, if that's all we have left." She picked up the pace. Clint yanked one of his own water bottles from his backpack and handed it to her. She spun the ice-cold bottle along the back of her neck. Clint took it and held it there. The coolness of it radiated through her and cooled her body.

The trees cleared out to farmlands and crops that had long since died when the Monarchs invaded America. They turned down a driveway, and she gazed at a beautiful farmhouse that had been vacant since the owner, Clint's uncle, was tortured and murdered at the hands of the Monarchs when he refused to deny his faith in God. Clint had told her where they were on their way to after Xander met his end. The story that Clint's uncle died the way he did crushed her heart, but she rejoiced in the fact that a martyr crown waited for him in heaven.

Clint stopped and slid a piece of siding over to the left of the front door, retrieving a key. It took a little wrestling to work the tarnished metal into the lock for the deadbolt, but he pushed open the door and went inside.

Casey took a seat at the table while Clint shucked off his packs. Clint mentioned going for the truck they had stashed supplies in and took off after grabbing another water. She protested, proposing he wait until morning, but he told her his military training was worse than a simple long walk in the woods

Casey took her time in the kitchen and familiarized herself with everything while she removed the food from

Clint's pack. She made sandwiches and chose a couple of bags of chips. Casey poured lemonade and sat down when she heard a truck. Her eyes flashed to the back door, the shield erupting to surround her.

She walked out to the back porch as Clint pulled around and shut the engine off. She dropped the shield and went down to help. They took the tarp off the bed of the truck; Clint carried a bag into the house. It landed with a thud when he put it on the floor. He smiled and sat down at the table to eat. He made quick work of the sandwich Casey put together and tipped the now almost empty bag of chips up and chomped on the last crunchy bits that fell into his mouth. They ate in silence; it was amazing how quiet it was without thirty more people in the house with them.

They thanked God for the food He provided for them and that they didn't fall short for anyone today. They prayed for their friends' travels to the new place and that they would understand why they left them and that they would be okay. She hoped this was their last stop for a while. It was cozy in Clint's uncle's house. She was already comfortable as if she'd lived there before.

Casey cleaned up while Clint brought the food in from the truck. Casey was almost done cleaning and wiped everything down, removing the layer of dust off the shelves of the cabinets, when he brought in the last one.

Dusk was on the horizon when they finished putting their food into the refrigerator, which was very cold, and Clint smiled and signaled to the solar panels in the backyard. They kept the house's electricity on while also keeping it off the grid.

Casey couldn't erase the image of the bugs attacking and killing Xander as she quaked again, tremors traveling down her spine. He may be on the wrong side of things, but no one deserved to die like that. The Monarchs probably believed it was easier to exterminate him than try to insert him into another group. Or was it his punishment for failing, and the Monarchs didn't offer second chances, much like the men they killed in the neighborhoods when they left them tied to a tree or fence. She remembered the guards they incapacitated were killed without a moment's hesitation where the Monarchs now lived.

They wanted a great night's sleep. It was exactly what they needed, and they journeyed upstairs to pick their spots and unpack to settle into their new home.

Casey took the room at the far end while Clint claimed the one at the front of the house. They figured it was easier to keep an eye on things with one at the front of the house and someone at the back. Casey was also glad to have the separation from Clint. She found it awkward with her and Clint being the only two in this huge house. She missed Ben and wanted him back. Oh, she trusted Clint with everything, but she was at a loss so many times on what to talk about. He didn't seem to be bothered by her nervousness and just let her have the time to work through their new situation. She knew he was also hurting with first Amanda and now Ben.

Their parents took it hard when Clint disclosed the news to them. She would never forget his mother's wails through the phone. She swiped at the tears that seemed to fall so frequently now.

Clint's uncle was the previous owner of the house they now occupied so he knew the ins and outs of every square inch of the property. Staying in the city was too risky, with all the buildings giving the Monarchs a way to hide and stage an ambush. The farmhouse in the open land that ran for miles was safe and they would be warned if someone or something approached. She did miss the small grove nestled into the trees unexposed from the road, but the robots that the Monarchs had created, overran them.

Closing her door, Casey dropped onto the bed and hugged a pillow. The mattress sank in as she sat on the end; she was happy with how comfortable it was. Uneasy feelings clouded her mind as she unpacked her clothes, adding to all the garments that still hung in the closet and overflowed from the dresser that no doubt belonged to one of Clint's family members.

Pulling out her pajamas and toothbrush Casey was the first to change and walk to the bathroom to brush her teeth. Clint waited outside the bathroom when she came out to head to bed. She smiled at him as he went in to get ready for the night.

Casey curled up under the homemade quilt and turned on her side. She fell asleep with the quietness of the house and no one else there except the two of them.

Thirty-Seven

The den was now home to the relic treasure chests that held all but one relic, the weapon that Clint used. Clint's uncle had kept the paperwork organized in the desk to keep the farm going, until the Monarchs murdered him eight years earlier. He left Clint everything and she glimpsed the personal connection he had with this house when he walked from room to room. It was exactly as his uncle had left it when he had willed it to him. Clint's aunt preceded her husband in death by twenty years when cancer stole away the possibility of a long life.

Clint turned as Casey watched him. "What?"

"Do you regret coming here?" Casey asked.

"Oh no, not in the least. Nothing but good memories in this house. Lots of love given by my aunt and uncle while they were alive." Clint grinned.

Clint left to take stock of what they had and how to best defend themselves here.

Casey secured the relics in the den where Clint wanted them stored. She looked at everything and tried to keep it as organized as Amanda had. She missed her so much. She was on a trip down memory lane with everything she touched while putting it away. The sphere vibrated as two fragments glimmered and bounced around in the case. The one piece was the larger piece that reclaimed itself, and now another piece was glowing. Casey thrust back from the desk and called to Clint. He ran in, gun drawn.

"Look!" Casey pointed to the sphere.

As they rounded the desk to look under the roll-top section, the new large portion had returned to its dull dormant state but the third piece had molded with the first two.

"What are we looking at?" Clint pointed the barrel at the floor switching the safety back on.

"The sphere," Casey whispered.

"And?" Clint's eyes narrowed. "Casey, there's nothing happening."

"Well, not now." Casey put her hands on her hips. "How about you tell me how many pieces there are?"

"Five." Clint snatched the case with the sphere. He counted again. "It was six last time we counted."

"And remember I said there were originally seven, which Ben confirmed?" Casey waited for the acknowledgment that she tried to tell him this before.

"Is it putting itself back together, fusing the cracks?" Clint positioned the case on the desk before pushing it away.

"The glowing shards vibrated and bounced around. But only the two that connected together, making the one larger solid piece." Casey rubbed her eyes. She was glad he finally realized she didn't imagine it. And if she didn't imagine this, what about the times her memories of Amanda seemed so real as if she was just living them for the first time?

"What does this mean?" Clint poked one of the shards.

"You're asking me?" Casey giggled.

"I'm heading back to see what's in the barn." Clint pecked Casey's cheek as a brother would kiss a younger sibling.

"At least you now believe me. I thought I was going crazy." She plopped into the chair behind the desk.

"Well, you *are* crazy, but aren't we all?" Clint dodged the wadded-up piece of paper thrown at him and laughed as he darted out the door.

She smiled as she listened to him laughing on the way out. She did a double take and saw Clint forgot his Glock. This may be the first time in history he didn't have a firearm by choice since being in the military. She remembered to check the safety to make sure it was on, then hid it against the back of the desk, knowing there were more hidden around the old house, and pulled out the parchment. She was eager to find out if anything changed since the sphere connected three of the pieces back together. What did all of this mean?

A clap of thunder brought Casey back from her daydreams of Amanda and meeting Ben and Clint two years earlier. The sky darkened as a clap of thunder shook the house, from a fierce storm rolling in.

Clint bounded in the back door, soaked from large raindrops that had started to fall. He laughed as he stomped his feet to knock off as much water as he could on the rug by the door, when an alarm went off somewhere in the house.

"I completely forgot about the weather data caster. Help me find it." Clint started down the hall, tilting his head this way and that, and stopping every couple of steps to try to narrow down the sound. They had to wait for every transmission as if they were playing the hot-cold game.

"Over here," Casey called from under the stairs. He opened the small door, and a red light harshly lit the small storage compartment where Clint's uncle kept what appeared to be a weather radio on a small shelf.

Casey was shocked that someone still manned the radio broadcast station for storm and weather alerts. Although they had made improvements since her time. It projected a map and path of the tornado. She had no clue where that was, but it sounded nearby with the howling wind that had started to blow, slamming into the sides of the house. The house groaned as it took the punishing onslaught of the storm.

"Did they say tornado?" Clint asked.

"Uh...maybe?" Casey didn't want to have this house destroyed. They had just gotten there. Where would they go if the storm devastated this place?

"Grab the relics. There is a storm cellar behind the house." Clint headed toward the den for the backpack they used to transport the relics from one place to the other.

"What about the shield?" Casey jolted as a shrill alarm sounded from the radio, interrupting them, and there were instructions for the impending tornado that told everyone to seek shelter.

"I seriously doubt that will keep us untouched from an act of God. I think he gave us the relics to fight evil not weather anomalies." Clint tried to smile but it came out more like a pained frown as he stared at the ceiling as if the sky was visible through it and he could see what was barreling toward them.

"It worked against animals with rabies. Shouldn't we give it a try? Why would God provide us with this perfect place to live, only to take it from us hours after we got here?" Casey reasoned, her heart racing hoping she wasn't putting everything on the line for a storm.

"Come on down to the cellar. We can test it out later." Clint just got the back door open when a large, fractured tree trunk with a few straggler limbs still attached slammed up against the house and knocked Clint into the kitchen.

Casey screamed as the shield exploded from her, placing the house in a bubble that thickened to become an opaque dome. The wind engaged in a full-scale assault on everything. The thunderous roar of what sounded like a train but she assumed was a tornado barreled toward the house. She concentrated on the shield, which became a solid cocoon around them. "God, let Your will be done."

Clint staggered to his feet while clutching his chest. The huge, contorted trunk blocked their exit with a very large funnel tracked across the field directly toward the house. Casey's eyes widened as her legs trembled. They didn't have time to run or take shelter; all that was left to do was pray. He blew out a breath and shook his head.

Clint kneeled. "Father, please stand guard for us. You put us here in this place for a reason. You know what Your plans are for us. We ask that Your will be done and that You help us through this trial that we're facing. We give this to You and our lives; we place them in Your hands." His eyes told her he thought of Amanda and Ben and that he would reunite with them soon if this didn't work. Casey smiled back; she would be with her brother and his family and parents again.

Casey mouthed amen to Clint's prayer. The tornado slammed against the back of the house first. Its deafening roar was too much. The air pressure dropped, and her ears popped when suddenly, it was deathly quiet. Casey scrunched her eyes and kept her hands up, projecting the shield, and sent out the request to cancel out the noise outside of its protection. Silence immediately greeted them.

"We're in the core. There's blue sky out there." Clint backed away from the door.

The second half of the tornado assaulted them with such a ferociousness they bowed their heads ready to be taken home but without the earsplitting racket. Clint locked eyes with Casey and nodded.

Darkness seeped into the house. A glance out of the kitchen windows showed nothing but swirling black. The air pressure in the house dropped again. She opened and closed her mouth, stretching her jaw.

Just as quickly as it began, it was over. The winds died down and the sky started to clear.

Casey withdrew the shield and stood. "Did we just dodge a bullet?"

"I think so." Clint glimpsed out the back door, shook his head, and then moved to the front. Casey followed, not sure what kind of damage they would have to clean up.

Clint hunched over. The temperatures had dipped considerably from the storm that rolled through. The sun pierced through the clouds and shone brightly on the side of the house.

Casey gasped at the same time Clint did. There, in the blinding rays of the sun, was the shape of a cross. The house was untouched by the tornado. The muddy fields were a mess while torn chunks of trees littered the woods on the other side. The tornado's path would be a reminder of what happened for years to come. But the bright, almost blinding cross of sunlight on the side of the house told them God wasn't done yet.

Clint coughed as he tried to straighten up.

"Clint?" Casey clasped her hand on his shoulder.

"I can't breathe," Clint wheezed as he tried to inhale.

Casey helped him remove his polo. A massive bruise mottled his skin from where the trunk knocked him back into the kitchen. Casey settled her hand against the damage. Bright blue diamonds surged to Clint, who still gasped for air. He shielded his eyes as the bruise faded before disappearing altogether.

She opened her eyes and blew out her breath.

"Thanks. I didn't realize it tagged me that hard." Clint tugged his jersey down over his head and placed his arms through the sleeves.

He walked around to the back, where he inspected the rest of the house. "No damage at all." He was in awe. Relief flashed across his face, softening his rugged features. There wasn't a part of this house that didn't hold a happy memory, and it was obvious from the way he took everything in. She was glad the shield worked and saved him from the heartache and loss of something that had more emotional value for him than a monetary one.

The rays from the sun faded and the cross vanished. She was astounded by the sign that He revealed, which demonstrated He would never leave them.

"Okay, that was remarkable." Casey shook her head.

"Guess we discovered the shield protects us through tornadoes." Clint smiled up at heaven as the sun shone on his face.

They both beamed and walked into the house. Clint informed her of his plans to cut up the part of the tree that blocked the back door to give them a boost in their firewood supply for the coming winter. He wandered down toward the barn, which luckily was not damaged from the storm's path, to find chainsaws with the best chains that would still start.

Casey stood at the back door when she projected the shield and surrounded the trunk that barred her from walking through. She put her hands up and the trunk inched back. She manipulated her hands to hoist it off the ground. Then she walked it back toward the backyard by the woodpile. She was overheated when she finally dissolved the shield, and the trunk thudded to the ground. She remembered she used the shield to move Ben in the tunnels and figured a trunk of oak would be easy to handle.

Clint stood, jaw open. She smirked as she brushed her palms against each other. The loud chainsaw cut through the calm after the storm. Before they knew it, everything was cut down to size. Even with the lower temperature, soon they were both drenched, and they'd shed their outer layers by the time they finished. Clint carried a large pile of logs as Casey wheeled a cart behind him. She moved the larger chunks to be cut down with the shield until they were a reasonable size that could be easily manipulated.

After unloading everything next to the fireplace, she ran to shower so they could work on putting together a meal. She was surprised how much food spilled over on the shelves as she took in the expired produce.

Canned homegrown food sat discolored in the clear canning jars. She piled them next to the sink, disturbing the sludge and seeds at the bottom of the jars, causing it to swirl through the liquid. She would take them to the copse of trees to dump them and then wash the jars. She'd never canned before but how hard could it be? Maybe his aunt owned a book to give her instructions on how to store foods.

They piled the logs in the holder by the fireplace. Clint cleaned out the hearth and inspected the flue. Casey smiled. She always enjoyed a fire in a wood-burning fireplace. It made the room cozier. This old farmhouse would feel like home with a fire going tonight.

Casey walked to the kitchen to think about what to prepare for dinner when she started when a throat cleared behind her.

"Sorry, I didn't mean to scare you." Clint chuckled. He always got a kick of how easily she startled.

"Uh-huh, sure you didn't." She turned around and saw he had already showered and redressed. Tree sap bonded to his skin, and she could see the red patches on his arms that matched her own after they scrubbed them clean.

He scratched at one of the red splotches. "What's for dinner?"

"Not sure yet. What do you think?"

"All I know is I'm ravenous," Clint said.

"Well, I can make lasagna if you want." Casey opened the pantry door for noodles.

"Oh, that sounds great. Did you need any help?" Clint looked down at her.

"No, go relax. You did the majority of the work. Least I can do is cook for you."

"You helped."

"No, I used the shield while you did the manual labor." Casey snickered.

Clint didn't say anything as he lumbered to the sofa.

She boiled the noodles and fried up some sausages and ground beef. In no time, she'd layered the ingredients in an old vintage dish, which she placed in the oven. Chopping up the vegetables for a salad killed some of the time waiting for the lasagna to cook.

By the time Clint rejoined her in the kitchen, he looked refreshed. She had no doubt they would be dead to the world tonight.

When the lasagna was ready, they sat down and ate in the living room in front of the fireplace. They listened to the crackling of the wood as it burned. The room was not only cozy, but it was also beautiful with the light bouncing and jumping from the fire. They decided to read some from the family Bible that Clint found while waiting for dinner.

His aunt's handwriting in the family tree she started when they had gotten the Bible on their wedding filled the front page. It was well kept but also worn from the hours spent reading from it. Clint said that was one of the best memories when he would spend part of his summers here was reading the family Bible after dinner and everyone had settled in to read God's word.

They decided to read from Exodus and how God showed His works and the miracles He performed to bring His people out of Egypt. He did so much for His people, and His protection kept them safe as they traveled to the promised land. There was no denying how much He loved them. They talked about how amazing it would have been to live back then and witness firsthand all the miracles He worked through Moses and Aaron. It astonished them how they wandered for forty years and their shoes and clothes never wore out.

The cross on the house after the storm was a boisterous topic, and they agreed on the strength from their Father in heaven. They treasured Him so much, and it was evident in the conversation they had after dinner. It was a nice change of pace for there to be only two people in the house instead of a couple of dozen.

"Did Ben ever tell you about the first time he was pulled through the sphere and met Mason?" Clint folded his hands behind his head and leaned back.

"What? No." Casey sat forward a little.

"I guess he came through some sort of small door you had at the back of the house and growled so low Ben thought he was going to have to change his pants." Clint chuckled.

The gasp and subsequent giggle that escaped Casey sounded weird in her ears. It felt like it had been so long since she had anything to laugh about. "I miss Amanda too. I never had a sister and she was the best."

"That she was. She would follow us everywhere when we were kids. For two boys to have a little sister who wanted to tag along was yucky." Clint didn't finish his thoughts.

"But she grew on you, didn't she?"

"When she said she wanted to be an archaeologist when she grew up, to a teenage boy she was the coolest girl in the world because she wanted to dig in the dirt for fun. I miss them every day." Clint became silent.

Casey let him have his moment. She hadn't known them half as long as Clint did.

They missed their friends, who they considered family, but it was so quiet, that every creak of the house from the wind was twice as loud as it should have been. It was coming up on winter and they worried if they had enough to last them through the season. At least it would be much easier to feed only two instead of thirty. The discussion turned to locating a safe food run route to last them all winter so they would only make the one run before the famous snow storms moved in that tormented the region every winter.

Clint got up and made a few calls and also contacted Doc about what options they had.

"How is everyone?" Casey prodded when Clint came back into the living room.

"Everyone's doing great; no issues and it's been quiet so far. Doc said he procured a site, and we can do a pickup in a couple of days. Shouldn't be a problem. Someone who did our food run when we lived in the warehouses can hook us up again. Able to make it out to the country, they offer supplies out here with fewer run-ins with the Monarchs."

"Great. It would be nice if we didn't have to worry about doing runs in the winter. Clint, how harsh was the weather when your aunt and uncle were still alive?" Casey glanced at Clint, who settled into his uncle's recliner and popped up the foot section. He looked like he belonged there and had always been the one to sit in it.

"Pretty bad. I heard stories when I was growing up about the electricity going out every winter until they put the solar panels in. The temperatures would get really low and if something did happen, he had a blower put on the fireplace so that air could be blown into the house and heat it that way. They also had an entire set of cooking dishes made for use over the fire for meals." Clint had a far-off look at his face as he gazed into the dancing flames.

Casey looked at him and she read the pain of Clint walking down memory lane on his face, eyebrows drawn together and the clenched jaw. She had had that look before when she reminisced about her family.

"So, we'll be fine is what you're saying?" Casey laughed.

"More than fine." Clint smiled.

"Well, I'm tired and I'll take a better look around to record the storm damage and what needs to be done. Are you going to bed soon?" Casey lurched off the couch.

"I'll be up later." Clint ambled to the fireplace and moved the logs around.

Casey watched him. There was still a lot of grief they both shared. They weren't even close to being okay.

Tomorrow was a new day, and she knew God was in control and everything happened for a reason.

Thirty-Eight

Clint tossed and turned and Casey listened while she counted the water spots above her head. Amanda's death brought with it nightmares. At first, he kept them from Ben, but it was hard to keep them from him when they shared a room so many times over the course of their running from the Monarchs. Ben then shared with Casey one night when she heard and knocked on their shared door asking if everything was okay.

Casey sat up as she heard Clint's voice. He was clearly having a nightmare; she recognized Amanda's name as he called out.

Not sure what to do, she grabbed a robe and secured it around her with the tie. Ben had always known what to do when he had them before, but since it was only the two of them, she didn't know how to approach the subject and hadn't asked what to do if he had one.

He was there for her more times than she could count, and she would be there for him too. As he seemed to settle and quiet down, her racing heart slowed in relief.

Casey fell back, and her head only just landed on the pillow when Clint started again. She shuffled from her room.

"Clint." Casey sighed.

"No!" Clint cried in anguish.

"Clint, it's me...Clint put down the...Clint!" Casey backed up as Clint raised a black matte-finish sidearm barrel, targeting dead center, his eyes distant, unfocused, clouded with confusion.

A shot shattered their quiet night. Casey's feet launched out from under her as the bullet slammed into her torso.

"OH MY GOSH. CASEY! I'm sorry. Casey!" Clint cried out. The gun in his hand clattered to the floor as he dropped it as if it was hot.

Casey slumped on the ground motionless. She didn't open her eyes as the blood spread on her top, seeping through the material.

Clint's voice shook. "Casey!"

"I'm...t-trying," Casey exclaimed.

She was cold. She should be warm if she was mending herself. Why was she so cold? The blood soaked into his pajama pants as he kneeled on the floor pressing over the wound.

Casey cried out from the pressure. Her dainty hands grabbed his wrists. "Father, please help me."

"Casey, you can do this! You can't leave me. Stay with me, sweetheart," Clint urged.

The room was saturated with a blue aura that pierced through his eyelids, snapping them open. The hard floor beneath Clint was saturated with her blood. Casey slowly stirred as light subsided and dimmed. When he opened his eyes, Casey let go and her arms fell to the floor, her eyes barely open.

"Case?" Clint checked her pulse. "This is why you can't approach me during a nightmare."

"Clint, I... I'm sorry," Casey stammered "But I'm okay. What had you going?"

"Amanda. I couldn't reach her. It was like the other dreams, yet there was something different. I swear she called to me." Clint scooped Casey off the floor.

"I believe the word you are looking for is night terrors," Casey murmured.

"No, this was different; I swear I heard her in my room." Clint's gaze told her he was lost in thought.

"Clint, I've had nightmares that seemed so real that I had to convince myself that they weren't when I woke up. You can't tell me you forgot about how I was after I used the shield against that man—"

Clint sat her on the side of the tub. "Casey, I'm so sorry."

"I'm okay. Gonna take a shower and go back to bed. It really is okay. I'm fine." Casey shook her head before taking a huge breath.

"I...man, I'm...seriously." Guilt flooded Clint's face.

"We're good. You'd never in a million years shoot me on purpose. Promise me you won't keep your nine next to the bed again, so you have time to wake up before you pull the trigger."

Clint only nodded as he secured the door behind him. The water started shortly after, and he slid down the wall so he was sitting with his knees drawn up. He wanted to make sure she wouldn't have to call out very loud for him to hear.

Not sure if she would be conscious enough to make it back to bed, he sat patiently as he replayed what happened.

The door opened shortly after. He hoisted himself to his feet and glanced into the bathroom at the pile of bloody towels and robe. "I'm going to lock up every gun in the house. I'm so sorry, Casey."

He assisted Casey to bed and kept watch until her breathing slowed and evened out, when she turned on her side. The blanket was under her feet, so he gently tugged the comforter out from under her to cover her. He stared down at her, knowing he owed her again. He was supposed to be her protector, but he couldn't even do that right.

With a change of wardrobe, he made his way to the shower after cleaning up the floor of his room.

"I almost killed her today, Father." Clint cast his eyes down. He dropped the ruined garments and towels in the trash bag and turned back toward the sink. Dark shadows below his eyes told of his sleepless nights. He had to get a grip on this, or it would lead to both of their downfalls.

He swore he heard Amanda through his communicator. Clint shook his head. He knew how crazy that sounded. It was impossible; she'd been gone for a couple of years. Maybe being back home would help.

Clint turned and started the shower. He stood under the spray for what seemed like an hour when the water started to run cold. He turned the water off and toweled off. His pajama pants were damp from him being in the shower for so long. He opened the bathroom door and was relieved when he stood outside Casey's room and didn't hear anything. He edged the door open. She hadn't stirred since he put her in bed. He gave her shoulder a squeeze as he passed before climbing into bed in his room and drifting off into deep uneventful dreams.

Thirty-Nine

Casey shuffled into the kitchen to make herself tea and poured water into the tea kettle. She never liked the smell of coffee much less the taste, so she preferred tea for caffeine than adding so much sugar to her coffee a spoon stood on its own. One thing she thought was so cute about Ben was the amount of sugar and creamer he added.

Clint scrambled eggs while Casey pulled out plates and silverware for the table. She removed the whistling tea kettle from the burner and made a very large cup of her favorite tea. Clint settled on juice and poured himself a glass before he put the eggs on the table and said a prayer before they ate.

They discussed what they wanted to do for the day, neither mentioning the night before. She wanted to clean more, going room to room dusting and washing all the bedding and drapes since it had been vacant for so many years. The house needed to be aired out. She frowned as she thought about the healing capability being so slow to react to her.

Clint talked about securing the guns they had brought and strategically placing them around the house. He planned to go through and take inventory of what was there and discussed planting a huge garden in the spring to start canning fruits and vegetables to lessen the worry about food next winter. Comfortable enough to think that they would be there the next season due to no one knowing about them, they planned for a future for the first time in a while.

It was a far-reaching dream, but they also discussed actually having dreams again, imagining their futures, and having a place to call home to stay for years. It was a lot to ask, but it was what they envisioned, and they agreed they both wanted to stay.

Clint trudged out while Casey cleaned the kitchen. He had offered to help her, but she had shooed him out and said to go get the guns in place and catalog what they had for supplies. She couldn't explain it, but she looked forward to learning how to can and store fruits and vegetables. There was something about homegrown that appealed to her. She never canned food before, but she would go through his aunt's cookbooks and hope she had one on food storage. She started in the living room and found the vacuum with no problem and set out to make the living room the nicest room in the house before Clint came back.

Humming one of her favorite songs reminded her about radio. They hadn't had music from an actual radio station in years, and she wondered if any were broadcasting anymore. She looked around and saw in a corner that she had yet to clean, a monstrously huge, ancient radio. She plugged it in and said a prayer that it worked. The lights came on and she turned up the volume until she heard static, turned the dial all the way to the end, and slowly scanned back across the stations.

It was about halfway through the scan when music came through the speakers. Not what she would listen to, she kept going crossing her fingers. She came across another station, horrified at what came out; she would never listen to that, so she kept going. Almost at the end of the dial, music that was a joy to listen to seeped into the room. It was a Christian station, and the song that played was one she didn't recognize, but the lyrics praised God and how much His children meant to Him. She smiled and wiped down the old radio with her dust cloth so that when she finished with the wood cleaner, it looked almost brand new.

She turned it up a little and kept going. There was something about music playing that encouraged her spirit and brightened her mood. She cleaned until her stomach rumbled. She looked at the clock, shocked it was after noon. She wondered about Clint, when she realized he hadn't returned. A sinking feeling stabbed at her that something had happened to him and she sprinted for the back door. There was another one of those large insects after Clint. Stepping from the back door of the farmhouse, she spied Clint frozen in place with one of the creatures down in between them.

"CLINT!" CASEY SCREAMED as another insect crawled out of the ground behind him and charged toward him. She thrust out the shield as it took a swipe; its claws cut long jagged gashes across Clint's back.

Clint arched his back as the barbs came into contact with his skin and knew he would more than likely be dead before he landed on the ground. That was when a blue orb raced across his field of vision—from where Casey stood—toward him. He had never seen her project it like that before. The shield propelled the mammoth bug with such force, that it was thrown into the grain chute on the tractor behind him. The bug dangled before he turned back around, unable to get itself off the chute.

Casey projected the blue light into the shield as it sailed toward Clint, faster than she had ever projected the shield. It enveloped him and held him as if in suspended animation. Clint kept an eye on the critter. Looking back at Casey, he saw the love and determination in her to save him, her head tipped forward, focusing all her energy on the single task of keeping her protector alive.

The other insect lurched toward Casey. Her eyes narrowed and she nodded to Clint as she whipped out another shield that froze the insect in place. Clint fired a static pulse from his relic. It crackled and sizzled through the air when it collided with the shield and almost disintegrated. The extra shield sailed back at Casey as she repaired him.

"Stay out of our lives!" Casey screamed, stalking toward his location.

The fabricated insect shuddered as it tried to remove itself again.

"Bring it if you think you can take me, but this stops now! Get off our property and out of our country!"

She threw another shield that encased the one on the chute as she sent a citrine orb, connecting with the shield. Static circled the ball. It coursed several times over and over as the shield shrank pulverizing it.

Clint's feet landed on the ground as he took in his shredded clothes.

Casey slumped to the ground, her knees and hands hitting at the same time.

"Look at me." Clint knelt in front of her, cupped her face in his hands, and tilted her head back to meet his eyes.

"I thought I was done with getting this tired after treating someone. I haven't had my energy drain like this in a long time." She smiled.

"Okay um, you hurled the healing power out in the shield. How long have you been able to do that?" Clint helped her up.

"I didn't know I could until I did it. I saw that thing go for you and I didn't think. I just imagined it gone." Casey's skin was flushed. Her lips quivered. "Do you think I could have done that to Ben?"

"No, don't even go there. Ben was gone before he hit the ground, remember? There was nothing left to revive without his soul. Let's get you back to the house before you collapse. You saved yourself last night, and maybe that's why you're so tired now." Clint wrapped his arm around her as she put hers around, grasping his belt loops with her fingers.

Clint couldn't take his eyes off the remains skewered on the equipment and decided they should probably burn it to destroy it. Not sure if the components would pose a danger and be able to transmit anything back to the Monarchs. Yes, a fire was the way to go. He had some magnesium in the barn that he could add to it and bring the temperature up high enough to melt everything in those creations.

Sitting Casey on the chair on the back porch, he vaulted into the truck to head toward the barn. Pulling in, he started loading firewood they had stored into the bed of the truck.

He wasn't sure how much he would need to completely consume everything, but it would need to be hot.

With the bed of the truck weighed down with firewood, he also added a gas can and a flare. Driving back out to the field, he decided he would build the fire under it, drop it off the chute on the pile, and light it when the tractor was far enough away.

Clint stacked the firewood carefully over a pile of magnesium inside the concrete blocks he placed in a circle, to create the most airflow through the base of the stack. That way, it would be hot enough to burn even the bare-bone components of this monstrosity. The Monarchs were a brutal bunch; they heard stories of how they caught humans to test the viciousness of the creatures. So many people lost their lives because they wanted to wipe out the Chosen Ones and take the relics to try to dominate the world.

Clint finished setting up the firewood. "Are you still tired?" he called to Casey.

"Not as much as I was before."

"Okay, I'm going to move the tractor and lower it to the stack. Go ahead and move the truck back to the house." Clint flicked Casey the keys; she caught them in midair.

She cranked over the engine. While she jogged back, Clint met her after moving the tractor back out of the way. Casey gulped at the bug that seemed to be so much bigger than the pile of wood. Clint never wanted that to be the way he died, and if it came to that, he hoped it would end him quickly.

Dousing gasoline on the wood, Clint emptied almost the entire pint of liquid and then leaped back several feet.

He pulled off the end cap to the flare and twisted the end, causing the bright red-hot flames to shoot out. He lobbed it toward the center. It landed with a thud on the side and started to roll. Clint sucked in his breath. He let it out when it came to rest on the wood, and the timber caught fire.

The flames danced in the air and licked at the wood doused with fuel. Casey and Clint sat mesmerized by the fire that increased in temperature when all the wood finally started to catch, and red glowing coals appeared on the edges of the wood. The magnesium glowed white. One by one, the plates and scales on the bug started to liquefy, dripping to the middle of the fire and hissing as they combined with the molten embers and white-hot fire.

"Hot enough fire can melt them." Clint couldn't take his eyes off the creature or what was left of it.

"Does that mean maybe one of our relic's powers could cause enough damage to melt them the next time they are sent here?"

"I don't know but I hope so. We also need to nose around on how they found us here. Someone may have placed a tracker somewhere." Clint looked down at his watch. It was early enough he could get a call in to Chloe and see about being sent something to scan for devices.

"How do we make sure they can't track us anymore?" Casey shivered next to him.

"Not to change the subject, but you directed out a second shield, another one than the one you guided to me." Clint frowned at the house. "I thought there was only one shield."

"Yeah, about that. You were on the other side so you didn't see it, but I created a second shield in the passageways when you were pulled down the tunnel." Casey followed Clint's line of sight.

"Seriously?"

"I moved Ben out of my line of fire when he stepped between me and the insects." Casey shrugged.

Clint's eyebrows practically hit his hairline. "Wait, the shield can't be used on the Chosen Ones."

"Well, I did to Ben, and I unleashed a second shield out here." She started back toward the house.

"I'm just now hearing about this. This could have been something we could have worked with before now." Clint climbed to the door at the back of the house.

He swept his phone off the kitchen counter and dialed his friend. He talked in hushed tones while Casey stalked above.

CASEY HAD NO DOUBT he was talking with his military contact about the information they had discovered. Maybe this would really make the Monarchs run scared.

Quietly knocking on the door to her room, Clint stared at an empty bed as the door swung open with his first knock. He tensed when she placed a hand on his back.

"You scared me." Clint turned around.

"Sorry." A mischievous smile played on her face.

"Come on down. I found out something." Clint steered Casey to the stairs and let her walk in front of him.

"Chloe got in touch with her uncle, and he is sending someone to our food pick-up location with a bug sweeper in two hours. I'm going to go meet them so they don't know where we are. Although, if the Monarchs have a tracker somewhere in our belongings, then it's a moot point, but I have an idea on drawing them away from this place."

"Don't those creatures showing up out there mean they already found us, so we have to leave?" Casey took in the kitchen. She knew Clint sensed her anxiety at the thought of moving again.

"That's unknown yet. I guess time will tell if it was random and they just happened to get lucky. With it being melted, since we burned it and there's nothing left to send out a signal, they may not know." Clint gazed out the window.

Clint answered his phone and had a hurried conversation before he hung up. "My friend found magnesium flamethrowers and said he would pass the information along to the military brass who can disseminate it from there. They will also test at what temperature it starts to melt the insects' plates."

Clint still had a lot of connections even though he resigned from the military years ago and didn't reenlist. He told Casey one night he saved a general's son from a sniper in a battle and the general told him that no matter when or where, he would have his back. His son rose in the ranks in the military until an aneurysm took his life years later.

They decided an early night was in order for Casey while Clint reunited with his contact to get the bug sweeper. Casey's head sagged as she tried to stay awake. She would be asleep in a matter of minutes after crawling into bed. Clint had done a lot of work in the fields earlier before coming face to face with the creature but decided finding the trackers was more important. After making an easy dinner Casey turned in and fell asleep quickly, not hearing when Clint left.

Forty

On the table was a weird device that must have been the bug scanner thing that Clint talked to Casey about the previous day. The house was too quiet. She tuned in her enhanced hearing and heard Clint snoring upstairs. She giggled, curious as to when Clint got home last night.

She pressed a button on the side and almost fumbled the gadget when green lights bounced across the screen. Cautiously, she moved around the room, but it never had more than two green lights at a time. She clambered to her room and pulled out the drawers that held her clothing.

She swept the device over her folded-up shirts and yelped when it flashed red. Did she already find a tracker? Moving the piles of shirts to the top of the dresser, she separated each of the three stacks and scanned one then the other. The second stack flashed red again.

Casey's heart raced as she unfolded each top and scanned them individually, finding the offending one that held a tracker. She felt around the collar and found a small sliver of a device in the corner of the collar.

She swept the rest of the room and came up with only one additional tracker. Adrenaline coursed through her as she ran downstairs to the kitchen. That room was clean so she worked her way across the lower level through each room. When she got to the den and the relics, she found another one in the parchment at the end of the paper that they hadn't unrolled in months, since she was concentrating on deciphering the new symbols that had appeared lately.

She found that the rest of the relics were safe when a shadow passed over the doorway. A scream erupted from her, while the shield popped up.

"Woah, Casey. It's me." Clint held his hands up. "What are you doing?"

Clint observed the device in her hands. She held up her finger over her lips and showed him a note. "Check this out. I've scanned every room down here but did find these in my shirts." She moved to the kitchen table to show him the two trackers from her laundry, then held up a second note. "And this one was in the parchment."

Clint frowned and grabbed the pen to scrawl below her writing. "Let's get the rest of the house inspected, and then we can initiate the second part of my plan."

"Second part?" Casey mouthed and put her hands on her hips. "You gonna let me in on the secret plan?"

Chuckling, he ruffled the hair on her head before taking the scanner from her hand. "Yes. Come on. You can help me." He pointed to the pad of paper and the pen and then motioned to his room.

Clint let her in on his plan while they debugged the rest of the rooms. They found two more transmitters in his clothes while they found three in Ben's that were still boxed. They sat at the kitchen table, staring at the nefarious small electronics that had caused them such heartache. They were small enough that she wondered if they could also hear them or just track them.

Commotion outside got Clint to sprint to the front door. "Creatures!"

"How many?" Casey sprang to her feet.

"At least three. Grab the flamethrowers." Clint smiled.

Casey shouldered through the door with two throwers.

At the front door, Clint nodded to her as he unlocked it and made sure the ends of their weapons were lit. The first insect immediately charged. Clint tugged the trigger and sent white-hot flames at the critter. The first blast didn't seem to faze it. The second set of flames seemed to be at just the right angle to get under several plates that immediately sloughed off, exposing the inner workings of the robot.

It charged Clint and Casey threw a shield out as a wall, tossing it back out of swiping distance of its front legs. Casey hit the exposed area and melted the joints for the back legs so it fell to the ground, unable to attack.

"That's one; two more to go. Casey, to your left there's one that's acting as if it's watching what we do." Clint took the one on the left as he darted around to the front porch. He sprang off the deck and pulled the trigger. The insect dodged and stumbled forward as Casey blasted it, melting the back plates again and disabling the components that worked the legs.

"Two down." They squinted into the fuel levels. They should have enough to take down the last one and incinerate them.

The third one spit several poison darts at Casey, who ducked in time for them to lodge into the front siding of the house.

"Casey, stay there!" Clint barked. "I have an idea. If we can trick them into thinking you are down, it may come closer."

Casey nodded and rolled on her back with her eyes on the other two.

The last one stalked toward her as Clint circled around, sidestepping the two that were on the ground but still had their front claws and poison darts to use.

Casey held her breath as the third one crept toward them.

Clint took the opportunity of the insect's distraction with Casey being down to fire at its back, melting several plates. It twisted around flames shooting higher as the inner workings combusted in the inferno and melted the electronics. White fire blasted out of the last couple of plates as it collapsed.

Casey vaulted to her feet and aimed for the first one while Clint finished off the second one. Using the rest of the fuel in the canisters, they easily melted the beasts into a liquid puddle.

"That'll be a mess to clean up." Clint shook his head. "We'll have to let the metal cool. Then, I can hook up the loader and carry it off to the rubbish pile behind the barn."

"Here, give me that." Casey took his flame thrower and set them against the railing and whispered, "Do you think this will work? Can they hear us through those small things?"

"If we do it right, yes, and the transmitters are very small." Clint raised his brows.

Raising her voice, she said, "I'm going to miss this place."

"Me too." Clint grabbed her hand and charged into the house.

After he swiped the trackers into a bag, Clint stormed upstairs with Casey right behind him. "Just take what you can. Be ready to leave in ten minutes."

"Got it." Casey separated from him and went to her room to toss clothes in a bag.

Clint met her at the front door. He turned one last time and took in the home she knew he didn't want to leave.

"Where are we going to go?" Casey skirted the piles of steaming metal.

Clint waved toward the truck. "I'm not sure but we can't come back here...ever."

Forty-One

They slowly made their way out of town. With their eyes on their surroundings, they didn't talk much except to discuss heading to the west coast where Ben's family offered them sanctuary.

Casey talked about how nervous she was to meet Ben's family. They knew so much about her, but she knew next to nothing except what Ben and Amanda had shared before their untimely deaths. Discussing the different perks of where they were headed, they kept the conversation away from Ben and Amanda themselves. Clint was still too raw to talk about Ben's death.

An hour later, a car up ahead flashed its lights seven times, then stopped for a count of three, and then flashed its lights seven times again.

Clint pursed his lips and shook his head. Pulling alongside the newer sedan, he noticed it was an unmanned vehicle. He got out and pulled their bags from the back as the trunk was opened. He slammed the lid and then said loud enough for Casey to hear in the truck, "Thanks for the lift. We're exhausted and going to crash most of the way there."

The sedan took off after Clint climbed behind the wheel of his truck.

"Do you think that will work?" Casey chewed at the corner of her mouth.

Clint shrugged. "Only one way to find out. Let's go home."

He turned the truck quickly, going off the road for only a second before they were on the way.

"I would feel better if we swept the house again. Did you sweep the truck?"

"Yes, when I picked up the device, we tested it but didn't find anything." Clint patted her knee.

They swept the house from top to bottom, even including the spaces they hadn't occupied since arriving. No additional bugs were found. Clint went to the loader and was in the process of moving the metal, and Casey said she would be working on the parchment.

"Father, please let us have some rest on all sides for a while. We need a reprieve for at least a bit." Clint sighed as he put the bucket under the last pile of metal. They had discussed it and decided together they were done running. This would be the last place they lived. If the Monarchs came to them with all their firepower, they would make their last stand here.

The engine cut out as he dumped the last piece behind the barn. Leaving it where it was, unable to crank the motor back over, he trudged back to the house. He would have to look at it another day; he was exhausted. Not just physically but mentally.

The light was still on in the den, but a pan with soup and a tray with sandwiches were on the sideboard ready to go.

"Are you ready to eat?" Casey faltered when his voice sounded behind her. "Sorry, I didn't mean to scare you."

"I'm fine just in my own world." She waved her hand around.

"Did you find anything?"

She dropped the parchment on the desk. "I'm not sure. But watch this." She folded the cuffs on her sleeves and held the parchment again. The symbols on her arms glowed.

Clint took hold of her arm and angled it this way and that, his eyes following the hieroglyphs as they wound around her skin. "Well, that's new. Is that what it did when they lit up on your skin to show how to use the relics?"

"Yes. Crazy, I know, but I can't figure out right now what it is trying to tell me." Casey pushed back from the desk and followed him as he proceeded to the kitchen.

Eating was a quiet affair. Neither had the energy to do more than that. A glow emitting from the office caught his eye. "Now what?"

Clint stormed down the hall; Casey had to run to catch up.

A green flash of light winked out under the roll-top as they ran into the den. Clint nudged Casey behind him.

Pushing around him, she heaved the roller up. "That is what it was doing before when you and Ben didn't believe me."

The sphere lay in four pieces. "There are definitely less now than there was before."

"And look, the largest piece is melded together where you can still see the seams of the previous breaks, Clint."

Casey put her hand on his arm. "Do you think we can get Amanda and Ben back?"

"Stop it. She's been gone for two years now. We buried Ben months ago. There is no getting *them* back." Clint stormed off toward the kitchen.

"But you felt something when you had your nightmare the other night. Don't lie to me, Clint. You are all that I have left in this world."

"It felt as if she's been here the whole time, didn't it?" Clint whispered as he scrubbed his hands down his face.

"Yes! How did you know that?" Casey couldn't believe what she was hearing. Clint felt it too. All her flashes of memories of Amanda! She thought were just that. Memories. Now she wondered if they were something more.

"That was part of my dream when I called her name. I swore she was physically here with us." Clint strolled to the back door. His large body was haloed by the setting sun. "Can we discuss this later? I need to lie down and then maybe we can go over the parchment together with clear minds. I know you have refused to look at it since Ben's death until now. We need to see what new developments were brought about with him gone."

Casey put her hand on his back. "I didn't want to admit he wasn't coming back. If I looked at the parchment it would only make it more real. I was afraid it would tell me that losing two of the chosen wouldn't change the fact that we still have to fight. But you're right. I can't just put my head in the sand and ignore what is going on around us. I think it's a great idea to go over it together."

Clint locked up as Casey retired to her room. He picked up the picture frame of the three of them as kids playing in the fields behind this house. His aunt had taken the picture while they were all on their way back. They had their arms looped around each other, trying to technically do the three-legged race but with three of them. The smiles on their faces was one of the happiest memories he had of them. They lived a carefree life before the Monarchs started their terror. He set the frame down and made his way to his room. Tomorrow, they would come up with a plan and surmise what the sphere piecing itself back together meant. For tonight though, he was done for. It was time to sleep. Hopefully without the nightmares.

Forty-Two

Clint woke and lay staring at the ceiling. There was a noise downstairs. A heart rate. Slow and steady told him someone wasn't stressed out or amped up by adrenaline. Papers moving across something like a desk alerted him they were downstairs. When he got up to check on Casey, light trickled to the upper level from the den. Darkness outside the windows told him it was too early for her to be up.

"What are you doing? It's the middle of the night." Clint stood there smiling at Casey, seated behind the desk going over the parchment. Her hair cascaded around her face as she studied the symbols.

"Just seeing if I can understand any more of this." Casey was in her pajamas and had her feet tucked underneath her in the chair. He didn't understand how women could pretzel themselves like that and sit comfortably.

Clint walked over and slowly ran his hand over the parchment he didn't have a clue how to read. He wished Chloe hadn't left, but he understood why, especially with what happened the last time. She was too young to have near-death experiences like that. She should be given the chance to grow old.

"I am no help there." Amanda was the one that deciphered this; Clint got a faraway look in his eyes he always did when he thought about his friend. There was still a void not having her around. The warmth of Casey's hand over his brought him out of his musings. She smiled up at him as he slung his arm around her. He still blamed himself for Amanda not being here.

"Well, I'm going back to bed. Are you gonna stay down here?" Clint nudged her shoulder with his.

"Yes, I wanted to take one more look and see if anything jumps out at me." Casey swatted at his arm, laughing.

CLINT DRUG HIS FEET as he climbed upstairs, and she heard the door latch. Looking back at the parchment, she wasn't sure where to start or what anything meant past what Amanda had shown her. Her heart ached that Amanda couldn't help them. Grabbing the parchment, she stuffed it in the tube they had gotten for it to help keep it undamaged. Opening the desk that had been in Clint's family for generations, she gasped as the tube fell from her hand and clattered on the floor. The case for the sphere shoved in the back seeped a faint blue light through the crystal lid that housed the shattered sphere. No, not again. She was tired of being the only one who was ever present when the sphere started its shenanigans that Clint had only witnessed partially one time.

Stepping back, she bumped into Clint. A scream erupted from deep inside her that shook the house. Clint sputtered, "It's just me, I heard your heart rate speed up."

Casey positioned him between her and the sphere. "Tell me I'm not imagining that?"

Clint glanced over her head. "Okay..."

The sphere no longer glowed. She curled her hands into fists. Why did it always stop when someone else was around? "Please tell me you saw the same thing or I'll think I'm going crazy."

"What? The sphere?" Clint yawned and plopped down on one of the chairs.

"Yes," Casey lifted the crystal case it was in and pulled it forward to the front of the desk.

"Um, yes?" Clint had a questioning look on his face.

"You saw it was glowing? Or I should say, several did, like before." She regarded Clint with hands on her hips. She was getting tired of this.

"Casey, that's been broken for over two years now. Even if it is putting itself back together, who is to say it will actually work and open the portals back up?"

"Yes, but how do you explain that there are only three now instead of the original seven? You even admitted there were at least six. I was putting the parchment away and thinking of Amanda and wishing she was here. I raised the secretariat and the sphere sparkled. This time not only a couple, but every one of them." Casey waved her hand toward the crystal case.

Clint walked up and squinted as if willing it to show some life. He looked down at Casey as if he didn't believe her. She didn't exaggerate and he wouldn't think she was now. She all but prayed he wouldn't think this was still part of her reaction to killing Monarchs. But this had nothing to do with that or the fear of losing them.

"Clint," Casey started. They stopped and held their breath as the last of the small fragments of the sphere started to glow. They vibrated and bounced around in the crystal case.

"Wait. How's this possible?" Clint's voice was almost too soft for her to hear, but she did because they thought the same thing.

Clint tilted the lid back as the sphere fragments rose from the case. They reformed as if a magnet pulled at the center and drew them into the exact place where they belonged before it shattered. As each piece connected, the blinding light that poured through the broken sides dissipated after it connected to the main piece. The sphere repaired itself and hovered a few inches above the crystal case with a blinding light radiating out in every direction. They shielded their eyes and turned their heads away as dots from the bright light danced behind her eyelids. The blinding light became a dull shimmering field around the perfectly repaired sphere. Not a single crack remained.

"Clint? Ben...he's..." Casey's barely whispered voice broke as the sphere projected a timeline with Amanda in the display. She was like she was before. She walked down the corridor with Ben while she looked up at Clint on her other side. There was no mistaking the way she looked at him.

He clenched his jaw and drew in a sharp breath. Pain clouded his features as she peered up at him. It was unmistakable; he did love Amanda and had for a long time.

Clint quickly shut off the sphere and slammed the lid when the sphere rested back in it. Casey wanted to scream at him, asking if he was crazy.

"Clint, we need to talk about this." Casey took in her friend's face.

"Casey, we can't do this. What would the ramifications be if we did?"

"Why would we be given this gift if this isn't what we're supposed to do? What were the ramifications when Ben took me?"

"She died. I can't go through that again." Clint put his head in his hands.

"Who said she dies this time?" Casey reached out to him, but he caught her and wrapped her arms around him.

"Would you want to be the one to tell her why we pulled her away from heaven?" Clint heaved a huge gulp of air.

Forty-Three

Clint fell into the chair behind the desk knowing he was right. His startlingly strong feelings for Amanda tightened the muscles in his chest, and he couldn't draw in a breath. When they were younger, she was the pesky little sister of his best friend. At the end of her high school years, she developed into a beautiful young woman. He was stunned when he came back from college one summer and laid eyes on her for what seemed like the first time in years with how much she had grown. He couldn't stop staring.

Yes, he was devastated when she died, and he hurt like never before. He only thought it was because he thought of her as a sister growing up and they had fought like brother and sister numerous times. Now, seeing her through the sphere, there was something more that he didn't want to admit to himself. Seeing her look at him the same way now crushed his heart with a heavy burden. She meant enough to him that he knew he had to let her stay where she was. And he would have to live with the pain; he now had to endure the feelings he finally admitted he had for her all these wasted years later.

Clint let a groan escape he hadn't planned on anyone hearing. Casey looked at him concern etched on her face.

"Clint?" Casey retreated to the chair behind the desk and perched on the edge, facing the chair Clint sat in.

"Seeing her like that...like she was two years ago, I—" Clint's voice cracked.

Casey put her hand on his shoulder. Clint didn't want her to struggle with the thoughts of what if she had saved her. He blew out a breath and wanted to reach for the sphere, if only to glimpse Amanda smiling and happy once again and not the dying woman he remembered.

It was a shock to see Amanda like that. Casey opened her mouth to say something but seemed to change her mind. Clint patiently waited until she was ready.

"Can I suggest a theory?" Casey cautiously started again.

"What?" Clint plopped the sphere in the air, catching it between his hands.

Casey pursed her lips and shook her head. "Would we technically be taking them away from heaven?"

Clint jumped out of his chair and towered over her, his face red, hands clutched into fists. "Are you saying that Amanda and Ben didn't go to heaven? Because I'm here to tell you they never loved anyone as much as they loved our Father in heaven! Believe me, I know when they each accepted Jesus into their hearts and the vow they took, to always put Him first."

"Clint." Casey put her hand on him and he stopped when he recognized how mad he was, it vibrated through every muscle. He put the sphere aside. She started again. "I'm not saying they didn't go to heaven; I know for a fact they'd be there waiting for us to join them. What I'm saying is we saw them in the sphere. It was *before* they died."

"Yes, I remember that day walking with her." Clint wished he had admitted to himself his feelings about her.

The feelings he denied back then flooded his heart. He flattened his palm against his sternum, trying to stop the painful throb behind his ribcage that kept time with the beating of his heart.

"Clint, think about where I'm going with this." Casey had a huge grin plastered on her face as she nudged his arm.

"What am I not getting?" Clint had hope on his face for the first time in a long time.

Casey continued, "They never went to heaven *yet* during that walk with you. So, would we really be taking them from heaven? Wouldn't it be like when I was brought here? I don't remember the years that I was brought forward. Also, look at what happened. The sphere, broken for two years, now regenerated itself while we thought about Amanda. It dialed up to a time with Amanda and Ben after I was taken, so they know who I am. Maybe this was part of His plan for us and what we may be about to face, and we need Amanda and Ben to do it." Casey took the shield bracelet from its crystal treasure chest case and set it on the desk.

"So, they wouldn't have memories of heaven if we bring them here before they died, and neither would have memories of what they went through." Clint hugged Casey. "I'm so sorry!"

"You're forgiven and exactly!" Casey returned his hug.

"Wait. Are we really thinking about doing this?" Clint guided Casey forward away from him, then walked toward the other wall. Casey observed the struggle he had wanting his best friend and best friend's sister back, but he couldn't wipe the smile from his face as emotions welled in his eyes. Clint contemplated getting them back, but he also struggled against what they dealt with now. Would they be able to bring both back?

"The prophecy does say four not two." Clint marched across the room and raised the lid on the crystal box containing the sphere again. It floated and shimmered without being activated by one of them.

The sphere showed a time with Amanda in her room with Ben, with her clothes set out for the next day. Casey remembered that day; it was the day Amanda died. Casey drew in a gasping breath as Clint gawked at her. "I remember her wearing that the day she died. Look, the picture of their parents isn't on her nightstand."

"Oh wow, you're right. Wait, we have to tell our other selves somehow so we don't ruin the plan and someone else dies. Do we need to leave the bracelet and ring with you somehow, Casey?" Clint took a notepad from the desk and fished around in the drawer, coming up with a worn-down pencil that held no eraser at the end of the crimped metal.

"I don't think so, since it will be an instantaneous time jump for them."

"Clint, please believe that we're okay. Ben and I will not be here to help you, but you will understand why in the long run. Please don't look for us and do the plan as scheduled. Casey, take the bracelet and ring; yes, it works for you. Watch out for hidden dangers in the parking garage. I'll be with you again soon, Amanda. Hint: Clint, this is in your own handwriting." Clint folded the piece of paper in half and looked back at the sphere showing Amanda getting into bed and Ben standing there as if saying goodnight. His pulse ramped up. They were going to do this. Get Amanda and

Ben back. How would this change the parchment? Casey had never told him anything changed when mentioning that they were reunited again.

"I WANT TO GO." CASEY watched Amanda in the sphere as she settled in for the night. "I'll have to do this quickly and quietly."

Clint grasped the note out of her hand, flicked the image in the sphere, and disappeared in front of Casey's eyes. She turned quickly to the image. She never saw it work from this side before. Clint had a very animated conversation with Amanda and Ben. Amanda shook her head and pointed to the door in her room. He pulled the note and placed it on her pillow. He seized her hand but she pulled her hand free to push at him.

Ben grabbed his shoulder to pull him away from Amanda. She tried to back away, but he held her face between his hands. Amanda eyed Ben, then Clint, and seemed to be listening. She nodded and looked back, taking in her room and the note Clint laid on her pillow, before taking his hand and holding out her hand for Ben. He reluctantly nodded before clasping her hand.

The sphere darkened and the light winked out, before the shards fell apart into the seven fragments that were there previously.

"No!" Casey wailed and reached for the sphere.

Her legs gave out. What just happened? The anguish radiating off Casey sent out pulses she couldn't see. He was her protector. He wasn't supposed to leave her! What was she supposed to do now?

The weapon that Clint never went anywhere without glowed from the cushion in the chair he was standing by when he went back in time. Casey carefully handled the relic; she couldn't stop the tears no one would know she shed.

With a flick of her wrist, she hurled it across the room only for it to vault back over the desk at her. She held up her hand to stop it from hitting her. The tendrils sought purchase and wound their way around her hand, searing into her skin. She screamed as the pain increased.

The weapon molded into her palm, sending the shield out in red sparkles while yellow-amber light flared behind her eyes. She lifted off the ground as the shield encased the entire house, turning into a solid, impenetrable mass.

Casey collapsed to the floor, alone. There was no one left. As the last relic absorbed into her, her reality hit home. Casey's nightmare of being left abandoned in a world where she didn't belong just became a harsh reality. Her anguished scream didn't penetrate the shield as unconsciousness crept toward her as if it were a living, breathing entity dragging her down. Where would her life go now?

Don't miss out!

Visit the website below and you can sign up to receive emails whenever K. A. Moore publishes a new book. There's no charge and no obligation.

https://books2read.com/r/B-A-MAMI-UQOUC

BOOKS 2 READ

Connecting independent readers to independent writers.

About the Author

K.A. Moore, born and raised in Kansas, is a retired 911 police dispatcher with over thirteen years of service and will be the first to tell you dispatchers are a special breed all their own. Her real passion is writing and putting her imagination into works of fiction. Faith-based Christian suspense is her preferred writing theme, with wild, crazy dreams as the backdrop to many scenes that seem to come alive in her writing. As she writes, her Chihuahua scampers for the coveted position of curling up in her lap while creating her stories.

www.ingramcontent.com/pod-product-compliance
Lightning Source LLC
LaVergne TN
LVHW050928080826
845145LV00001B/252

* 9 7 8 1 9 5 7 2 2 3 1 4 8 *